ROC

ROBERT M. KERNS

KFP

Published by Knightsfall Press
PO Box 280
Mineral Wells, WV 26150

ABOUT THIS BOOK

A woman on the run. An unexpected meeting. Rising tensions.

Sloane happily worked as a farmhand for an elderly couple in Nebraska...until people arrived in blacked-out SUVs asking about a woman who turns into a giant bird. When Sloane refused to go with them, they killed her elderly employers and razed the farm to the ground. Then? They pinned the crimes on her. Sloane's been running ever since.

Karleen returns to Precious after a meeting with her sister. She's within an hour of home when a woman stumbles out of the underbrush lining the road and collapses on the yellow line. The woman whispers one word as she passes out: hunters.

There's only one thing for Karleen to do...

To Janice Miller, Carolyn "Nana" McClellan, and all the other grandmas who touch their grandchildren's lives.

A light breeze blew through the cafe's outdoor seating area, and the sun shone down from a cloudless sky, warming everything it touched. Mouth-watering scents wafted out of the cafe as staff carried drinks and food to their guests, whether inside or out. It was a busy time for the cafe, as people occupied most of their tables, and no one suspected that two of their number were not technically human.

Nadine looked across their table, taking in all the subtle changes in her sister's demeanor and presence since she called Karleen out of the woods to help her with the abduction of her friend's child. Her sister sat in a crowded patio of a *city* cafe, and she seemed at ease and relaxed. The Karleen of even three months ago would have been fidgeting and checking sight lines and sniffing the air, but now? She leaned back against her seat in a comfortable pose with her legs crossed under the table.

"Have you heard from Mom and Dad lately?" Karleen asked.

Nadine broke off from her consideration of her sister and

nodded. "They're doing well. They're visiting Rick and his family right now; newest grandchild and all that."

"Seriously?" Karleen asked. "How many nieces and nephews do I have now?"

"Uhm…" Nadine's voice trailed off as she pursed her lips and started some mental math. *Let's see. There are my two. Jack's three. Will's four. And this one makes three for Rick.* "I think twelve all told, if my math is right."

Karleen gaped at her sister. "Twelve? Are you kidding me?"

"Sis, we've been out of high school for sixty years, and it only takes nine months to make a baby. Twelve is kinda low for shifters in that amount of time."

Nadine watched the weight settle around her sister's shoulders, before Karleen asked, "Do they know about me? I mean, I know I walked away and all, so everyone would be well within their rights…"

"We would *never* do that to you, Karleen. Mom and Dad always ask if I've seen you lately, and the kids all ask if Aunt Karleen will come to the next family get-together. The boys never really knew you well, but they hang on every word when I tell the family how you're doing. You have a family waiting for you, whenever you're ready for us."

A single tear escaped Karleen's iron self-control, and she casually dabbed it away with a napkin that she placed in her lap. "When is the next family get-together?"

Nadine smiled. "A couple weeks from now, actually."

"A couple weeks? That's… wow… that's really short notice. Would I be able to bring Wyatt?"

Nadine fought to maintain her non-expression and hide even the barest hint of a reaction. A shifter named Wyatt had recently come onto the public scene in the shifter world in a big way. Thomas Carlyle no longer sat on the Shifter Council because of him, and she did not want to make *any* assumptions. "Wyatt? Who's that? Do you finally have yourself a man, sister dear?"

Nadine felt her jaw drop when her sister *blushed*. Karleen looked away and tried to hide her face like an embarrassed schoolgirl, and neither of them had been a schoolgirl for several decades now.

"Oh, you do!" Nadine gushed. "I have *never* seen you blush before, sis. You have to tell me simply *everything* now. Come on; spill."

"Hush already!" Karleen said around a still-embarrassed smile. "I don't think they heard you in the next state over."

Nadine evolved her smirk into a full-blown predatory smile. "Would you like them to? Hubby-dearest says I have a good set of lungs in me."

In the blink of an eye, Karleen's coloring resembled a ripe tomato, and she buried her face in her hands. "I did *not* need to know that, Nadine. Whatever your husband thinks or doesn't think is no business of mine at all. But yes, I am finally seeing someone. And he's really nice. I don't need you going all 'big sister' on me or him. I can take care of myself. You know that."

"You're right. You've always taken care of yourself. You've always forged your own path, but that doesn't change the fact that I want details on this Wyatt of yours. Did you meet him during the abduction thing?"

Karleen nodded. "He's dreamy, sis. I will rub my wolf up against him anytime he lets me."

Now, it was Nadine's turn to gape. "Karleen! Do you know what that means to shifters? Please, tell me you know what that means."

She shrugged. "I didn't, really. Not at first, but my wolf explained it to me. Then, I rubbed my wolf against him for the first time, and it was everything my wolf said it would be."

"You are such a shameless hussy," Nadine shot back amid giggles. "I can't wait to tell Mom and Dad."

"Don't you dare!" Karleen replied through a huge grin. "That's *none* of their business."

"Oh, it's not? How is it not our parents' business that little Karleen finally found herself a guy?"

Karleen arched an eyebrow. "'Little' Karleen, is it?"

Nadine beamed. "Well, you *are* the baby of the family. At least for now, anyway. Once they get tired of being grand-parents, Mom and Dad might go for another round of parenting. I've heard whispers that we're not their first litter. Which is also common among shifters."

"Seriously?"

Nadine nodded in response. "Oh, yeah. We're basically immortal, sis, with shifter healing. But… you've stalled for long enough. Tell me about this dreamy Wyatt of yours."

Karleen blushed again and shook her head. "You are relentless."

"What… you think I'll let you surprise *all* of us by just showing up with him? Come on; give, already. I'm the family reconnaissance. I already know he's a decent guy, or you wouldn't be chasing his tail. But you gotta give me more than that, sis. Just think of how our brothers will respond. Do you *want* them all to do the 'big brother' thing with Wyatt?"

Karleen snorted a laugh, and Nadine had never heard her sister do *that*, either. Then, Karleen said, "I think I'd like to see that."

"Why?" Nadine's eyes narrowed. Karleen had that mischievous twinkle in her eyes that hadn't changed one bit since they were kids.

The mischievous twinkle evolved into full-on amusement as Karleen spoke, "You remember Shep?"

"Shep?" Nadine blinked at the non-sequitur and searched

her mind. Then, she frowned. "The Arenbergs' Rottweiler? What does he have to do with this?"

"Shep wouldn't chase Wyatt, either."

Nadine's frown deepened. Shep had no fear of shifters—unlike most animals—and chased every shifter in the town where they grew up... except Karleen. Even when Karleen was just a toddler, that damned Rottie rolled onto its back and bared its throat at the mere scent of her. It wasn't until Karleen revealed herself to be the first modern primogenitor that... no. It couldn't be.

"This Wyatt you're chasing... he's that new feline primo-genitor everyone's been hearing about? The one that cost Thomas Carlyle his seat on the council?"

Karleen's grin turned into a flinty glare in the space of a finger-snap. "First, I don't know anything about that, and second, what I know of Thomas Carlyle tells me he doesn't deserve a council seat. I've lost count of the number of wolves who have tracked me down over the years and asked —almost begged—me to end him."

"The word among wolves is that your beau goaded Carlyle into a challenge and then humiliated him in the arena," Nadine explained. "More than a few aren't too happy about that. He did choose not to take Carlyle's seat on the council, which was a good thing. That kept things balanced, but he's none too popular in certain circles, regardless of his primogenitor status."

"Would our brothers or father be among those wolves?" Karleen asked, not *quite* giving Nadine the Stink Eye.

Nadine chuckled and shook her head. "Dad doesn't care about any of it. He goes about his daily life and never gets involved in politics."

"So, it's our brothers then." Karleen almost growled. "Which ones? All of them?"

"Jack and Will seem the fiercest in their dislike of the

5

Wyatt circulating in the shifter news. Rick has a new baby; not much competes with that."

Karleen leaned back in her seat and crossed her arms, glaring at the tabletop. It was clear to Nadine that her sister considered the situation, and it wasn't lost on her that the two brothers who disliked the public perception of Wyatt the most were their two *oldest* brothers.

After several moments, Karleen snorted; only this time, it didn't come from amusement. She unfolded her arms and uncrossed her legs, placing her palms on her knees as if she meant to stand. "If they have a problem with Wyatt, then they have a problem with me. Hell with it. I've lived this long without my blood family."

"Karleen! Wait!" Nadine hissed, trying to keep her sister from leaving and not cause a scene at the same time.

"What? If Wyatt isn't welcome, neither am I. He isn't some weekend boyfriend, Nadine. How many guys did you bring home for dinner that we only saw once? After the fourth or fifth, I stopped caring about their names unless I saw them a second time. Do you think I *want* my first time seeing the family in sixty years to be some kind of rude pissing match between Wyatt and my brothers that sets everyone on edge? None of us need that, sis. I've been just fine all these years without the family; I can go a few more. See you in a year or two. Call if you need help."

Before Nadine could say another word, Karleen stood, dropped some bills on the table, and walked away. Nadine watched her sister leave the cafe, and she fought the urge to slam her fists on the arms of her chair. Thirty years! She'd been slowly working her sister for thirty years to get her to come back to the family, and her damn fool brothers sent all her hard work up in smoke.

The engine of a well-tuned chopper erupted in a furious rumble from the cafe's parking lot, and Nadine watched her sister ride away as feelings of dread formed a pit in her stomach. She didn't want to have the conversation about this with her parents. Dad would be hurt; he missed Karleen something fierce. Mom... Mom would probably be livid and have a none-too-quiet word with the boys. Either way, Nadine didn't want any part of what came next.

KARLEEN FOUGHT the rage that simmered inside her. How could people who seemed like such upstanding, worthwhile souls as her *brothers* support someone like Thomas Carlyle? The man gave misogynists a bad name. She didn't have *proof* that the man forced himself on weaker female shifters, but too many of the women who came to her showed signs of surviving brutality. Her conscience wouldn't let her simply challenge and kill him. She needed actual proof of what he was supposed to have done, which she didn't have.

The city around her transitioned to suburbs and up-scale, middle-class housing developments. Then, the suburbs and communities became more hilly and forested terrain, and Karleen felt a tension fade from her body and soul she hadn't realized she held. She was glad Precious didn't have a city vibe or even big town feel to it. As much as she wanted Wyatt and wanted to explore having him in her life, she doubted she could enjoy her time with him if he had chosen a city. But whereas most wolves *might* be able to hide in cities or suburbs and have people mistake them for weird dog breeds, Wyatt had no chance. No one would mistake a Smilodon for a pet cat.

Despite herself, Karleen chuckled at the thought of taking Wyatt to a pet park in his cat form. Every animal in a square mile would probably piss themselves in submission. A few humans might, too.

The absurd thought went a long way to banishing the ire Karleen felt over the situation with her brothers. As much as she felt the yearning all shifters did to be near and with family, Karleen still thought that the proper path was leaving them to their own devices. She didn't feel like she belonged in their lives, no matter how much she wanted otherwise.

A little over an hour later, the Godwin County sign flew past her right side, and the feeling of being home surprised her. She hadn't thought of anywhere other than her cabin deep in the Oregon wilderness as home in a very long time.

Movement on the side of the road up ahead drew Karleen's focus. A woman burst out of the underbrush lining the rural road. She wore a flannel shirt, denim jeans, and sneakers of some kind. The shirt and jeans possessed numerous jagged rips and tears. She ran into what was the oncoming lane for Karleen, her speed slowing to a stagger, and she collapsed laying halfway across the double yellow line.

Karleen applied the brakes and eased her ride to a stop on the berm. She hit her hazard lights before she put the kick-stand down and removed her helmet. She left the bike idling in neutral as she rushed to the woman's side. Still, five feet or more from her, the scent of a shifter reached Karleen.

As she knelt beside the collapsed woman, Karleen saw the woman's eyes fluttering as she breathed heavily.

"Do you need help?" Karleen asked.

The woman moved her head in a minute fraction of what might have been a nod in normal circumstances.

"Hunters," the woman whispered so faintly even Karleen's shifter hearing almost didn't catch it.

Well... that tore it. Karleen almost felt like moving her chopper out of sight and leaning the woman against a tree with a water bottle while they waited for the hunters. It had been a while since she had a good fight. But she didn't know how many hunted her or how well armed they were. While she knew she would win the fight, how much of her would be left afterwards?

No. The better path in this instance was to take her back to Precious. Doc could fix the woman up, and she could tell Wyatt what happened. The tricky part would be getting the woman back to Precious via motorcycle in her half-conscious state.

Karleen scooped the woman into her arms and carried her across the road. She placed her on the back seat and let her slump forward to rest on the gas tank. Then, she went to her saddlebags. She unlocked the left one that held her emergency supplies, like tire patches, a spare chain, bungee cords, and such. The right was her utility bag. Its contents changed with Karleen's needs, and it had been quite a while since she'd even looked in there.

The lid rolled back, and Karleen snorted at what she saw. Emergency climbing gear—including two harnesses—and a bag of carabiners. Huh. Was the search and rescue job for those missing hikers the last time she used this? That was something like eight months ago. Still, she wasn't about to look a gift horse in the mouth. Those harnesses might take this from being a forlorn hope to something vaguely feasible.

Karleen hustled into her climbing harness before she put the other one on her rescue. Then, she sat on the bike and pulled the woman against her back, clipping the two harnesses at each shoulder with two climbing-grade carabiners. Then, she locked the right saddlebag and pulled a red bungee cord from the left saddlebag before closing it. Karleen lifted the woman's legs and bent them around her waist, like she was giving her rescue a piggy-back ride. She used the bungee cord to secure the woman's ankles. The last thing Karleen wanted was for the woman's feet to flop around and get caught on the chain or the rear tire; that would be a bad day for all involved. The good news was that shifter healing would handle any minor injuries incurred from this.

She took hold of the handlebars and leaned side to side. It wasn't perfect, but if she kept her speed down, it should work. She shifted into first gear. Then, she eased back onto the road that hadn't seen any traffic since stopping and resumed her return to Precious.

2

I sat at a table in Gladys's diner, my attention divided between my amazing meal and my equally amazing—yet for different reasons—and very attractive meal companion. Gabrielle sat ninety degrees around the table to my left, so we both could watch the windows and door.

If I was prepared to be one-hundred-percent honest with myself about her, I was already smitten. Gabrielle had the dusky complexion of Middle Eastern or eastern Mediterranean ethnicity, and she kept her dark hair short. It wasn't buzz-cut short, but it didn't have the long side strands of hair that I saw in pictures of 'page boy' styles. Tall and lithe, she moved her athletic form with an innate grace only a born shifter possessed, and her personality made her a joy to be near.

Yeah… I was a lost cause.

"So what do we have on the docket after lunch?" I asked between bites.

Gabrielle took a few more bites before she replied, "I was thinking we'd spend an hour on responsibilities of being an Alpha and another hour on shifter stuff. I don't want to push you too far too fast, because that's no way to learn anything. Honestly, given you're two months into being a shifter already, I may just call it good and help you learn as you go. You've done really well so far with the few times you've needed to adjudicate things as Alpha, and you have Alistair and I for meeting prep in the future."

I nodded around another bite. When did steaks—and medium-rare steaks at that—get to be so tasty? This was my third one, and I kind of felt like I wanted a fourth.

"So… do we get to have another game of 'Catch the Cat' tonight?"

Gabrielle blushed. Honest-to-goodness *blushed*. "Let's see how Karleen's doing when she gets back. She said her sister sounded a little off when they set up the lunch date, and if she needs us, I'd rather focus on that."

"Naturally," I replied. "Sometimes, I think Karleen needs us as much as I need the two of you."

A haunted look took over Gabrielle's expression for a moment, and I wondered what all she and Karleen talked about. I knew they went for runs sometimes that turned into talk sessions as they swam in Gabrielle's lake.

"Yeah, she really does. She hasn't told me a lot, but what little I do know… well… she had a rough childhood."

Ouch. Rough childhoods either screwed someone up for life or set them on the path to success because they fought against their experiences. Karleen hadn't told me all the whys and wherefores that led her to abandon shifter society for however long she had, but I didn't see how it could've been good. And yeah… I didn't know how old she truly was yet, either. In the long run, age didn't really matter, since shifters only died from wounds and not from old age or disease. What blew my mind about that was Alistair *choosing* to look as old as he did; come to find out, he didn't have to.

The roar of a chopper reached our ears, and Gabrielle and I grinned at the same time.

"She's back," I said.

Gabrielle nodded, and we *devoured* our food so we could go welcome her back. As soon as our plates were clean, we stood, and I tossed a handful of bills on the table. We turned toward the door, and I blinked at the sight of Karleen having someone behind her on her bike that looked unconscious. Gabrielle didn't freeze; she crossed the space to the door in the blink of an eye and was halfway across the street by the time I shook off my surprise. I hurried to catch up.

"...ran out of the underbrush along the road," Karleen was saying as Gabrielle helped her release her passenger from the harness. "I have no idea who she is or where she's from, but she scents of shifter. Normally, my wolf tells me what breed a shifter is, especially if I haven't met the breed before, but she's been silent the whole time."

"Here, tough guy," Gabrielle said, gesturing to the unconscious woman. "You can carry her into the infirmary."

I chuckled and scooped the woman up in a bridal carry, following Karleen and Gabrielle as they opened doors for me. The last set of doors—the ones that led to Doc's triage area and the rest of the infirmary—swooshed open on their own at Gabrielle's approach.

"Doc," Gabrielle said, "we have an unconscious woman here. She scents like a shifter."

Doc looked up from a book of some type just as I followed Gabrielle through the automatic doors. "Ah, yes. Put her over there on the bed where you woke, please, Alpha Wyatt."

By the time I had the woman laid out on the bed, Doc was across the bed from me. He started his exam with two fingers pressed to the side of her neck. "Hmmm... she's alive, yes. Pulse is steady if a little weak."

I picked up on the shifter scent as well, and I agreed with Karleen. I didn't know what breed she was.

Well? I directed to the part of my mind that was no longer human.

My cat sent back a mental image of a massive Smilodon yawning, the growly voice asking, *What?*

You've always identified shifter breeds for me before. What is she?

Trouble, the growly voice immediately replied. *Very yummy but still trouble.*

Seriously? That's all *you're giving me?*

What? A mental image of total innocence formed in my mind. Then, an almost-human shrug. *All cats think birds are yummy.*

Birds, huh? So, she's an avian shifter?

Sure... why not.

My cat sent an image of a massive Smilodon lazing in the shade of an enormous tree on a bright, sunny day. I felt pretty certain that was code for 'not talking anymore.'

"My cat hinted that she's an avian shifter," I said while Doc continued his exam.

Karleen scoffed. "Well, that's no fair. My wolf doesn't even acknowledge her existence. The last time I asked, she sent back an image of us playing in the woods."

Just then, the woman's stomach growled. Most people hear 'stomach growled' and think of the fairly tame growling human stomachs do. Yes, for the most part, ours are the same way. Except this one. It wasn't a growl so much as a roar. Doc even took a small step back from the bed.

"Should we go get a couple platters of food, Doc?" I asked.

Doc nodded. "Yes, that might be good."

HER HEAD HURT. Her stomach ached. The last thing she remembered was... what? Running? Right. She ran through the forest after they found her at that campground. But where was she now?

She laid on a... well... it almost felt like a hospital bed. Her back angled slightly upward. The smell of strong disinfectant assaulted her nose, and she heard a heartbeat and breathing close. *Very* close. Whoever was with her knew she was awake if the person was a shifter. Might as well get it over with.

She opened her eyes and saw a curtained off space. The drop ceiling and florescent lighting screamed hospital of some type, and terror threatened to overtake her that they caught her at last.

"Hey, relax," a new voice said. A woman's voice.

Turning toward the voice, she saw a woman in a flannel shirt, blue denim jeans, and biker leathers. Her dark hair brushed her shoulders. Her expression—her entire demeanor—conveyed concern.

"I don't know where you think you are, but I'm almost certain you're wrong," the woman said. "You're in Precious, the infirmary there. My friends went across the street to get some food for you, and they'll be back shortly."

At the mention of food, her stomach growled again. Growled so fiercely it sounded like it might attempt escape to get its own food. Then, her senses finally caught up to her; the woman in biker leathers was a shifter. Hints of wolf but nothing like any wolf shifter she'd ever encountered.

"I'm Karleen Vesper," the woman continued. "You stumbled out of the forest about an hour west of here and collapsed right on the road's yellow line. I brought you here. Doc says you're okay overall, just malnourished and dehydrated. We're going to fix you up, okay? You don't have to run. You're safe here."

No. She wasn't safe anywhere. She didn't see how she'd ever be safe again. Not since the Higgins farm outside Pitawqua, Nebraska. Goodness, that was what... a year ago now? But how much was safe to tell? She always avoided large settlements before—regardless of human or shifter. Except now she was one of two places she never wanted to be.

She opened her mouth to speak, but her throat and mouth were parched. She cleared her throat and licked her lips. "How long?"

The woman calling herself Karleen lifted one eyebrow. "About ninety minutes since I found you. It's been maybe twenty minutes since my friends went for food. They should be back very soon."

"Who else is here?"

"If you mean the infirmary, no one; Doc went to get a bite once he finished making sure you had no injuries that required his immediate attention. If you mean the town, I have no idea. The whole county is shifter territory, and the only humans we have in town are those who know about us."

The sound of an automatic door opening preceded footfalls and a cornucopia of lovely food smells. Two silhouettes approached the curtain, and Karleen moved to pull it back and revealed two people—a man and a woman—both carrying platters piled high with food.

"Oh, hello," the young man said, his expression one of warm greeting. "Welcome to Precious. I'm Wyatt, and for my sins, the Shifter Council named me Alpha. This lady to my right is Gabrielle, and I see you've already met Karleen."

It was all she could do to bob her head in acknowledgement of his words. Her eyes remained locked on the food, almost drooling at the thought of it all. But then, reality returned.

"I don't have any money."

Wyatt placed the platter on the foot of the bed and gave her a dismissive wave. "Don't worry about it. If anyone gets grouchy, the infirmary can reimburse me, since Doc said you needed food."

That was enough for her. She leaned forward as far as she could, grabbing the platter and moving it to rest on her lap. The woman Wyatt introduced as Gabrielle placed her platter on the now-vacant foot of the bed.

Gabrielle touched Wyatt's upper arm as she said, "I'm going back for drinks. What do you want?"

"Something fizzy... no ice," Wyatt replied, handing her a card.

"Karleen?" Gabrielle asked.

"I'll have what Wyatt's having but with light ice."

Then, Gabrielle turned to her. She paused mid-bite as a wave of *something* passed through her. Sorrow? Regret? She wasn't sure what she felt, but these people opened up their lives and town to her. Fed her. And she didn't want to tell them her name. She didn't want to tell them anything about her. She feared it would only get them killed.

She swallowed her bite and answered, "Uhm... water, I guess."

"You sure?" Gabrielle asked. "There's tea, coffee, pretty much any kind of soft drink you can imagine."

"Water's fine."

Wyatt added, "If you don't mind, swing by Hank's and see if he still has any of those hydration packets left. Besides just getting more water in her, she may be low on electrolytes."

Gabrielle nodded and left, leaving the other two watching her eat.

"You were back kind of soon," Wyatt remarked, looking at Karleen. "Everything go okay?"

Karleen grimaced. "It went. 'Okay' might be stretching things. Nadine wanted me to come to the next family get-together, which is something like next month or two weeks or something. I don't really remember right now. What pissed me off is how two of my brothers apparently have *opinions* about you from whatever gossip the wolves around there are spreading over the Thomas Carlyle thing."

"Why would that matter?" Wyatt asked, his face scrunching up to show his confusion.

"Because… well… I was going to invite you along."

Wyatt's confusion vanished. "Oh. You mean like a 'meet the family' situation?"

"Yeah. I mean, it's been a while since I've seen any of them, and we seem to be building something, so I'd like them to meet you if I'm going to be back in the shifter world from here on out."

Karleen's words clicked with something in the woman's mind, mid-bite, and she fell into a coughing fit as she almost choked on her food. When she cleared her airway at least, she almost gaped at Karleen.

"Are you okay?" Wyatt asked.

She only had eyes—or focus—for Karleen. "You said '*back* in the shifter world.' Does that mean what I think it means? Are you the North American dire wolf?"

Karleen blushed. Then nodded.

"Oh my goodness," the woman gushed. "I've been chasing every rumor and suspected sighting up and down the Pacific coast looking for you for something like six to eight months now. I need your help. Will you teach me how to go completely off the grid?"

Karleen glanced at Wyatt, then said, "To be honest, I'm not sure how much my experience will help you. Number one, I never had people hunting me, so you should really deal with that first. At least, I assume you have people hunting you, since it seemed like you were running from something before you collapsed. Number two, I didn't *leave* shifter society so much as ignore it. I built a cabin deep in the Oregon wilderness and just let the world do its thing. I went into towns for supplies I couldn't make when I needed them and sold pelts and traps and whatever for money. We don't even know what *breed* of shifter you are, so even after the first point, it's kinda difficult to know if I can help you at all. You haven't even told us your name. I get that, and I don't want you to feel like I'm being pushy or nosy. But at the same time, are we just supposed to shout, 'hey you?'"

And there it was. She would've liked to get through both platters of food before having to give them her name. Every time she gave it before, it was a toss-up whether people tried to run her off or turn her in. She took another bite to stall. When the silence extended quite a ways past awkward, she looked at the platter in her lap.

"My name is Sloane Martinez."

Karleen looked to Wyatt; he shrugged. Karleen turned back to look at Sloane, adding her own shrug to Wyatt's and saying, "You said that like we should recognize your name. Should we?"

When Sloane didn't answer, Wyatt produced a phone from his hip pocket and tapped at the screen. Just a few seconds later, he whistled. "It says here that a Sloane Martinez is sought by police as a person of interest in connection to the murder of Jerome and Beatrice Higgins and arson at their farm just outside Pitawqua, Nebraska. That you?"

Sloane continued to eat. Neither Wyatt nor Karleen looked tense, so she held out hope. But maybe they were just letting her finish the food before they called the police.

"It's about me, yes, but I didn't do it. And I know every criminal says that. But I really didn't. I worked for Jerry and Betty as a farmhand, their only farmhand. Been there for years. Then, one day, three blacked-out SUVs rolled up while we were at the kitchen table eating dinner, and people in suits and sunglasses stepped out. They demanded I come with them, never showed any ID or warrant or anything. Just demanded I go with them. I didn't even get the chance to say 'no.' Jerry was all over them like a bulldog on a T-bone. While Jerry and the lead guy argued, one of the guys pulled on a pair of blue latex gloves and went to Jerry's gun rack. He pulled down a shotgun, loaded it, and calmly blasted Jerry into oblivion. Then, he went to the kitchen and did the same to Betty. I booked it out of there. A few of them chased me, but I managed to get away. They've been chasing me ever since."

"She's telling the truth," Karleen remarked.

Sloane frowned at her. "Seriously? You believe me just like that?"

Karleen returned a patient—almost motherly—smile. "We're shifters, honey. We can hear variances in people's heart rate when they lie. You're not lying."

Sloane nodded her understanding and went back to eating.

"So, what do we do?" Wyatt asked. "Figure out who's hunting her and why?"

Karleen leaned back against her chair, looking up at the ceiling tiles as a grimace took over her expression. For several seconds, the only sounds came from Sloane finishing the first platter and switching it with the second.

"I want to say yes," Karleen answered at long last. "The problem is that we have to be very careful about how we do so. We don't want to give humans the impression we're sheltering a murderer and arsonist."

"Get Alistair's opinion, then?" Wyatt asked.

"Yes, I think so."

The infirmary door activated, and Wyatt grinned at the sound of a second woman's voice. Gabrielle arrived with a drink carrier and two gallon-size jugs of water. A woman who looked about Wyatt's age with wavy blond hair and a curvy yet athletic build carried a brown paper grocery bag.

"Look who I found loitering on the street," Gabrielle said as she handed off the drinks in the carrier. "She arrived just as I was going into Hank's store."

"So, what brings you to visit, sis?" Wyatt asked.

The blond Wyatt claimed as a sister beamed. "I'm looking for Karleen."

"Oh, and before I forget," Wyatt interjected, "this is Sloane Martinez. Sloane, this is my sister, Vicki."

Sloane waved her greetings as she continued to eat.

"Why are you looking for me?" Karleen asked.

Vicki turned to her after waving a 'hello' to Sloane. "A couple of government fops pretty much demanded a meeting with the family, and Grandpa and Grandma don't want me going alone. All of our people are in the Magi database, but have you let Doc put you in the shifter one yet?"

Karleen shook her head. "He won't even if I agree to his primogenitor exam. I made very clear what his fate would be if any of my information ever reached a government database."

Vicki beamed. "Sweet! So, do you mind going with me?"

"Nope. When are we going?"

Now, a slight blush colored Vicki's cheeks. "Uhm… is tomorrow too soon?"

3

I watched Sloane reach her food limit about two-thirds of the way through the second platter. She drank a couple glasses of water with electrolyte packets dissolved in them, then laid back against her bed.

"Oh, my." Her voice had an almost dreamy lilt to it. "I can't remember the last time I felt truly full. That was so yummy. Thank you."

I smiled. "No problem. So… as long as you promise that you won't try running off, I'll go ask Doc if he'll sign off on you getting a room at the hotel here in town."

"But… but… I can't stay. I simply *can't*. They'll come for me. They always do."

Karleen, Gabrielle, and I all shared a look. Karleen spoke. "Let them come."

Sloane blinked her astonishment.

"You're sure?" Her voice was soft and quiet, almost as if she feared their answer would change in a moment.

I nodded. "Very sure. Let's get you set up in the hotel for now. While Karleen goes with Vicki tomorrow, we can start working on clearing your name." I grimaced. "If I'm going to be honest, we'll probably lose most of tomorrow just figuring out who all is after you. I kinda hope those nameless suits show up, too; it would help us to understand who they are and what they want."

The infirmary door slid open, and I turned to look. Buddy Carrington stepped through and headed straight to me.

"Alpha Wyatt, there are a handful of suits over in the diner hassling everyone about some woman they were chasing through the woods west of town. They look pretty rough, too. All mud-soaked and ratty. I think they had some problems."

"How'd you get away?" Gabrielle asked.

Buddy grinned. "I was across the street. Saw 'em get out of some blacked-out SUVs and heard 'em start with the questions when the lead guy only had one foot in the diner's door."

I turned to my sister. "You feel like helping out with an interrogation?"

Vicki scanned the faces looking at her, then turned back to me. "I won't be helping you start a war with the Feds, will I?"

"I don't see how," Gabrielle replied. "If they're honestly Feds, they're violating the treaty we have with them, because we police our own. They should've passed word to the Shifter Council. If they're not Feds, then they're guilty of quite a few crimes."

Karleen snorted a laugh. "They're guilty of crimes, either way. They killed the Higgins couple and burned down their farm. Besides, with the way Sloane's case appears to be on the surface, there's no way the Council wouldn't call the Huntress to handle it. So, no matter who they are, they're ours."

"Huntress?" Sloane squeaked. "You all know the Huntress?"

Gabrielle hung her head as Karleen pointed at her with a thumb. Sloane's eyes went wide.

"Relax," Karleen said, placing a hand on Sloane's. "We know you're telling the truth about what happened."

I looked Sloane right in her eyes. "Will you wait here for us? We can help you get all this sorted out, but only if you stay here with us and don't run off."

Sloane held my eyes with her own for several moments before she looked down at her lap. "You promise you're not just going to hand me over to them?"

I gave her my best encouraging nod. "Yes, I absolutely one-hundred-percent promise they will not get their hands on you. We, however, will absolutely get our hands on them."

Vicki beamed. "Let's go interrogate some people. I've always wanted to practice my Charm spell."

WHEN WE LEFT the infirmary building, we found a sight that made my blood boil. The muddy suits had Gladys pressed up against one of their SUVs, telling her all the various ways impeding federal agents would go poorly for her. The guy talking waved his hand with his index finger pointing in Gladys's general direction, emphasizing his points.

In a way, though, it was kind of funny. We were down-wind of them, and the scents carried on the breeze told us they were plain-jane, vanilla humans. I had no idea how old Gladys was, but even a newly adult pup could ruin ten humans' day; the six surrounding her wouldn't be much of an obstacle if she decided to end the farce and go back to her diner.

I eased to a stop behind the suits and crossed my arms,

putting on what I hoped was my best 'unhappy Alpha' expression.

Gladys pointed at me, saying, "Boys and girls, the one you need to speak with is right behind you. I just run the diner."

One of the suits—a woman—glanced behind her and saw us. The suit standing closest to Gladys tilted his head to the side and replied, "Come on. That old trick?"

The woman who saw us tapped the talker on the shoulder, but he brushed her off.

"Child," Gladys said, her voice almost weary, "I'm getting tired of repeating myself, and you're keeping me from my business. You have no concept of what I am or even how old I am, so I suggest you get your finger out of my face before I bite it off and make you regret ever being born. Or... I suppose I could just stand here and watch the guy who runs the town wipe the asphalt with you."

"Now, see here," the man replied, "that kind of attitude will only—"

"Gladys," I interrupted the man, "go back to the diner. I'll handle this."

One of the suits moved as if to stop her, and I raised an eyebrow. Our eyes locked. He let Gladys pass.

"Show me some identification," I said, my arms crossed over my chest.

The man who had been accosting Gladys took a few steps toward me. "You are impeding—"

"I'll do more than impede you in just a few seconds unless I see ID."

"You do not have the authority to—"

I said one word, "Sis."

Vicki recited something that made me think of Ancient Sumerian, and each of the people in muddy suits swayed on their feet as rings of pastel-colored light particles swirled around their heads in halos.

"Who are you?" Vicki asked.

"I'm Ronald Tomlinson," the man said, gazing at Vicki with unbridled adoration in his eyes.

"Okay. Who do you work for?"

Ronnie shook his head. "Oh, I'm not supposed to tell *anyone* that, Mistress, but you are such a wonderful person. We're United States Black Ops. Deep, deep Black Ops. Our unit existed before the big merger that created the Joint Special Operations Command, and somehow, everyone kind of missed us. I'm not really sure who we answer to anymore, if anyone."

Vicki nodded. "What brings you to Precious?"

"You will not believe this, Mistress. You won't believe this at all. We have credible intelligence that there is a woman living in the country who can turn into a giant bird. We have been tasked with capturing her and returning her to our facility for study."

My sister and I shared a look, and I nodded my head for her to proceed. "What about the treaty between the United States and the Shifter Nation of North America? I thought it was one of the country's oldest treaties. What you're doing kind of violates that, right?"

The man blew a raspberry and made a dismissive wave. "You really believe that old wives' tale? We haven't been able to get anyone to verify that such a treaty ever existed, let alone *show* it to us. Next, you'll be telling us there are actually Magi and Fae and all that other stuff."

"So, where's your facility then?"

Ronnie beamed. "A couple hours north of the Grand Tetons. We're buried under one of the mountains in the Rockies. I've seen builders' plaques dating back to the early Cold War, and we've added and expanded over the years since then."

"Why don't we go to the town's admin building?" I

pointed to it down the street. "We can be much more comfortable and discuss things further."

We could also set up the conference room to record everything. I wanted everything safely stored away somewhere it could be retrieved and verified at will.

"Oh, that sounds like a lovely idea, sir," Ronnie chirped. "I'm sure Mistress is getting tired, standing out here in the sun."

I turned and moved close to Gabrielle, whispering low enough that the humans around us couldn't hear. "Get everything set up to record in the conference room."

Gabrielle nodded and jogged ahead of us.

Then, I asked Karleen to wait until we were inside the conference room, then get Sloane settled in the hotel. It didn't look like clearing her name was going to be as much of a chore as I first thought.

OVER THE NEXT FEW HOURS, we collected an obscene amount of information about who these six individuals were, who their overall unit was, and what they knew or didn't know about Sloane and shifters in general. One of the men confessed to murdering Mr. and Mrs. Higgins, and the apparent leader admitted to setting the fires. The fact they thought the greater shifter community was a hoax perpetrated on the fledgling federal government struck me as either rather odd or rather sad, possibly a little of both.

Once we had the pertinent information, we took them to the county jail, where the sheriff and his deputies processed them before providing each person a set of pleasant orange sweats. More than one deputy couldn't believe how compliant they were. The second each person occupied their own individual cell, having willingly surrendered any and all hidden items they might have used to attempt escape, Vicki canceled the charm spells and left them to stew in despair over how much information they gave us.

Outside the jail, I thanked my sister for her help with a brotherly hug. The moment she teleported back to our grandparents' house, I headed off in search of Alistair.

I FOUND him just as he locked up his office for the evening. He took one look at me and unlocked the door, waving for me to join him. Then, invited me to sit. I sat in the one my grandfather had occupied when he came to Precious looking for me, and Alistair sat in the one opposite it.

"All right, lad. Even as old a wolf as I am can tell you have something on your mind. How can I help?"

I took twenty minutes outlining everything we knew at that point, starting with seeing Karleen return to town with someone on her motorcycle and carrying through to turning the six suits over to the sheriff.

When I finally ran down, Alistair leaned back against his seat and shook his head. "Damn, lad. You don't do anything in half measures."

I shrugged. "So, what do you think? How should we handle this? Take this to the Shifter Council for them to take to the Feds?"

Alistair looked up at the ceiling, his eyes flicking side to side. I had only seen him this deep in thought one other time. After several moments, he brought his eyes back to me and nodded.

"Yes, Wyatt. That is exactly what we do. It's the only response that doesn't at least carry bad connotations for us. I'll need to check a map to be sure, but it doesn't sound like this facility of theirs is inside one of our territories. So, if we attack them in response to what they've done, we're de facto attacking the United States. That's not an anthill I want to kick over."

I nodded my understanding and sighed. "Okay. I'll get you the recordings for you to take to the—"

"Oh, no, lad. For something like this, *you* need to be there and present the recordings. We might even want to take this Sloane Martinez, so the council can hear that she's honest when she tells her story. Where is she now?"

"She should be in the hotel. Karleen was supposed to take her there from the infirmary once we had all the suits in the admin building's conference room."

"That's good," Alistair remarked. "She should be comfortable until I can get a meeting with the council. It's already too late to make those calls tonight. We might as well get some sleep and start this fresh in the morning."

I smiled as we both stood. "Thank you, Alistair. I appreciate all your help and counsel."

Alistair clapped me on the shoulder as we left his office. "Think nothing of it, lad. Your grandfather saved my life many times over during the war. The least I can do is help you find your way."

4

K arleen and Vicki stood on the sidewalk outside a massive high-rise in the heart of a major urban center. People lined the sidewalk around them, and the first thing Karleen noticed was the ambient assault on her sense of smell.

"Goodness," Karleen growled, fighting the urge to scowl, "where are we? The very air reeks."

Vicki scrunched up her nose and nodded. "It's bad enough even I can smell it, and I'm not quite sure where we are. A city, obviously, but they just gave me the building's coordinates where they wanted to meet me."

Karleen shot Vicki a look, her eyebrows inching upward. "You can teleport to geographical coordinates? Can all Magi do that?"

Vicki grinned and bobbed her head. "As long as they're Master-certified or higher. I passed my Master exam about three weeks ago now."

"Congratulations," Karleen replied. "Now, come on. Hopefully, the inside smells better than the outside."

MITCHELL CAVENDISH STEPPED into the security office and walked straight to the staffer who summoned him. "Report."

"Sir, Victoria Magnusson is here, and she's right on time," the young woman said. "She has someone with her, but whoever it is doesn't come up in any of the databases we can access. Nothing on the shifter or Magi databases, FBI facial recognition, DOD search, NCIC, VICAP, INTERPOL... nothing."

Mitchell looked at the dark haired woman standing beside Victoria Magnusson. Part of him wanted to know who she was and where Magnusson found her. He certainly wished he knew what her capabilities were. Whoever she was, she moved like she knew her body. Ex-Mossad, maybe?

In the long run, it didn't matter. One woman would *not* stop them. As soon as Magnusson stepped into the room they had specifically for meetings like this, the conclusion was foregone. If Victoria Magnusson ever wanted to breathe air as a free woman again, she would turn over all data and information related to making the various types of -bane ammunition.

"Bring the cell jammer to standby," Mitchell said. "Activate it the moment Jettrey ushers them into the room."

"Yes, sir."

THE BUILDING INTERIOR didn't smell as bad as the outside. For that, Karleen was thankful. But something was... not right.

She and Vicki arrived on the 30th floor without any problems, and the sign by the door said these people were State Department. The more people Karleen encountered, though, the more she was certain these people were not run-of-the-mill government staffers. For one thing, when they passed someone, the person's heart rate kicked up. Not a lot, and certainly not close to the level of a fear response. Maybe momentary shock of recognition? Like maybe they *knew* who Vicki was?

Total speculation, but Karleen needed something to do besides watch angles and corners and doors as she followed Vicki through the corridors.

Jeffrey, their guide, stopped in front of a door labeled 'Conference Room 4' and opened the door for them. He was handsome enough for a human in his late 20s to early 30s, but when Karleen put him beside Wyatt in her mind, poor Jeffrey just couldn't compete. The poor kid couldn't give a decent roar, and he smelled like he bathed in some pungent kind of cologne.

A large oval conference table dominated the space. It looked like natural wood with a dark stain, and it was big enough that thirty-odd chairs ringed it. The walls were a pleasant off-white, and the carpet was the commercial stuff that might have been a centimeter thick, if that.

Vicki staggered a bit as she stepped into the room, and Jeffrey closed the door behind them. The sound of the door's lock clicking was so loud, even Vicki should have heard it. Vicki seemed very unsteady on her feet as she went straight to a chair and sat.

The first thing Karleen noticed in the room's almost unnatural quiet was the faint hum of electronic devices. Humans couldn't hear it. Either too faint or a frequency outside their range. But that faint hum was either listening or recording devices or both.

Karleen pulled her phone out of her hip pocket and saw it showed no signal. She put that aside and brought up a notes app and typed out a message.

I can hear electronics. Assume they're listening, watching, or both.

Vicki read the text and nodded. Then, she held out her hand for the phone. Karleen obliged her and watched her tap out her own message.

There's some kind of anti-magic field in this room. Felt it right inside the door.

Well, damn. Someone was serious about something. Karleen looked at the wall across the room from them. It *looked* like simple, painted sheetrock. But there was no way to know if that was true without trying to break through it.

Karleen made a slow scan of the room with her eyes. No obvious cameras or even pin holes that might hide them. No smoke detectors. Just drop ceiling and florescent lights. Two doors: the one they entered and a second almost directly opposite it.

The far door clicked, then opened. Two people entered. One man and one woman. Both wore suits and neutral non-expressions. Karleen couldn't smell any gunpowder, so they must not have been armed. Probably trusting in the anti-magic field to protect them. Idiots.

Before anyone spoke, Karleen picked up her phone and opened the voice memo app. She already had a bad feeling about the entire situation and wanted a record of what transpired.

"Good afternoon, Miss Magnusson," the man said. "I am Mitchell Cavendish, and this is my associate, Leah Brenner. We're here today to discuss the Magi Assembly's repeated refusal to supply -bane ammunition to various countries around the world."

"The recent unpleasantness in the Pacific Northwest," Leah interjected, "has proven beyond any doubt that humans are at a disadvantage when confronting Magi and shifters."

Mitchell nodded his agreement before returning his eyes

to Vicki. He reached inside his suit jacket and produced a folded document inside a blue manuscript cover.

"This is a court order requiring you to hand over all information necessary to create -bane ammunition or weapons. If you fail to do so, the order also grants us authority to classify you as an enemy combatant, giving us the authority to hold you without due process until such time as you comply."

Vicki lifted one hand and waved a finger in a 'send it here' gesture. The man slid the document across the table, which was so glossy and polished the whole surface was near frictionless. She read through the document. Then, she produced her phone and flipped through the document again, taking a picture of each page.

"What are you doing?" Leah asked.

As soon as she had a high-res picture of each page, Vicki sent the document sliding back across the table. "I wanted a record of it in case that document disappears when you realize just how big a pile you've stepped in."

Mitchell and Leah shared a look. Then, Mitchell turned back to us. "So, you won't comply?"

"No," Vicki answered. "That is Magi-proprietary information. Beyond that, you need a Magi to do it. A hedge wizard or witch can't."

An almost-predatory smile curled Mitchell's lips. "We have a Magi to do the work, and I don't mean you. We only need you to provide the information."

Vicki and I shared a look. Almost like we planned it, we lifted our phones in unison and snapped pictures of Mitchell and Leah.

Mitchell frowned at us. One of his hands curled into a fist. "Look... stop with the pictures already. We have anti-Magi restraints that we will use when we take you out of this room. You seem to think you're just walking out of here, but that's not the case. Until you give us what we want, the only place you and your mercenary friend are going is prison."

"Mercenary?" Karleen asked. "You think I'm a mercenary?"

"Ex-Mossad, probably," Leah remarked, "but yes."

Vicki erupted in laughter. "Oh, that is priceless. So, you're telling us you plan to hold us against our will if I do not agree?"

Now, Mitchell and Leah shared a look as if they questioned Vicki's mental capacity.

"Yes," Mitchell answered, "that is exactly what I'm saying."

"Even though you realize doing so violates the US-Magi treaty?"

Leah made a dismissive wave. "The Magi Assembly won't care about some slip of a girl, even if she is Connor Magnusson's granddaughter. The information is more valuable to us than whatever settlement we have to make with the Assembly to smooth this over."

Vicki nodded. "Well, I certainly take exception to *that*. I am not 'some slip of a girl.' But so be it. I think we're done here." She turned to Karleen. "Do you mind?"

Karleen stood, grabbed the closest chair, and turned to the wall. Most wall studs used sixteen-inch centers. She had no idea if that was the case in city high-rises, but it seemed like the perfect opportunity to find out.

"Hey!" Mitchell shouted as Karleen drew the chair back over her shoulder like a batter in the World Series.

"What are you doing?" Leah added.

Karleen paid them no mind as she swung the back of the chair at a spot she hoped held no wall studs. The chair's strike cracked the sheetrock, and Karleen tossed the chair aside.

"Stop right there!" Mitchell shouted, standing and placing

clenched fists on the tabletop. "If you persist, you'll only have more charges added."

Karleen peeled the sheetrock back, revealing insulation beneath a mesh of wires. She reached out and touched her fingertip to it. Electricity zapped her, but it wasn't anything she couldn't handle. The problem was that the wires were almost piano wire. They would shred her hands if she tried to... wait.

Mitchell and Leah jumped to their feet and hustled to the door on their side. They both started pounding fists on the door, demanding attention.

Karleen grabbed another close chair and snapped off one of its legs. The chair leg tapered from wide up by the seat to barely wider than a quarter where the leg rested against the floor. She rammed the narrow end of the chair leg into the wire mesh and pulled it down toward the floor with all her might.

The thin wires couldn't stand up to her strength. Sparks crackled and flew as wire after wire snapped. Some kind of alarm started blaring.

"Hey... my phone has signal now," Vicki said.

"Call your grandparents," Karleen replied. "I'm still working on getting us out of here."

The wires no longer carried electricity, and Karleen was able to use the chair leg to bend the mesh back away from the insulation. All that was left was the nasty business of pulling out the insulation. Karleen grimaced and shook her head. She *hated* fiberglass.

She jabbed the chair leg into the insulation as high as she could reach against the backdrop of Vicki calling her grandparents while Mitchell shouted for her to put down the phone. It took some work, but Karleen managed to rake most of the insulation out of the wall. She found what looked like more sheetrock. Lifting the chair leg one more time, she swung the thick end against the sheetrock and broke through. She saw a glimpse of what looked like the hallway where they followed Jeffery to the conference room.

Karleen turned back to Vicki. "Come on. I see the hallway."

"You'll never make it out of the building alive," Mitchell snarled.

Vicki made no reply as she stepped to Karleen's side, and Karleen pushed her through the wall first. Strands of the wire mesh tugged at her clothing as she passed. Then followed. As soon as Vicki passed through the wall, she felt her magic again... just as six or eight men in suits with earbuds charged around a distant corner. Karleen pushed through the wall behind her, and Vicki took her hand. She recited a series of words in Ancient Sumerian, and both she and Karleen vanished from the hallway.

KARLEEN STOOD in what appeared to be a study or office. A massive desk that looked sturdy enough to prop up the Empire State Building despite being older than dirt dominated the space. Woven rugs lined the floors, and wood paneling with a light stain lined the walls, minus the ten-feet-tall windows with arched tops. Hints of citrus hung in the air.

Connor Magnusson paced from wall to wall behind the desk, a phone held to his ear while he gestured with the other hand. "No, Pierre, this wasn't some kind of mistake. Vicki sent me pictures of the document once the cell jammer went down. Yes, she's fine. She and her friend just popped into my study. But as much as I appreciate your well-wishes, that's not the point. We have a *treaty* with these people. This is not how friends act, let alone allies, and I vote we convene the Assembly to determine our response."

Connor paused for a moment. "No, Pierre, I don't really care what the vampires think of it. They will just try to spin the whole situation to their advantage and turn their coats mid-discussion if they feel that's the most advantageous for them. Let's just leave them out of it."

Another pause to listen. "Again, Pierre, I think you may be underestimating the amount of support we have among shifters. At least shifters in North America. I've already informed the Assembly that my grandson is the feline primo-genitor, and he's growing into a rather proficient leader. He and Alistair are taking another matter to the Shifter Council in a couple days, so we could ask him to add a point to the agenda."

Another pause. "Yes, yes... I understand that you lost family in the last Shifter-Magi war. So did I. So did Maeve. And so did almost every other Magi family. But the shifters lost people, too. I've said for years that there's no point in fighting old wars. There never has been. That hatred you carry will be a poison to your soul, Pierre."

Another pause. "Thank you. I need to speak with my granddaughter before I continue making calls. I want to hear about it from her. Thank you for your time, Pierre."

Connor pulled the phone away from his ear and thumbed the control to end the call. He dropped the phone on the desk and crossed the room to pull Vicki into a tight hug. After several moments, he released her and stepped back, turning to Karleen.

"Miss Vesper, I do not have the words to express how grateful I am that you were there for Vicki today. I have no doubt at all that your presence enabled her to remain free and get word of this back to us."

Karleen blushed and looked away for a moment, shaking

her head. "It was nothing, sir. Even if I didn't think of Vicki as a friend, she's Wyatt's sister, and Wyatt... well... Wyatt is rather special to me."

"I'll make sure he knows what you did today," Vicki interjected, adding a conspiratorial wink. "Should make him *very* happy and grateful."

Connor chuckled at his granddaughter's antics, then gestured toward seats. "If you don't mind, I'd like for you take me through it, step by step. Tell me everything."

5

In the end, we couldn't devise a method of getting Sloane into Chicago with any kind of timeliness. The warrant out for her made most forms of transportation unwise, and trying to make a road trip of it seemed equally inadvisable. So... when Mohammed can't go to the mountain, the mountain goes to Mohammed.

Three days after Alistair contacted the Shifter Council, twenty-four councilors arrived in Precious. I had two local volunteers per councilor waiting to help them to the hotel with their luggage and show them around town if they wished. As the councilors stepped out of their respective luxury SUVs, none of them seemed particularly enthused about the visit, but none of them seemed outright hostile, either.

One of the feline councilors who brought Thomas Carlyle to Precious made a point of approaching me first. Her expression seemed a mix of playfulness and weary traveler.

"Alpha Wyatt," she said, extending her hand, "were you aware there are shifter towns and territories that have *never* seen even one councilor visit?"

I gave her a respectful handshake and grinned. "They must be very boring places, then, Councilor. We have you rooms at the hotel here in town, and I trust you've had a word with your associates about what will happen if they mistreat any of my people?"

The feline councilor laughed. "No need to worry. The councilors who came with me are the only hardy souls willing to brave your potential wrath. *Everyone* remembers Thomas Carlyle. I give my word, Alpha Wyatt, we'll be on our best, most polite behavior."

I gestured to the waiting volunteers, and they descended upon the councilors with smiles, handshakes, and welcome. The feline councilor watched the happy chaos for a moment or two, then turned back to me.

"You certainly have a way to make people feel welcome. I'm not sure any town has ever welcomed us like this."

"Well, I made sure everyone knew *why* you're here. Sloane has spent most of the time since she arrived here in her hotel room, regardless of anyone's attempts to draw her out. But on those rare occasions we have succeeded in getting her outside, she's made a good impression. The people who have interacted with her like her."

The feline councilor's vibrant blue eyes locked on me. She held her silence for a few moments. "And you're so sure she's a victim in all of this? You're sure she had nothing to do with what happened in Nebraska?"

"Oh, she was very much involved in what happened in Nebraska," I countered. "None of us are denying that. But those black ops people came for her. She was just living her life as a farmhand. Wait until you hear the interviews we had with them. They wanted Sloane because they believed she could turn into a giant bird."

"And can she? Shift into a giant bird, that is."

I shrugged. "No clue. Haven't asked. In the long run, it's immaterial to the situation. All this happened because of what those black ops people *believed*. It doesn't matter if it's true, and I'd think we would be very interested in stopping people from hunting shifters for research anyway."

"You're right about that. We will not be humans' lab experiments."

"Come on. Let's get you settled. We can hit this fresh in the morning."

KARLEEN FOUND SLOANE WATCHING THE COUNCILORS' arrival from the lobby of the town's admin building. The woman stood at the window with her arms wrapped around her midriff, and Karleen could see the tension in... well... not just Sloane's shoulders but her whole body as soon as she laid eyes on the woman.

"Hey," Karleen said as she arrived at Sloane's side. She maintained a respectful distance, aiming for supportive but not crowding or pressuring. "How are you holding up?"

Sloane never took her eyes away from the scene unfolding outside. "Will they help me?"

"I don't know, honestly. In the long run, though, that doesn't really matter."

Now, Sloane pulled her gaze away from the window to look at Karleen. "How can you say that? They're *councilors*. They govern the Shifter Nation."

"And Wyatt does not care. They're not holy or untouchable to him. He's already unseated one of them, and it was the guy most of them are—or were—afraid of."

"Thomas Carlyle."

Karleen nodded. "Yep. So, you see, I'm not sure 'Will the councilors help me' is the right question. I think the better question to ask is, 'Will *Wyatt* help me,' and there's no doubt of that in my mind at all."

Sloane turned back to the window, where Wyatt and one of the councilors were just now leaving the street to walk toward the hotel. After a few seconds of no response, she absently nodded.

THE QUESTION of where to hold the meeting with the councilors proved to be an interesting one. On the one side, everyone would technically fit in the town hall. *However*, if they asked Sloane to shift, would she still fit inside the space? It was an older building, and the ceilings were only eight feet. Sure, it seemed a little odd to be worried about a shifter's animal form not fitting inside the town hall, but no one in town had ever seen Sloane shift.

In the end, I settled on the amphitheater in the park behind the town's admin building. Anyone who wanted to attend the meeting with the councilors could sit in the stands, and the performance area was more than sufficient for all the councilors and anyone they might call to give testimony.

I stood at the top of the amphitheater stands, overseeing the preparations, when I felt the presence of someone at my side. I glanced that way and saw Sloane.

"Morning." I tried for pleasant, genial tone... but it was difficult when all I really wanted was to go back to sleep. I was not a morning person, not by any stretch. Waking up with Karleen and Gabrielle snuggled against me certainly didn't encourage me to leave the bed, either.

Sloane nodded. "Yes, it certainly is. Karleen said it didn't matter if the councilors didn't want to help me."

"That sounds like her, and... well... she's not wrong. I'd

like to work within the accepted channels of shifter society, but if that isn't possible, I have a few other contacts we can use to sort out your situation."

We fell into a companionable silence, and people started arriving for the 'festivities.' After several minutes, someone arrived on my right, and when I turned, it took all my willpower not to gape.

"*Miles?*" I'm sure my tone betrayed my utter shock at seeing the old groundskeeper from my grandparents' estate. He stood a respectful distance off my right side, his thumbs hooked into his belt loops. His beard still touched his sternum, but there was no mistaking the intelligence or the intensity behind his eyes.

"Mornin', lad. Young Miss said ye be havin' some excitement around these parts today, and since I haven't seen yer town yet, it seemed like the perfect time."

The last time I'd talked with Miles, he strongly hinted that he was the Merlin of myth and legend. He didn't come right out and say it, but I left the exchange certain that's who he was. So, given that... what could possibly be in store for today that *Merlin* would call it excitement?

Talk about something not boding well...

"Well, you're always welcome here, Miles. Once we sort out this business with the Council, I'd be happy to show you around town."

Miles scoffed and made a dismissive wave. "Lad, don't ye have better things to do than show an old man around a town you're still getting to know yerself? I've been exploring the world on me own for more years than ye'd believe. I think I'll be just fine."

Of course, *he* would be just fine. This was the guy whose response to Vicki's abduction Alistair said would be 'apocalyptic.' I wasn't worried about Miles. I was worried about *the town*.

"Well, just let me know if anyone gives you any grief." Very fervent hope, there, that no one would.

Miles smiled. "Again, lad, ye've no need to worry. I'll be fine."

I really, really hoped I had no need to worry, but Miles was definitely right about having other things that required my attention. This meeting not the least of them. From the looks of it, Alistair's people already had the conference table with an appropriate number of chairs in place.

A few townsfolk meandered into the amphitheater and chose a seat. Over the space of an hour, the few became several.

"Well, lad," Miles remarked, as he watched the milling mass of people approaching the amphitheater, "I should seek a seat, lest the choice pickings get claimed ahead o' me."

With that, the old groundskeeper—who looked like Santa Claus after a crash diet—made his way to the front row and chose the seat in the very center of the entire space.

"Where should I be?" Sloane asked, her voice hesitant.

That... was a very good question. She was the star witness, as it were. Not a good idea for her to be too far.

I gestured toward Miles. "Might as well have a seat somewhere on the front row. It'll simplify matters when it's time for you to tell the councilors your story. If you're nervous, you could always sit with Miles. He's a childhood friend of mine."

Sloane nodded her agreement and walked to the opposite staircase from the one Miles used. She was halfway to the front row when the feline councilor arrived at my side.

"Good morning, Alpha Wyatt." She almost purred the words.

"Morning, Councilor."

After a few moments, she said, "You've arranged quite the venue here."

"From what everyone tells me, the amphitheater is normally used for outdoor entertainment, but since none of us have seen Sloane shift, I figured it presented the least risk to her. I don't know what happens to a shifter whose animal is larger than the space they're shifting in."

The feline councilor shuddered. "Nothing good. I promise you that." The other councilors began trickling in, and the feline councilor sighed. "Well, if you'll forgive me, I must leave you to officiate this affair. Maybe we could chat over food later?"

I wasn't sure what to make of her question. I suppose it could have been a thinly veiled advance, but at the same time, maybe all she wanted was to talk about how I was settling in. Might as well find out.

"Sure. I do believe I could spare the time, and shifters are always hungry."

"Oh, you have *no* idea," she replied over a playful wink. Then, she sauntered off to take charge of her associates.

A familiar scent heralded the arrival of Gabrielle right before her arm snaked around my waist and pulled me tight. I leaned over and kissed her in greeting.

"She's going to be trouble," Gabrielle remarked, after returning my kiss with one of her own. "I'll have to speak to Karleen about her."

"Where is Karleen? I thought she'd be here to help soothe Sloane's nerves."

Gabrielle leaned into me for a moment, then took a half-step back so she could lift her gaze to meet mine. "She was still finishing breakfast when I left the diner, but don't worry. She'll be along."

A big yawn took me by surprise.

"Bored with us all so soon?"

I chuckled. "Not even a little bit. I didn't get a lot of sleep after the two of you spent several hours wearing me out."

"Go get some food; there's still time. You still skip breakfast too much. A human can get away with it for the most part, but shifters can't. Seriously… do you *want* to pass out while you're addressing the councilors?"

There was no denying she had the right of it. Or even worse, what if I sat down to await the call to speak and nodded off? That wouldn't look so good, either. "Okay. You win. I'll dash over to the diner for some quick food."

"No need," Karleen said, and the smells of Gladys's diner accompanied her words.

I turned and found Karleen standing a few feet away. She held two food containers that Gladys used for to-go orders. Right that second, I wasn't sure which I was happier to see: Karleen or the food.

"Gladys told me she hadn't seen you in the diner yet," Karleen continued, "and she wouldn't let me leave without sending your breakfast favorites with me."

I gave Karleen a quick kiss as I snagged the food and flopped in the aisle seat of the top row. The world soon faded around me as I sated my hunger. By the time all the councilors arrived, the sustenance had buoyed my spirits, and I no longer felt like finding a convenient shade tree to go back to sleep. I conveyed the containers to a convenient trash receptacle and joined Gabrielle, Karleen, and Alistair in the stage-left side of the front row.

"The councilors will expect you to present the case, as it were," Alistair said as I arrived. "Are you ready?"

I nodded. "It's not that difficult. My favorite advantage shifters have over humans is our ability to tell when a person lies. I'll explain the circumstances as I know them and turn the floor over to them to go where they will with it."

"Is Sloane aware they'll ask her to shift? I don't see how they'd go through with all this without it."

Karleen took this one. "Yes. We've spoken about it.

Frankly, it's been so long since she's felt safe enough to shift without it being an emergency that she's looking forward to it. You might want to whisper to them that they should hold off on that request until they've asked her everything they want. The way she talked, I wouldn't put it past Sloane to go for a joy ride... er, flight... with it being her first shift in quite a while."

The sound of a gavel striking a surface drew my attention, and I saw the feline shifter tapping a striking block.

"Be it known to all present," she spoke in a hall-filling voice, "that I hereby call this exigent crisis council to order. Alpha Wyatt, please approach and present the matter that called us here today."

I took the few steps necessary to stand at the unoccupied edge of the conference table and conveyed all that I knew of Sloane's situation, including both my and Karleen's assertion that we detected no lies when Sloane told her story. When I played the recorded interrogations of the black ops people, I saw a wide range of reactions: fear, anger, anxiety, amusement, and more.

After I concluded my remarks, the feline councilor said, "Regardless of whether Sloane is one of us, we have a treaty with the Americans for just this reason. I personally feel there can be no doubt that this requires a direct and unambiguous response, and neither do I feel we should dawdle in delivering it."

Another councilor—this one a bear shifter—nodded her agreement. "Undoubtedly. I for one would rather go to war than be some scientist's experiment in a lab. Beyond that, I would like to hear from the aggrieved party, but I want to be very clear in that I am not doubting Alpha Wyatt's honor or integrity at all. It is simply that I feel all of us need to scent and hear the truth of her words from her own mouth. It is one thing to challenge Alpha Wyatt's veracity, however stupidly foolish that might be, but no one would challenge all of us."

Heads nodded around the table, and the feline councilor looked from one side to the other before nodding as well. "So be it. By general acclamation, this crisis council calls Sloane Martinez to speak her piece."

I yielded the floor and returned to sit between Gabrielle and Karleen, and each was quick to claim one of my hands with one of theirs, despite the formal ambiance of the proceedings.

Miles leaned close and whispered something to Sloane, then she nodded and stood. She approached the conference table and adopted a relaxed stance.

"Please, begin," the feline councilor said, adding a gesture.

Sloane recounted her story, taking the councilors through her time at the Higgins farm including the arrival of the black ops people. Then, she described the following months she spent looking for Karleen because she wanted to disappear from the world, and finally concluded with the events that led her to collapse on a road outside of Precious.

"Is there any truth to the belief that you are an avian shifter?" a councilor asked. She seemed especially earnest on the topic, but I guessed that had something to do with her being an avian, too.

"Yes," Sloane answered simply.

Now, the councilor's poker face slipped, and eagerness suffused her expression. "Will you show us… please?"

Sloane took a deep breath and nodded. Without waiting any further, she proceeded to strip and crouched. When she shifted, I felt like I knew what Gabrielle must've felt all those weeks ago when I had my first shift in the diner. Sloane's bird was *huge*, easily twelve feet tall if she was an inch. Each toe of her feet looked at least as thick as the business end of a Louisville Slugger, and her feathers were a russet brown with faint black mottling. Her head and beak held hints of hawk, falcon, and eagle, but it was like recognizing a child in the child's great-grandparent.

The councilors' expressions all betrayed shock, with hints of a wide range of additional emotions. The avian councilor gazed at Sloane in rapt adoration. The audience looked on in thinly veiled interest, but their exposure to a Smilodon trotting through the town's park and hills might have adjusted the bar for what it took to produce shock.

"She's beautiful," escaped Gabrielle's lips in a loud whisper tinged with awe.

Sloane turned to look at us and bobbed her head in an exaggerated nod of thanks.

Before I realized what was happening, Miles stood at Sloane's side, his hand held up as if to touch her as he said, "May I, lass?"

Sloane turned back to him and bobbed another nod. Miles stroked the feathers along Sloane's side as his eyes trailed from her head to her feet.

"Och, such a beautiful *èan* ye are, lass. It's been long, long years since I last beheld one of yer kind, and I feared I never would again. A beauty like ye deserves to be in the air. Go. Enjoy yerself."

Sloane cast a glance at the assembled councilors who were only now regaining their composure.

"Never ye mind about them. If they have an issue that persists past Wyatt's defense of ye, they'll face me, and I promise ye they do not want that at all. So, off wi' ye now. 'Tis a beautiful day for flying methinks."

It didn't escape me that Miles slipped as he spoke with Sloane and allowed his odd accent to color his speech more than usual.

Sloane bobbed her head in one last nod, and Miles backed away to give her room. Sloane stretched her wings, shadowing a span of at least thirty feet, and leaped into the air. Each flap of her wings carried her higher, and when she was far enough away, she cried her joy to the world, a powerful *scree* that would've ruptured eardrums if she were still in the amphitheater.

It was Buddy Carrington who filled the awed silence that blanketed the area after Sloane's departure.

"At least she flew toward the forest and hills. As big as she is, she'd crack a windshield if she dive-bombed a car."

6

S ilence reigned in the amphitheater for several minutes while we all watched Sloane fly into the distance. Once she was little more than a speck on the horizon, the feline councilor cleared her throat and tapped her gavel once more.

"I think it's safe to say we have just witnessed the first avian primogenitor in recent times. I open the floor to my esteemed fellow councilors to begin debate on the best course of action regarding Sloane's situation with mortal law enforcement."

The avian councilor was quick to speak. "It should go without saying that we defend her. I mean... would any of you let some shadowy black ops group railroad Alpha Wyatt or Primogenitor Karleen or any other shifter into a black site's laboratory?"

"No," the bear councilor—a sassy, no-nonsense woman from Manitoba—replied. "If we allow them to do that to one of us, it won't be long until they're doing it to *all* of us, but we also need to handle this respectfully and with care. The black site identified in Alpha Wyatt's interrogation lies outside shifter territory, and if we gather the Nation and attack, we will be committing an act of war against the United States. We have shed blood, lost shifters, lost friends, lost family protecting the United States ever since its founding. Attacking them now—even over something like this—is not how friends, let alone allies, treat one another.

"Now, I may be an old bear who isn't current on all the new fads and phases of global society, but I try to live my life according to one axiom that is as fundamental as water being wet and the sky being blue: treat others as you want to be treated. I think that should be our first step. I think treating them like we would want to be treated—in this instance—takes the form of telling them what's happening and giving them the chance to stop it."

Whether the other councilors agreed or were just reluctant to challenge a polar bear shifter, they soon nodded their assent.

"Should we take that to mean you support sending a delegation to Washington, D.C., to speak to someone in the US government?" the feline councilor asked.

The bear councilor replied with a sagely nod. "Yes. We might want to read the text of our treaty with them to see who our point of contact is and start there."

I immediately saw a potential pitfall with that idea. I stood and raised my hand.

"Yes, Alpha Wyatt?" the feline councilor asked.

"Councilors, it is possible that the point of contact specified in our treaty may no longer exist. I don't know precisely *when* we signed the treaty with the United States, but the government has gone through a lot of shuffling and re-organization down through the years. We may have to track whatever office is specified in the treaty across the successive years to learn where the responsibility now lies."

The bear councilor frowned. "It hasn't been *that* long

since we signed the treaty. Surely, someone would know who's responsible for maintaining relations with us."

It took all my willpower to keep from grinning. "Esteemed Councilor, while I would never be so rude as to ask a lady's age, the United States Constitution has been in effect for around two-hundred-thirty to two-hundred-forty years. Sure... that's nothing to shifters or even some Magi, but regular humans even three generations back didn't personally experience the founding of the country. I give it even odds that whoever we're supposed to contact doesn't even *know* shifters exist, let alone that we have a treaty with the United States. Does the Shifter Nation of North America even have an ambassador to them? That's who would normally handle approaching the government about this."

Now, the councilors all looked to one another. I heard whispered questions back and forth on the ambassador issue, but apparently, none of the current councilors' tenures extended back to World War II, which was the last time the Shifter Nation had any formal contact with the United States government.

After several minutes, the feline councilor turned back to me. "Alpha Wyatt, you raise excellent concerns. It seems we must examine the text of the treaty before we can proceed. Will you shelter Sloane Martinez until such time as we can devise a best path to rectifying this matter?"

"She will always have a place here with us as long as she's a good citizen," I replied, "but if I may, I would ask that the Shifter Council not take too long determining the best path. It won't be long before the black-ops people's superiors question why they haven't checked in, and I would hate for the matter to escalate due to simple inaction."

Several councilors' eyes narrowed at my statement and implied challenge.

"Should we take that to mean you intend to act on your own after a given period of time?" the bear councilor asked.

I gave them my best innocent grin as I said, "Esteemed Councilor, I would like nothing better than to live my life separated from all the politics and stupidity I have witnessed since becoming a shifter... just like Primogenitor Karleen did for many years. But since the Shifter Council decided in its supposed wisdom that I should be Alpha of Precious and Godwin County without my consent and against my wishes, I see no reason to act in any other way than how my conscience and personal values dictate. If that means using my contacts to approach federal law enforcement on my own, then I shall do so utterly unconcerned with how ineffectual or pointless it might make the Shifter Council appear."

The bear councilor's expression shifted into an angry glare. "You *dare* challenge us in such a manner? Especially no older than you are? I will—"

"Before ye finish that sentence, lass," Miles said, moving to stand beside me, "ye should take a moment to step back and consider just how precarious yer intended path may be. Polar bear or not, I would put my money on the lad here in any confrontation between the two of ye. It might not be the wisest course to see a challenge where none exists. Instead, perhaps this be merely a consequence of forcing a primogenitor into your power structure."

"And just who are you to be inserting yourself into these discussions?" the feline councilor asked. "This is the second time you've interfered."

"Lass, I be known in this time and place as Miles. I work as a groundskeeper on the estate of the lad's grandparents."

Miles lifted his left hand and wove his fingers and thumb through an intricate series of gestures that he made seem as nothing, a well-trod path he knew as well—or better—than his own face. When he finished, I noticed a sigil etch itself into the conference table's surface, though I was at the wrong angle and distance to see it.

The councilors, however, saw it just fine. By the time the sigil completed its appearance, every councilor was pale. The feline councilor's jaw trembled. The bear councilor's eyes looked wider than a saucer in a tea service. The avian councilor looked primed to sprout feathers and flee the area.

"As for who I be, ye may consider *that* me calling card."

After several minutes of silence interrupted only by the sounds of Nature around the amphitheater, the feline councilor took a breath, saying, "Please, sir, forgive any slight we may have given you."

Now, I really wanted to know what that sigil was *and* what it meant.

"Lass, after ye reach a certain age, all but the most grievous of insults becomes little more than the pitter-patter of raindrops. I would ask ye, though, not to discuss what ye've seen. Ye've no idea how insistent annoying youngsters can be with their worship when they think yer one of their heroes." Miles started to turn away but stopped and turned back to the councilors. "And no, I am *not* a hero, just in case any of ye be thinking otherwise."

With that, Miles turned and left the amphitheater. When he was halfway up the stairs, the sigil carved into the tabletop vanished as if it had never been.

"At this point," the feline councilor said, "I believe the only thing we can do is adjourn this discussion until we have examined our copy of the treaty. Alpha Wyatt, I ask that you give us three days to do so and formulate a response. If you haven't heard from us by then, you may feel free to handle this as you see fit."

"That's fair. I have no problems giving you three days."

"Then, we're adjourned," the feline councilor replied, adding a crack of her gavel.

The councilors all stood, and by the time they reached the stairs out of the amphitheater, half the audience was already gone.

I leaned against the conference table in silence as I watched everyone leave, thoughts swirling through my mind about the situation. Both the potential, snarled furball over our official contact with the federal government and just the whole situation in general. I couldn't shake the feeling that this was not going to be a simple matter, and I feared Sloane might be lost amid the impetus to normalize relations between the shifters and Uncle Sam.

The arrival of Karleen and Gabrielle at my side pulled me out of my concerned thoughts. I leaned close and kissed the neck to my left—Karleen—before turning to kiss the neck at my right—Gabrielle. Not too long after we decided to try a formal relationship between the three of us, Gabrielle and Karleen sat me down for a discussion about how shifters viewed female shifters in relationships, especially females in relationships *with Alphas*, and I left the conversation even less enthused to be shifter than I was going into it.

One of the big things that didn't sit well with me was the perception of the female's status based on position and proximity to the Alpha. The senior or more-dominant female in the relationship would always be closest to the male—or in my case, Alpha—no matter what. I didn't like that at all and wanted no hierarchy, whether actual or perceived, between Gabrielle and Karleen, so we settled on the simple expedient of changing up who was closest to me in any given moment. Some days, Karleen would be on my right and thus appear to be the senior of the two, and other times, it would be Gabrielle. No formal events in the shifter community had happened as yet, so we didn't have any feedback on how the solution would play out in the greater shifter world. But the people of Precious and Godwin County seemed comfortable with it, and honestly, they were the only people I cared about.

The rest of the shifters could just as easily get glad in the same pants they got mad in.

THERE WAS nothing like the feeling of wind whistling through her feathers. Catching a thermal and letting it lift her higher and higher in an ever-widening spiral. It had been so long since Sloane felt relaxed enough—and safe enough—to enjoy a simple flight for nothing more than the sake of flying. For the first time in so, so long, she felt *free*.

A pang of hunger radiated outward from her stomach, and she considered how long it had been since she hunted, something the predator part of her nature dearly loved. Directing her attention to the forest floor, she sought convenient sustenance. The tree cover below ended, and several deer grazed in the revealed meadow. Perfect! She always had loved the taste of venison.

Her enthusiasm overtook her, and a hunting cry escaped her beak as she tucked her wings to her sides and began the dive. Every deer in the field looked up, and moments later, each and every one did something she had never seen before. They all lifted their left forelegs and waved them like they were saying hello. Why would they do that? How would they even know what a 'hello' wave looked... oh, no. Those weren't animals, at least not proper prey animals. They were *shifters*!

Sloane threw her wings as wide as she could and locked her joints. Just like a parachute, they caught the air and ended her dive. She circled the meadow a couple times, doing her best to wave a wing or rock side to side as she soared… anything to communicate that she understood they weren't food. A few of the deer gave her another wave before they resumed grazing like the others.

As she swept through a wide spiral and considered her options, another odd sight caught Sloane's eye. A speck of blaze orange in the next meadow over. As she concentrated on it, the speck resolved into a man carrying a rifle; he wore a blaze orange vest and ball cap. No one had ever discussed rules for humans hunting in the forests around Precious, but those deer—including the three or four bucks with impressive racks of antlers—in the next meadow over were fellow shifters at the very least, maybe even people she knew from her limited explorations of town. She didn't know if she had time to fly back to town for Wyatt, and she wasn't sure if a shifter might survive an accidental headshot. That left only one option… and she'd accept whatever scolding or punishment Wyatt or the councilors felt appropriate.

Once more, she folded her wings to her side as she kept her beak pointed toward the hunter and her eyes locked on him. He was moving slowly and cautiously, and the better part of fifty yards extended between him and the tree line that would've saved him.

As the poor soul grew ever larger in her view, movement in the right corner of her vision drew her attention. A doe stepped out of the forest in front of the hunter. Sloane pulled her focus back to the hunter in time to see him lift his rifle.

No. Not on her watch.

It didn't matter that the doe might not be a shifter. She was only a couple miles from town and easily still within shifter territory, and shifter territories were always no-hunting zones regardless of where they were. She needed a distraction. She filled her lungs with crisp, cool air from a deep breath.

Just as Sloane shrieked a hunting cry to the heavens, the doe threw her legs wide and dropped to the ground as the hunter squeezed the trigger of his rifle. Sloane saw bark explode from a tree trunk a few yards behind the doe as she scrambled to her feet and darted off toward town.

The hunter jerked his head to look toward the sound, and she watched his eyes widen and his jaws drop at the sight of her oh so close. She saw his shoulders tense, and she knew she had to time this just right, lest he escape her. She pushed her feet forward—toes spread wide—and the moment she felt resistance on her hallux talons, she clamped *all* her talons tight and flared her wings, then flapped for all she was worth.

The high-pitched, incoherent scream—not to mention the weight hanging from her legs—told Sloane she was successful. As she gained altitude to keep her prize above the treetops, a thought struck her out of nowhere: she didn't remember if the hunter had his rifle on a sling.

7

As he crossed one of the many meadows in west-central Godwin County, Lewis Mitchell reflected on the state banning hunting in several counties, Godwin being one of them. It made no sense to him. None of the counties had a military base or any structure that the government might want to keep random citizens from approaching. There were no reported geological problems, like random sinkholes or anything like that. The state hadn't marked any of the counties as nature or wildlife preserves or designated them as parks. He simply could not see any reason to ban hunting here.

And so, when Paul bet him five-hundred dollars that he wouldn't have the nerve to hunt and kill something from one of the no-hunting zones, Lewis finished off his beer, crushed the can, and thought, *Why not?*

Now? He damn well *knew* why not.

The talons digging into his back sent hot spikes of pain radiating across his torso; how this dumb bird managed to slip its talons around his arms at his shoulders and only stab him with one talon each—while missing all the major arteries—he didn't know, but he was grateful all the same. The overhead view of the terrain sent his mind swirling through a vicious cycle of vertigo, panic attacks, and disbelief that this was even happening. Oh… and to top it all off, he'd messed himself—both #1 *and* #2—as he felt his feet leave the ground.

This day was shaping up to be just lovely all the way around.

At least he still had his rifle. It hung from the sling diagonally across his body. He wasn't stupid enough to try shooting this crazy bird while he hung hundreds of feet in the air, but it had to land *sometime*. He'd be ready when it did. Lewis Mitchell was not on the menu—not on any menu—if he had anything to say about it.

After what seemed like an eternity but was no more than thirty minutes or so, Lewis watched the outskirts of a town pass under him. Given where he'd been when this bird snatched him and the direction they flew, the only town this could be was Precious, the county seat. Oh, shit… if someone saw this bird flying away with a person, would they take a shot?

Before Lewis's thoughts could spiral out along that thread, the bird started shrieking some kind of cry as it began circling over what looked like the center of town, at least as far as Lewis could judge. People soon gathered along the main street, filling the sidewalks as they laughed and pointed at him.

This made no sense. What was this dumb bird doing? It wasn't behaving like an animal at all.

The bird must have seen what or who it wanted, because it swung out wide back the way they came before looping around and coming in like a 747 on a glide path to land. His heels striking the pavement created just enough of a drag that the hot fire of the two talons piercing his back renewed and intensified. Then, at some point that only made sense to the bird, it released its grip on him and continued to glide ahead of him until he stopped sliding on the pavement.

Lewis fought to remain conscious as pain unlike anything he'd ever felt raged through his body. Part of him felt like just giving up. Just go ahead and pass out, not caring whether he woke again. But he cared too much for his family to let that happen. His little girl would be five soon and start Kindergarten next year.

The crowd around him parted, and a man that didn't look any older than his younger brother Wes stood over him. Brown hair. Clean-shaven. Unhappy expression. The man's fists rested on his hips as he looked down at Lewis, and soon, the damned bird leaned into view beside the man, looking down at Lewis as well.

What the hell was going on? Was he dreaming? Was this an hallucination from major head trauma? He didn't remember falling, but if he had and this *was* an hallucination, would he know it?

"Well, what have we here?" the young man said, then looked at the bird standing beside him as if that was a normal occurrence. "Sloane, Karleen has your clothes. She should be along any moment now."

The bird bobbed its head in an exaggerated nod of all things, then backed away and disappeared behind the crowd. This definitely had to be some kind of hallucination. Did he get into a patch of happy 'shrooms without realizing it?

Just then, he heard a young voice shouting, "Alpha Wyatt! Alpha Wyatt!"

A girl with a runner's build—plus wearing running shorts and the local school jersey—burst out of the crowd and almost skidded to a stop at the young man's side. As she gasped for air, she said, "Alpha Wyatt... there's a... hunter..."

The young man—Alpha Wyatt, apparently—lifted a hand and pointed at the ground. Lewis watched the girl look down and lock eyes with him. Then, she said, "Oh. Okay."

"Thanks anyway, Sally," the young man said. "Sloane dropped him off."

"I was so scared," Sally replied. "If Sloane hadn't been there, I think he would've shot me."

Say what now? Okay. He *had to be* hallucinating. He would never shoot a person, not intentionally at least. Was this girl in the forest behind that doe and he didn't see her? Was that what made her think he was going to shoot her?

"Excuse me?" the young man—Wyatt apparently—asked. His tone dripped offense and disbelief. "He did *what* now?"

"He was in the middle of lifting his rifle when Sloane shrieked. He did fire, but I dropped flat, and the shot went over me. If she hadn't been there, I'm afraid he would've shot me."

Wyatt's expression shifted from disbelief and surprise to heated anger that looked fit to vaporize lava. He crouched to the point that he was little more than a foot or so above Lewis, and the look in Wyatt's eyes told Lewis in no uncertain terms he was a dead man. And when he spoke, Wyatt's voice was colder than an arctic graveyard... at night... in January.

"Neighbor, you have no idea how difficult it is for me to resist ripping off your head for someone to use as a chamberpot. If you'd like to have even the slightest hope of living to see the end of the week, you will use two fingers to unlatch and withdraw the bolt of that rifle. You will then unclasp the sling from each attachment point. You will then grasp the rifle with one hand on the stock and one hand on the barrel. If you do *anything* other than what I've directed,

I'll smash your skull into pudding right now. Do you understand me?"

All Lewis could do was nod in the affirmative.

Wyatt's eyes narrowed. "I didn't hear you."

"Y-y-yes, sir. I understand." Lewis almost didn't recognize the sound of his own voice. He'd never sounded like a coward before.

"Do it now."

Lewis slowly and deliberately performed the actions Wyatt instructed... and *only* those actions. When he pulled the bolt back, the spent casing from his shot flew out and pinged as it struck the asphalt. There was something about Wyatt that frightened him to the very core of his being. His lizard brain that hadn't evolved past the Stone Age—otherwise known as the amygdala—was gibbering in uncontrolled terror.

"Good. Maintain that pose and do not move." Wyatt stood and scanned the crowd, then said, "Anyone know where Sheriff Clyde is?"

"Right here, Alpha Wyatt," a man replied. The man in a sheriff's uniform who pushed his way into view looked to be a tall, no-nonsense block of granite right out of a John Wayne western. The hand-cannon that rode at his right hip had to be either a .454 Casull or .44 Magnum. Oh, shit... might even be a Smith & Wesson .500.

Wyatt pointed at Lewis. "Book this idiot for trespassing, hunting in a restricted zone, and assault. I'll leave it up to your judgment whether to escalate it to assault with intent to kill and attempted murder, once you have statements from Sally and Sloane. You better hose him down, too; from the smell, he failed potty training."

Sheriff Clyde looked down at Lewis for a moment before lifting his head to look at Wyatt again. "Well, damn... I'm kinda surprised I don't need to clean up his corpse. You have a tendency to be a mite overprotective."

"It's taking everything I have not to turn him into bloody vertical blinds. Maybe use his skull for a soccer match afterward."

Sheriff Clyde erupted into a huge grin. "There we go. That's the Wyatt we all know and love."

All this talk of dismembering or rending him wore on Lewis to the point that his last nerve snapped. "Okay. Can we tone down the threats a little? I don't see what the big deal is. I never saw this girl. A buddy bet me $500 that I wouldn't go hunting in one of the prohibited zones, and I took a shot at a doe that looked like it just grew out of its spots. This kid was nowhere in sight; I don't care what she says."

By the time Lewis ended his tirade, everyone in sight glared at him, and more than few growled. Wyatt and Sheriff Clyde included.

Clyde shook his head as he scooped the fired casing from the hunter's rifle into an evidence bag. "You just confessed to attempted murder and signed your buddy up for rough ride."

"What? How? Are you deaf? I'm telling you... that girl *wasn't there*! It was just a young doe and that ginormous bird!"

Clyde growled as he took Lewis's rifle and grabbed the collar of his shirt and vest, then started dragging Lewis away. "You stupid bugger, she *was* the doe. Alpha Wyatt, I'll send one of the deputies to locate the slug this idiot fired and another over with a mop and bucket for the trail he's leaving on the pavement."

"Thanks, Sheriff," Wyatt responded. "Book him and hold him for now. Might want to have Doc look him over, too."

"You might want to call your sister, while you're at it. I doubt this guy's dumb enough to cough up his buddy's name, now that he knows I want to charge the guy for accessory to attempted murder. The Attorney General is going to *love* us; there hasn't been a case like this in forty or fifty years."

COME TO FIND OUT, shifter society averaged a case like that of the hunter about one every eight to ten years. On the one side, that kind of blew my mind; I would've thought there'd either be at least one every hunting season, or it would go for decades between them.

Then, a rather chilling thought occurred to me. Were cases like these only *reported* every eight to ten years? I seemed to remember something from radio or TV a few years back—one of those 'random facts about our society' segments—that listed a surprising number of hunters that go missing every year. No body. No blood. No trail. No 'hunting accident.' Just… gone. Did these missing hunters run afoul of a shifter or shifters? Is *that* why they vanished?

My thoughts spiraled down that rabbit hole as I crossed the distance to the hotel. Through the front doors' windows, I saw a collection of councilors lining up at the front desk, and as I opened the door, I heard the feline councilor at the front of the line say that she was ready to check out.

The polar bear councilor saw me before the others did, and she gave me a respectful nod of greeting, which I returned, and said, "Hello again, Alpha Wyatt. Have you come to see us off?"

"I planned to do just that, but I'm afraid a matter has arisen that I would like to discuss if any of you have twenty minutes."

By now, the feline councilor turned away from the front desk and adopted a playful smile. "Raising more hell already, are you? Why, Alpha Wyatt, you are incorrigible."

I laughed. "Unfortunately, I can't claim this one at all, but I will if you really want me to."

The deer councilor who had been silent through much of the presentations regarding Sloane's situation stepped forward as he said, "Well, young man, you have our attention. You might as well lay everything on us."

"Sloane and one of our deer shifters encountered a hunter a couple miles outside of town. According to the would-be victim, the hunter took a shot at her while she was in deer form, but Sloane interrupted him, scooped him up, and flew him back to town. Sheriff Clyde has him right now, and I hope he's hosing the guy down before he puts him in our jail."

Several councilors frowned their confusion. The avian councilor asked, "Why is that?"

"I guess being scooped into the sky like a fish out of a river by a huge raptor was sufficient grounds for the fellow to void himself. He smelled rather nasty when I was standing over him outside in the street."

The councilors all replied with understanding nods and a few grimaces.

"I'm willing to hear the matter," the feline councilor said, looking to her associates. "What of the rest of you?"

The deer councilor and the bear councilor both gave firm nods, the deer councilor saying, "Oh, I absolutely want to hear this case. I do not appreciate such a violation of our territory, which ultimately is another violation of our treaty with the United States."

Nods of agreement began rippling through the assembled councilors until all of them had agreed to stay.

"Thank you for your help," I said. "If any of you will miss your flight over this, I'm happy to cover a replacement ticket out of county funds."

The polar bear councilor made a dismissive wave as she

said, "Sonny, we flew two of the Council's jets out here, because there were so many of us. Those planes won't leave Spokane International until *we* say they do."

"Oh. Well, in that case… if this lasts long enough that you'd rather spend one more night, the rooms are on me again."

The councilors turned to take their luggage back to their rooms. When the feline councilor turned, Melody lifted the room key she had just turned in and smiled as she said, "Here you are, ma'am. I haven't completed the check-out paperwork yet, so it's like you never left."

THE PASSAGE of about twenty minutes found me and the councilors in the town hall of the city's administration building. As it had every other time I'd been in the room, the space's resemblance to a courtroom seemed uncanny. On our way into the administration building, I stopped at the reception desk and asked the staffer to call Sheriff Clyde to let him know the councilors decided to stay and hear the hunter's case. We spent no more than ten minutes in the town hall when the doors opened to admit Sheriff Clyde, Sloane, Sally, and the hunter in question—wearing blaze orange scrubs and handcuffs.

The sheriff parked his detainee in a chair as Sloane and Sally sat across the room from him.

"I still say you have no grounds to hold me," Lewis grumbled. "I ought to stand up and just walk out of here."

Clyde chuckled, and it held no mirth. "Son, you do whatever you feel you need to do, but you should know that there's more than one predator in the room and we all love a good chase. So, go right ahead. We'll probably play with you a little bit before we catch you, just to break up the monotony of the day."

"Predator?" Lewis asked. "What do you mean? Like child predators? Sex predators?"

The sheriff shook his head. "Not quite. Alpha Wyatt, would you mind educating him on the nature of his accusers? You're the most spectacular predator we have."

I simply crossed my arms. "Not until you go out to the custodial closet and get one of those thick contractor-grade trash bags for his feet. The custodial staff doesn't deserve to clean up after him if he voids himself again."

Clyde nodded and turned to his detainee. "Please, feel free to run while I'm gone."

Then, he trooped out to the hall and came back shortly with *three* contractor-grade trash bags and some thick twine. He had Lewis lift each foot in turn and fed the lifted foot into the trash bag, pulling it up as high as possible, then tied it off with a piece of twine. Then, repeated everything for Lewis's other leg. *Then*, Clyde had Lewis to stand and rolled the third bag so that it was open with a rolled ridge around its diameter; he placed it in the seat and had Lewis sit on it.

"Well, Alpha Wyatt," he said, "I think we're about as good as we can be."

I didn't really want to shift and ruin my clothes, but I wasn't about to strip down in front of Sally—as she was underage and all— or the councilors and the hunter. Ah, well... surely, Hank would have another shirt like this in the general store, right?

I moved to stand in the large space between the conference table and the wall, then touched the part of my mind that was no longer human and willed the shift. Fabric exploded all around me, and by the time the threads settled, the hunter looked like he was catatonic. He stared at me with wide eyes, a gaping mouth, and absolutely zero movement beyond the basic, autonomic functions.

An idea popped into my head, and it was something only

my sister would consider, let alone do. But I couldn't resist. I took one step toward the hunter and snapped my jaw like I was biting something, then licked my lips.

Lewis Mitchell's eyes rolled back in his head as he went limp and slithered to the floor... terrified into unconsciousness.

8

The councilors all performed some variation of looking back and forth between me and the unconscious hunter for several moments, before the feline councilor cleared her throat and tapped her knuckles on the table.

"I call this hearing to order. We gather here today to deliberate the matter involving Lewis Mitchell, a human hunter illegally within Godwin County—which is a duly recognized shifter territory by the State of Washington. It is most commonly the case that the subject of the hearing is conscious and present to participate, but proving the nature of the situation to him seems to be more than his constitution can bear. No matter. We will proceed. Sheriff Clyde, we deputize you to present the case against Mister Mitchell in Alpha Wyatt's stead. Alpha Wyatt, I trust this meets with your approval?"

I stood and bobbed my large head in a nod, then promptly laid back down. I had to stack my paws, one on top of the other, to act as a chin rest that was tall enough to prevent my curved incisors from poking into the floor.

"Let the record reflect that Alpha Wyatt nodded his

assent," the feline councilor continued. "Sheriff Clyde, please present the case and call any witnesses you deem appropriate."

Sheriff Clyde stood and cleared his throat as he approached the conference table.

"Esteemed Councilors, earlier today, Sloane delivered this man to Main Street. He wore the garb of a hunter, including a blaze orange vest and ball cap, and he carried a scoped hunting rifle, chambered in .308 Winchester. Just as I arrived on the scene, I heard Sally Poole arrive at Alpha Wyatt's side and report a hunter in the woods outside of town. At this time, I ask Sloane Martinez to tell us her experiences."

The feline councilor nodded, saying, "Ms. Martinez, please step forward."

Sloane stood and told the councilors everything she experienced from the moment she started to claim a deer for food up through delivering the hunter to Main Street in Precious. At no point did her heart rate, breathing, or any of the regular tell-tales indicate she lied.

"Thank you, Ms. Martinez. Sally Poole, will you tell us what you experienced?"

Just as Sally approached the table, our intrepid hunter rejoined the land of the conscious, starting to mumble even before opening his eyes, "Wha... didn't think you could pass out inside a hallucination."

"Mister Mitchell," the feline councilor said, "you are most certainly *not* inside a hallucination. Now, be silent. You will have your turn to speak in a moment. Miss Poole, if you please?"

Sally described how she, her family, and few of the other local deer shifter families went out for a run and some grazing. Everyone kept to the ranges set aside for prey shifters, and everything was going well until she saw the hunter. When she realized he was actually going to shoot her, she did the only thing she could think of, which was throw her legs wide and fall to the ground. She finished her re-telling by describing her flight through the forest to alert Alpha Wyatt or at least get *some kind* of help and arriving in town after Sloane brought the hunter in.

Like Sloane before her, none of her biometrics that shifters could sense indicated she told a lie.

The feline councilor gave Sally an encouraging smile. "Thank you, Sally. Sheriff Clyde, is the accused able to speak?"

By now, Lewis was back to staring at me. He remained in the same posture and position that he assumed when he passed out, as if he feared moving would spur me to attack him. Sheriff Clyde approached him and hauled him to his feet.

"But... what about that... that *thing*? It'll eat us all!" Lewis wailed.

"Oh, shut up, you ninny. That's Alpha Wyatt. You've already met him, and he won't attack you unless you attack someone else."

I bared my teeth and nodded. Then, I took a long, deep sniff and licked my lips again... like there was a very savory meal just within reach. Lewis pissed himself like I'd turned a tap, darkening the crotch and upper thighs of his orange inmate scrubs, and the unmistakable bouquet of fresh urine filled the town hall.

Clyde looked down, then looked up at the ceiling as he released a very put-upon sigh. "Dammit, Wyatt..."

"Alpha Wyatt," the feline councilor began, "while I understand your evaluation that this man deserves as much punishment as you see fit to deliver for attacking one of your citizens, I'm sure I can speak for all assembled councilors when I ask you not to terrorize Mister Mitchell until we've finished these proceedings. Chicago is a long way off, and we'd like to leave by the end of the week."

"Oh, I don't know," the deer councilor opined. "I'm enjoying Alpha Wyatt terrorizing him."

The feline councilor shot her associate a frown. "You're a deer shifter, too, so you're biased. Matter of fact, you probably shouldn't even be sitting this case."

"Too late. Let's get on with this." The deer councilor rolled his hand in a 'hurry up' gesture.

The feline councilor turned back to Lewis. "Mister Mitchell, do you have anything to say on your behalf?"

By now, the state of affairs seemed to be sinking into Lewis's mind... at long last. He gaped at the deer councilor in a horrified stare before looking over his shoulder to give the same expression to Sally.

"Deer shifter?" he asked, almost too quiet to hear. "You mean, they can turn into deer? Like a buck or a doe?"

"I'm rather proud of my twenty-point rack," the deer councilor said. "I've been growing it a while."

Any hint of a defensiveness or defiance vanished from Lewis's posture. "Oh, my... I'm so sorry. I didn't know. My buddy and I have never understood why there are so many prohibited-hunting zones across the country. Wait... are they all...?"

"Shifter territory?" the feline councilor asked.

Lewis replied with a weak, horrified nod.

"If the prohibited-hunting zone is not inside a state or federal park, it's almost guaranteed that those zones are shifter territory. Most shifter communities normally have predator shifters policing the borders, but it just so happened that most of the shifters in Godwin County—whether predator or prey—gathered in Precious for our impromptu visit. You see, my fellow councilors and I represent the government—for lack of a better term—of the shifters. And I'm afraid, Mister Mitchell, that we need your buddy's name."

"Paul," Lewis answered as he bowed his head. "Paul Burkett. What will happen to us?"

"Well, I think it's clear to everyone involved that you violated the no-hunting zone of Godwin County for the explicit purpose of hunting. The treaty between the Shifter Nation of North America and the United States gives us complete authority to do as we will. In a normal situation, you wouldn't even be alive right now; one of the shifters guarding the county border would have killed you for taking that shot if you somehow managed to get past them in the first place. You attempted premeditated murder at the urging of your associate. Your lives are ours now to do with as we please."

Lewis nodded as he hung his head and his shoulders slumped.

"Alpha Wyatt," the feline councilor continued, and I stood and turned to face her, "you and Sheriff Clyde will contact the state's Attorney General to report this incident and request a warrant for the apprehension of Paul Burkett under the terms of the shifter treaty. As has been established in precedent, both Mister Mitchell and Mister Burkett are yours to do with as you see fit." She glanced among her associates. "Does anyone wish to comment or move for a vote toward a different outcome?"

The other councilors remained silent, a few shaking their heads 'no.'

"Very well," the feline councilor remarked and rapped her knuckles on the table once more. "We're adjourned."

Clyde collected Lewis and helped him step out of the trash bags. He took the bags with him as he left with Lewis in tow. The councilors stood, and the feline councilor approached me. She held out her hand as if to pet me, and I nodded.

The feline councilor stroked the fur along my head and spine as Sloane, Sally, and the other councilors filed out of the town hall. Once we were alone, she said, "You are such a strong and beautiful cat, Wyatt. I want to discuss the possibility of a courtship… once you can discuss things again. It's such a shame that we have no way to communicate in our animal forms."

She gave me one last head-to-tail rub and patted my shoulder before we walked out of the town hall; she was kind enough to help me with the doors.

GABRIELLE LOOKED up from whatever held her focus as I padded into the Alpha's house through the back door. "Decide to go for a ramble after the councilors left?"

I shook my head and headed for our bedroom. Halfway down the hallway, I shifted mid-stride and went to my closet. Gabrielle followed me and bathed me in appreciative ogling and suggestive sounds that shifted to pouting that may (or may not) have been fake as I dressed.

"The councilors were leaving, but Sloane brought in a hunter who violated Godwin County. He took a shot at one of the deer shifters."

Deadly seriousness subsumed Gabrielle's demeanor in an instant. "Who was it? Are they okay?"

"The deer in question was Sally Poole, and yes, she's fine… aside from having a good scare that'll make a fun story for her grandchildren. She thought fast enough to kick her legs out wide and fall to the ground just as he took the shot, which gave Sloane the time to pluck him out of the meadow like other raptors catch fish. He—the hunter in question—is now very well aware of *why* the no-hunting zones exist around the country and is coming to grips with the idea that he is guilty of attempted murder. His buddy set him up to it on a dare, so we're going to grab that guy, too, when we go to the Attorney General about this."

"Any idea what you'll do with them? And why did you come back as your cat?"

I gave Gabrielle a very predatory smile. "I was thinking on the way over how fitting it would be for this guy's buddy to experience just what it means to be defenseless against a master hunter; I've decided we'll pick him up in the dead of night, dose him with a sleeping agent, and bring him out here in the woods somewhere... probably some place deep in the predator ranges. Then, strip him naked and tell him if he can get out of the county without being caught, he's a free man."

"Okay... so who's hunting him?"

"You."

Now, Gabrielle shared my smile. "Do I get to kill him?"

I sighed. "It depends on the background check I'm going to have Sheriff Clyde do. If this guy's a bad dude who's left a trail of harm and ruined lives, you're welcome to do with him as you will. But if he's just a guy who had a bad idea and set his buddy off on this mess, I'd rather talk to him after you let him experience what it's like for the regular deer every hunting season."

Gabrielle shook her head as she muttered. "You're too damn good for us, Wyatt."

I pretended like I hadn't heard and then remembered something. "Oh, hey... what do you know about the feline councilor that came out with the group?"

"Not much, really. I know she's a lioness, and she's always seemed to be a decent person. Why?"

I leaned against the wall and rubbed my face as I sighed. "She hung back while everyone else left the town hall, where we held the hearing for this hunter. She told me she wanted to discuss a courtship once I could talk again. What do you think?"

As I pulled my hands away from my face, I caught Gabrielle in an unguarded moment. Her shoulders were tense, and her expression communicated worry to me. Aw, shit...

"Hey, none of that." I pulled her into a hug and held her tight. "None of that, now. Even if something happens with this councilor, I'm not trading up, and if she tries to run you off, she'll face me." After several moments of silence, I stepped back from the hug and kissed her cheek as my lips passed. "I don't want you thinking you're leaving this relationship any other way than by *your* choice... and hopefully after you've let me try to talk you out of leaving. Okay?"

Gabrielle bobbed a nod. "Sorry... sorry. It's just that most guys would drop a jaguar in a hot minute if he had a chance at a lioness or a tigress, especially if the guy wasn't strong enough to have his own pride. They're the elite of feline shifters... like marrying intelligent and super-attractive royalty."

I leaned back in and gave her a quick peck on the lips before pulling back to meet her eyes with mine. "If I could have only one cat in my life, she would be you, and that's not going to change."

"What's this?" Karleen said as she walked into the bedroom. "Is something wrong, Gabby?"

Gabrielle scoffed. "Only my insecurities. The lioness councilor made a pass at Wyatt. She told him she wants to discuss a courtship."

"The way you say that makes me think there's something special to a courtship. What did I miss while I was out of touch building a cabin and chasing rabbits?" Karleen asked.

"Courtships among shifters are most often used as a

prelude to becoming an Alpha mate and establishing a pride," Gabrielle explained.

Karleen frowned and looked to me. "You mean you didn't set her straight about us?"

I chuckled and shook my head. "Nope. I couldn't. I was a saber-tooth cat at the time she declared her interest. I just came back to shift, get dressed, and find you two."

"Well, you've shifted, and you're dressed. Let's go tell this lioness what the deal is." Karleen turned and led us out of the Alpha's house. As we stepped onto the sidewalk, she frowned. "Oh... do either of you know anything about Sloane bringing in a hunter? I saw a couple deer shift to human out in the park and overheard pieces of the conversation."

"Yeah, that's a whole *thing*," I replied. "I'll explain on the way to the hotel."

9

The closer we were to the hotel, the more I felt like I was marching to the gallows. I was not looking forward to this conversation, especially since I didn't want to make an enemy of the feline councilor. It would be nice just to slink off and let Gabrielle and Karleen handle it, so I voiced that thought.

"Nope," Karleen replied as Gabrielle slipped an arm around mine and held it tight.

"You have to establish our authority to have the conversation, at least," Gabrielle added. "If we just show up without you, it could mean anything."

Well, damn. So much for sneaking off...

We were maybe fifty yards from the hotel when I saw salvation. Sheriff Clyde stepped out of his office that doubled as the jail and headed straight for us. We crossed half the distance to the hotel by the time he arrived.

"Ah, Alpha Wyatt," Clyde said, "I was looking for you. I've heard back from the Attorney General's office. We can present our case as soon as we can arrive in the capital. She

81

has arranged for the state's Supreme Court to take us in as soon as we can be there."

That didn't add up for me at all. "Why would the state's Supreme Court hear our case? I thought issuing warrants and such happened at the magistrate level."

"It's because we're shifters. Since someone has to have a security clearance just to know we exist and what the no-hunting zones really mean, any cases involving humans and shifters go straight to the Supreme Court."

That set me back on my heels a bit. "Wow. That's... that's kind of daunting."

Clyde replied with a dismissive shrug. "This won't be my first rodeo, as the youngsters say. It's no biggie. With the evidence we have, including Lewis's statement, that Paul fellow is already ours. He just doesn't know it yet. Do you think your sister might portal us over there? It's about a four-hour drive, otherwise."

"I wouldn't see why not. I'll give her a call right now."

"Uhm, no," Gabrielle interjected.

Karleen agreed, saying, "You have something else that requires your attention, at least for the next few minutes. *Then*, you can call Vicki about the portal. Twenty minutes won't make much difference when they're expecting you to take hours."

Clyde chuckled. "I'll have everything ready, Wyatt. Just come by the jail when you're finished."

Karleen and Gabrielle smiled sweetly to Sheriff Clyde, thanked him for understanding, and resumed our journey to the hotel. It didn't take us long to arrive, and we found the feline councilor sitting in the lobby. That's when I realized I hadn't seen any of the other councilors' vehicles in the parking lot out back or outside the hotel.

My confusion must have shown on my face, because as she

led us to a quiet seating area, the feline councilor said, "The other councilors are already on the way back. I told them I'd be fine flying commercial, but I won't lie that I'm hoping you might prevail upon your sister for a quick portal to Chicago."

I chuckled. "Well, she'll probably be here anyway to portal Sheriff Clyde and I to Olympia, so I wouldn't see why not. The last time I visited our grandparents, I found a scratching post in my old room, so she owes me if she wants to escape retaliation."

The feline councilor's eyes shot wide. "A scratching post? Really?"

"Oh, yeah, my sister's an imp. A one-hundred-percent, fully verified, mischievous imp. I thought I smelled kitty litter through the door of *her* bedroom, and she doesn't have a cat, so there's probably a litter box in store for me, too. Vicki has a rhythm to these things, which means the litter box will appear around our birthday… unless she has a rough day and needs a distraction."

The feline councilor just shook her head. "Well, at least your family's doing well with the change. Normally, when a human becomes a shifter, they have to cut all ties, and that's always difficult."

I nodded my understanding. I was afraid the small talk might become awkward, so I tried to stave that off. "So, you said you wanted to discuss a courtship, but I wasn't in a position to respond. The thing is that I'm kind of already spoken for."

Then, I gestured to Karleen and Gabrielle like a gameshow hostess displaying a prize.

"We thought we should come back with Wyatt so that we all could discuss the matter," Gabrielle explained. "Karleen and I have told Wyatt we don't mind the pride growing, but we want a say in who joins."

"And what are your thoughts about all this?" the councilor asked me.

I grinned. "Well, at the very basic, I'm a guy, and I haven't seen a female shifter yet who is ugly. So, yes… I think you're attractive. You also seem like a decent person, which is important. The major thing for me is that there will *not* be a hierarchy or anything similar. Karleen, Gabrielle, and anyone else who joins will be too special to me for that kind of thing to happen. Oh, and she—meaning any new prospects—will have to be fine with me coming from a Magi family and still having close ties to them; having an issue with Magi—especially my family—is a deal-breaker, right there."

"Have you three discussed children?" the feline councilor asked.

I blushed as Karleen and Gabrielle beamed. Karleen answered, "Oh, we all want children, but we thought it best to wait maybe a year so that Wyatt truly has become accustomed to life as a shifter."

"And we won't be doing any of that silly rotation stuff some shifter families do," Gabrielle added. "Once we decide to pursue children, any member of the pride who wants to try is welcome."

"Hey… weird question," I interjected. "How do shifters differentiate between the Alpha's pride and the overall pride? Like, I thought a group of shifters led by a feline is called a pride, whereas it's a pack when led by a wolf."

All three ladies smiled. Karleen laughed. The feline councilor explained, "We don't tend to organize along pack or pride lines. Normally, there's an Alpha over a town, county, or region, and that Alpha's family is often called a pack or pride. But how it often goes is that people identify with the location rather than the Alpha."

I leaned back against my seat and relaxed. "Whew! I was worried about that."

"Your principles and how you stick to them are two reasons I find you so attractive," the feline councilor said. "I like strong men who stand by their convictions against all challenges. That you are like this when still of such relative youth makes you all the more remarkable."

I couldn't keep from blushing again, and the feline councilor returned a predatory smile.

"Well, anyway, I'm not opposed to exploring the possibility of you joining us, and if you don't mind, I'll leave you to work things out with the ladies while I arrange that portal for you."

The feline councilor gave her assent with a slow, regal nod. I stood and left the hotel, trusting Karleen and Gabrielle to handle matters.

"He is such an innocent sometimes," the feline councilor said as she watched Wyatt leave. "I wonder how he manages remaining so."

Gabrielle was quick to say, "He's a genuinely good person. He cares about people, and he believes in discharging his responsibilities the best he possibly can. I know being named Alpha wasn't his choice or even to his liking, but he's been very good for Precious and Godwin County."

The feline councilor nodded her agreement as she took a breath. "Well, we should probably get to this. I am Lyssa Veronica Westridge, and I am the third daughter of my litter. I have never been married, and neither have I sought a mate before. And yes, I am a lioness, in case you didn't know."

"So, why Wyatt?" Karleen asked. "If you've never sought a mate before, why choose to pursue him?"

The regal and reserved demeanor of both a lioness *and* a councilor faded. Lyssa dropped her eyes to the floor for several moments before she lifted them back to look at Karleen and Gabrielle. "Because I was never sure my previous would-be suitors wanted *me*, instead of a lioness. I promised my father not long after I became a woman that my mate would be someone who appreciated me for me and not my breed or whatever successes or accolades I accumulated in life. And besides all that, Wyatt is simply a beautiful cat. There's just something about him that makes me want to rub against him all day long. I resisted saying something as long as I could, especially since events draw Wyatt more and more into the world of shifter leadership."

Karleen and Gabrielle both chuckled. Karleen said, "Oh, trust me; we know *that* feeling very well. I still haven't forgotten what it felt like to be standing in a kidnapping scene, just having shifted to my wolf, and all she wanted to do was rub against Wyatt from snout to tail."

"So, is there any way we can work this out?" Lyssa asked.

I STEPPED outside the hotel and turned toward the sheriff's office, but I stopped and leaned against one of the columns supporting the hotel's portico. Then, rubbed my face with both hands. Was this really happening? Were Karleen and Gabrielle really negotiating a potential courtship for me? And what was with the feline councilor pretty much throwing herself at me? I didn't see how I would ever get used to this part of being a shifter.

The lioness would make a good addition to the pride, the growly voice remarked.

Where have you been? It's been over a week since you talked to me.

My cat sent a strong feeling of exasperation. *There is no 'you' or 'us.' There is just 'me.' I haven't made too many mistakes, so*

I didn't need significant comments. But I want to go for a long run. Soon. I miss my fur and claws. Today was frustrating in its brevity.

That sounds excellent. As soon as we get Lewis and that Paul guy dealt with, we'll go on a long run. Maybe even spend a couple days in our fur.

Good. Then, my cat sent an image of lazing into an afternoon nap in the shade of the sole tree on a prairie or savannah, and I took that to mean he was finished talking for now.

I reached to my back pocket for my phone and then remembered it had been in the pocket of the pants I shredded when I shifted in the town hall. Oh, well… at least the administration building was close.

WHEN I STEPPED through the door of the admin building, the staffer sitting at the reception desk grinned and held up my phone. "Forget something, Alpha?"

I returned his grin with a smile of my own. "Yes, thanks, Jeff. I appreciate it."

He handed it to me, and I unlocked it to call my sister.

She answered on the second ring. "Hello, my furry sibling. How are you today?"

Jeff couldn't keep from grinning, and it looked like he fought back an outright laugh. Shifter hearing… yay.

"Hi, sis. So, I need a favor. You mind hopping over here and making a couple portals?"

"Not a bit, brother mine. Who's going where?"

"A group is going to Olympia to speak with the Attorney General on a matter, and the feline councilor stayed in town to handle a couple matters and hoped you could save her from flying commercial. Oh, and we'd appreciate a portal *back* from Olympia when we've finished there."

"By 'we,' I take it you're going to Olympia, too?"

I nodded, even though she couldn't see it. "Yeah, we have

a bit of a mess over here, and the resolution path involves discussing the matter with the Attorney General and a presentation to the state Supreme Court. Sheriff Clyde wouldn't let me deputize him to act in my stead, so I'm going too."

There was a brief pause, and then, I heard, "Grams, I'm going to Precious to help Wyatt with a few things. I'll be back later."

The next thing I know, the call dropped and Vicki stepped out of nowhere and into the lobby. She slipped the phone back in her purse and pulled me into a tight hug. "Grandpa and Grams send their love, and you're not going to Olympia without me. The government's been weird enough lately that I'm not going to risk you. Granted, my run-in was with the federal government, but I'm of the mind we should approach all governments with caution and healthy skepticism right now."

Vicki stepped back and seemed to notice Jeff. He was about our age, and I felt like handing him a paper towel to clean up the drool on the desk, given how he gazed at my sister.

"Oh, hello. I'm Vicki, Wyatt's sister."

"Uhh… I'm Jeff. Uhm, nice to meet you."

I suppose, if you didn't grow up with her, Vicki *was* rather stunning. She'd pulled too many pranks on me, though. I saw past the gorgeous cheerleader captain facade and knew her for who she really was. An incorrigible, unrepentant imp.

"Nice to meet you, too," Vicki replied as she fell into step beside me. Then, she waved her fingers over her shoulder as she said, "Toodles!"

Vicki and I headed down the street to the sheriff's office. As we walked, we saw Karleen, Gabrielle, and the feline councilor leave the hotel. When they saw us, they changed course to meet us, and they caught us two doors down from the sheriff's place.

"Hi, I'm Vicki, Wyatt's older sister," she said, holding out her hand to shake, "and you are?"

"By all of eight minutes, sis…" I grumbled.

"Lyssa Westridge," the councilor answered as she shook hands with Vicki. "I stayed behind to talk about a possible courtship with Wyatt and have been discussing the matter with Karleen and Gabrielle."

Vicki beamed. "Well, I love Karleen and Gabrielle like sisters, and I trust them to watch out for Wyatt. Just so you know, though…" all semblance of the happy, up-beat cheerleader vanished "…if you hurt my brother, no one will *ever* find what little remains of you. Do you understand?"

"Seriously, Vicki?" But the two ladies went right on like I'd never spoken.

Lyssa gave my sister a firm nod. "The wrath of a Magi is something no one in their right mind would risk, and I'm glad to see you value Wyatt so much."

The beaming cheerleader was back. "Well, of course, I do. He's just the purr-fect brother. So, you wanted a portal somewhere?"

Karleen and Gabrielle snorted a laugh, while I just shook my head. I loved my sister, but sometimes, she was a handful.

"Yes, please, if it isn't too much imposition," Lyssa said. "The other councilors are already on their way back to Chicago by now."

"Okay. I'll need a reference point. A street address or GPS coordinates will do."

Lyssa rattled off an address, and Vicki lifted her hands to trace a series of complex gestures as she recited words in an ancient language. Soon enough, a portal winked into existence.

"Is that the place?" Vicki asked.

Lyssa poked her head through before turning back to us. "Yes, thank you."

Then, she took the few short strides necessary to approach me and tip-toed to kiss my cheek. When Lyssa turned and stepped through the portal, and Vicki closed it.

Now that it was just 'us,' I gave my sister a scolding expression. "Did you really need to threaten her like that, Vicki?"

"Nope, not at all, but you would've done it for me." Her impish smile was positively gloating.

10

Vicki's portal delivered our odd group to a nondescript entrance to the building where we should start by meeting the Attorney General before moving on to the state's Supreme Court. Given the dramatic reversal of Lewis's understanding, we dressed him in casual clothes for this trip. He seemed to be a decent enough individual that I was considering him becoming a shifter. But... I wasn't about to offer that without getting to know him a little more.

Sheriff Clyde approached the door and pressed the button marked 'Ring for Access.' Within moments, a uniformed officer opened the door, his demeanor stern.

"Hello, young man," Clyde said, "I'm Sheriff Clyde Wilson of Godwin County, and the Attorney General is waiting for me and my party."

The officer looked at each of us in turn. After a moment, he nodded once and stepped back from the door. Sheriff Clyde motioned for all of us to follow him, and a second officer standing a few feet back from the entrance took up the rear while Clyde chatted with our greeter during the walk.

We stopped at a checkpoint in front of a bank of elevators about sixty feet into the building from our point of ingress.

"These people are for the Attorney General," the lead officer said, addressing the officer at the checkpoint.

The checkpoint officer lifted the handset of a nearby phone and dialed an extension.

A mousy voice answered, "Attorney General's office."

"This is Side Checkpoint One," the officer said. "I have a party of six for the Attorney General, led by a Sheriff Clyde Wilson of Godwin County."

"Hold please," the mousy voice replied.

Over the two months and change since the rogue cougar attacked me, I had grown to appreciate the enhanced senses a shifter possessed. It's unlikely the officer that led us to the checkpoint heard the other side of that phone call, and I stood some fifteen feet away from the desk yet heard both sides of the call like they were at a table with me.

"Officer?" The mousy voice came back on the call. "The Attorney General said that Sheriff Wilson and his party are sufficiently ahead of their expected arrival time that you should conduct them straight to the Supreme Court. He has already called to inform the court of Sheriff Wilson's arrival, and they are ready to hear his case now."

"Thank you," the checkpoint officer responded and returned the phone's handset to its cradle. Then, he looked to our guide. "The Supreme Court will receive Sheriff Wilson and his party now."

Our guide nodded once and gestured for us to follow him, saying, "Follow me."

He resumed chatting with Sheriff Clyde as we walked down the hallway. We spent maybe twenty minutes navigating hallways and elevators before we approached a set of double doors bearing the seal of the state's Supreme Court. Our guide led us through the double doors and into a courtroom with an expanded bench, a large gallery, and no jury box. Exquisite wood paneling lined the walls, and our feet sank into fine carpet as we walked down the aisle.

A side door on the opposite wall from where we entered opened, allowing another uniformed officer to enter. Our guide told her that we were the Sheriff Clyde Wilson party, and she nodded once before disappearing back through the door.

The officer guiding us gestured to the first row of the gallery, then said, "Feel free to sit here while you wait for the court to convene."

He then walked back to join his associate standing at the doors where we entered.

"You didn't tell me we'd be appearing before the state's Supreme Court," Vicki hissed in my ear as she grabbed my arm. "I am *not* dressed to appear before the Supreme Court, Wyatt."

"Sorry, sis. I didn't expect you to tag along."

Vicki glared at me for a moment before delivering an exasperated huff. She pivoted on her heel and strode back to the officers, stopping about ten feet away.

"Gentlemen," she said, "my darling brother failed to inform me that the purpose of the trip today was to appear before the Supreme Court, hence my everyday attire. I would like to correct this lack of respect before the court convenes, but I didn't want to alarm either of you. With your permission, I'll adopt more formal attire, part of which includes my staff of office."

The officers glanced to one another before the one who served as our guide shrugged and said, "Uhm, sure."

I don't know what they were expecting, but I'm sure what happened next wasn't it.

Vicki lifted her left hand and traced a complex pattern with her fingers as she recited words in that ancient language she used for her spells. A kaleidoscopic halo appeared about six inches above her head and rained a cascade of light particles to the floor. When the shower of light faded, Vicki stood in the aisle garbed in a tailored conservative pantsuit, the slacks in black and the blouse in gray. A black robe of glossy velvet hung from her shoulders, serving as the suit's jacket, and stopped just above her ankles. The robe did not close, nor was it designed to, and silver runes ran down the vertical seams and circled the cuff of each sleeve.

Vicki now held her staff in her right hand as well, and while the contours and physical dimensions matched the staff I'd seen in the past, the look of it and its sheer *presence* was unlike anything I'd ever experienced. Always before, Vicki's staff had seemed a dainty thing, little more than a garnishment to help her meet the vision people expected of Magi. But this staff? Even twenty feet away, I felt it in my very soul. It seemed alive to me... alive and *hungry*.

The officers gaped at the change. Both sets of eyes were almost comically wide. The officer who'd brought up the rear as we walked through the building edged his hand toward his sidearm.

Without another word, Vicki turned and walked back toward the front of the courtroom. She chose to sit across the aisle and two rows back from us. She gathered her robe around her as she sat and leaned the staff against her shoulder. I wondered who this regal dignitary was and what she'd done with my imp of a sister. As soon as she was settled, Vicki met my eyes and smiled, and as the smile lit her eyes, I saw the sister I loved and had known my entire life.

AFTER A FEW MINUTES of waiting so that we understood the gravitas of the people whose day we interrupted, the side door in the far corner opened. The same uniformed officer stepped through. She walked to the 'stage-right' corner of the bench, squared her shoulders, and spoke in a hall-filling voice, "All rise! The Supreme Court of the State of Washington is now in session."

Nine individuals filed through the side door behind the officer and ascended the bench. The justices assumed their seats, and the center justice cracked a gavel. She said, "Be seated. Sheriff Wilson, it's been a while since you appeared before this bench. Please, step forward and introduce your associates."

Sheriff Clyde stood and stepped to the speaker's podium, placing his case file on the lectern. "Your Honors, as the Chief Justice intimated, I am Sheriff Clyde Wilson of Godwin County. The young man sitting at the aisle is Wyatt Magnusson, Alpha of Precious and Godwin County. To his right is Gabrielle Hassan, and to her right is Karleen Vesper. To *her* right is Lewis Mitchell, who is one of the principals involved in the case that brought us here today."

"Thank you, Sheriff, but you seem to have missed someone."

Before Clyde could turn, Vicki stood and approached the gate in the balustrade separating the gallery from the court. She said, "Your Honors, please forgive my lack of preparedness. I am Victoria Catherine Magnusson, Heiress to Clan Magnusson, Heiress to the House of Merlin, and bearer of *Requiem*, the Black Staff of Ruin. I provided my brother and his party transportation today, and he neglected to inform me he was coming to address the Supreme Court."

The justices cast nervous glances to one another before the Chief Justice asked, "Forgive me, but did you say Heiress to the House of Merlin?"

"Yes, Your Honors," Vicki replied. "He was—or possibly is —my grandmother's grandfather."

"May I ask the purpose of the qualifier?"

"Well, Your Honors, no one is one-hundred-percent certain Merlin is actually dead, so I hedge my bets."

I fought to keep a straight face. If Miles hadn't seen fit to introduce himself to Vicki, I didn't want to be the one to let the cat out of the bag, so to speak and pun very much intended. But that raised an even bigger question. How did Grandma not recognize her own grandfather? As far as I knew, she hired everyone working the grounds personally and managed the crew as a whole. Did Miles change his appearance prior to becoming one of the grounds staff? Or did Grandma just not tell anyone that the Merlin of legend routinely weeded her flower beds?

"That is a very interesting thought, Lady Magnusson," the Chief Justice remarked, drawing my attention back to the proceedings. "You are the first Magi to grace the Court in any of our tenures; be welcome."

Vicki nodded graciously and side-stepped to sit by the aisle in the row opposite me.

"Sheriff Wilson," the Chief Justice continued, "present your case, if you please."

Sheriff Clyde took the justices through the case he had assembled, culminating in the request for a warrant to apprehend Paul Burkett to face shifter justice.

"And why are neither this Sloane Martinez nor the girl Sally Poole present?" one of the justices—a middle-aged man sitting on the far stage-left side of the bench—asked into the silence after Clyde completed his presentation.

I didn't like the expression on this justice's face, so I stood and approached the balustrade's gate. "That was my decision as Alpha of Precious and Godwin County. We are working out a misunderstanding between Sloane Martinez and the State of Nebraska and didn't want that mess to affect our purpose here today. Regarding Sally... well... she's been traumatized enough during all this, and I wanted her to be free to begin putting it behind her."

"I don't approve of you making decisions for us, Mister Magnusson. I'm tempted to request a recess until such time as these witnesses can be brought before us."

"If I am to address you and your associates as 'Your Honor,' I expect the same courtesy and respect in turn, sir. The proper form of address is 'Alpha,' 'Alpha Wyatt,' or 'Alpha Magnusson.' As far as you not approving of me, I don't care. It is my understanding that this hearing is largely a formality, and if you drag this process out over your inflated ego being a little butt-hurt that we didn't bring a traumatized adolescent here so you could traumatize her further, I have no problem going over your head. I already need to talk to the feds anyway, and I have no problem making sure the Shifter Council is aware of your petty obstructionism."

Before the justice could respond with what his expression implied would be rather heated, the Chief Justice cracked her gavel. "Enough, Lyle. Alpha Wyatt is very much correct that this process is a formality, and unlike you, *I* was a justice of this court the last time the Shifter Council removed one of our number with cause. I recommend you not attract their attention in a bad way."

I sensed movement to my left just before Vicki said, "And I would like it to be a matter of record that Clan Magnusson and the House of Merlin will stand with their wayward son, even if he has hopped the fence to the shifters."

Damn... Vicki didn't *quite* throw down a gauntlet, but I suspected—out of everyone standing in the courtroom—she was by far the most dangerous person here. I wasn't all that anxious to find out what 'the Black Staff of Ruin' meant, either.

"Lady Magnusson," the Chief Justice responded, "I appreciate your steadfast defense of your brother—"

"Forgive me for interrupting, Your Honors, but I wish to correct your implied misunderstanding. Yes, Alpha Wyatt is my brother, and I personally would defend him no matter what. However, in this instance, I am speaking on behalf of Clan Magnusson as a whole *and* the House of Merlin. Both families—in their entirety—consider Alpha Wyatt to be one of our own and will defend him or any cause he believes in as if he stood within our ranks as a respected Magi."

And… there went the gauntlet.

"Very well," the Chief Justice concluded. "I feel as though we've wandered a bit from our reason for being here. Mister Mitchell, do you have anything you'd like to add?"

Lewis stood. "No, Your Honors."

"Does anyone feel that we should deliberate the case?" the Chief Justice asked her associates.

The justice on the far 'stage-left' side of the bench looked like he was about to speak but pursed his lips and remained silent.

The Chief Justice nodded once. "Very well. I call for a vote. Raise your hand if in favor of issuing the warrant for Paul Burkett that Sheriff Clyde and Alpha Wyatt have requested."

Eight hands went up, and I wasn't surprised at all to see the argumentative sourpuss was the only hold-out.

"The request for a warrant is hereby approved. The court's clerk will issue said warrant within ninety minutes. Court adjourned." Another crack of the gavel, and we all rose as the justices stood and filed out of the courtroom.

As soon as the side door closed, Vicki recited words as her left hand traced a complex gesture, creating another kaleidoscopic cascade of light particles. When they faded, she was back to everyday, casual attire.

"I'm glad that's done," she said. "I hate the formal robes.

Whoever designed them hasn't realized it's the 21st Century and that there are more breathable materials than velvet."

IN THE END, it only took the Supreme Court's clerk a little over thirty minutes to deliver the warrant. Once we had that, there was no reason for us to remain, and Vicki opened a portal back to Precious.

11

The damp coolness brought Paul out of his peaceful sleep more than anything else. He pawed for the covers in a half-awake state and found thistle, grass, and a rock. That finished what the cool dampness started in rather short order.

"Wha—" Paul vocalized his confusion as he sat up and blearily examined his surroundings.

A full moon illuminated the countryside almost as bright as day, and no clouds occluded the stars. He sat on a small grassy rise about twenty-five yards from a forest's tree-line. A slight breeze blew across the field, and he shivered as the dampness—now recognized as dew—pulled heat from his body as it evaporated. Faint wisps of pine, mint, and other forest scents wafted along the breeze.

Then, he realized he was nude.

A sound drew his attention, and he looked over his shoulder to see a group of people emerge from the forest. A young man led the group, and he held something in his hand. But it was too dark to see what it was.

"Oh, thank goodness," Paul gasped. "I don't know what's

going on. I went to sleep in my apartment and somehow woke up here. I don't even know where I am."

The young man stopped about fifteen feet away. He lifted his hands, and Paul heard the crackle of paper as he unrolled whatever it was in his hand.

"Paul Burkett, you incited your associate—Lewis Mitchell —to violate a prohibited-hunting zone wherein Mister Mitchell attempted premeditated murder against one of the locals. You are now within a few feet of the geographic center of Godwin County. It will be midnight in twenty minutes, and starting then, you have until dawn to reach the county line—in whatever direction you choose. If you reach the county line, you will be free and clear."

"And what happens if I *don't* make the county line?"

"Then, you won't be free and clear."

Paul frowned at the lack of further explanation. "Well, what about clothes and a GPS or a compass or something?"

"We caught your friend in the act of attempting to murder one of my people who possessed nothing more than you do right now. As such, that is all *you* shall have for this challenge. But don't despair. We took a vote and decided on giving you a fifteen-minute head-start."

Paul shook his head as he fought the urge to freak out. "This is crazy. What you're doing... this can't be legal."

The young man chuckled. "Oh, yes, Mister Burkett... it's very legal. We have a warrant from the state Supreme Court granting authority to apprehend you to face our justice. Since you and your friend are such expert hunters, we decided our justice was for you to know what it felt like. Meet your hunter... or should I say... huntress."

For a heartbeat or two, Paul didn't notice any difference. Then, he saw it. A shadow slinked out of the night, and it took everything he had not to break down into gibbering terror. A black panther—the night too dark to determine jaguar versus leopard—stalked up to the young man's side. Its eyes remained fixed on Paul as its tail lashed side to side, expressing its opinion of the captured hunter. In that moment, Paul knew this was his last night alive. Even with the best gear and a thirty-minute lead, he couldn't outrun one of Nature's apex predators.

The young man leaned far enough to the side to stroke the cat from neck to tail, then scratch behind its ears. The cat's tail abruptly switched from lashing to a languid swish. When the young man's hand stopped scratching its ear, the big cat proceeded to rub its length along the young man's leg.

Movement on the young man's left side drew Paul's attention, and an outsized wolf stopped to stand beside the young man and leaned against him. The young man stroked the wolf—whose shoulders brushed the young man's hips— and scratched its ears, too.

"So, as I said earlier," the young man said, "you get a fifteen-minute head-start. Then, Gabrielle starts." He indi- cated the black cat. "At thirty minutes, Karleen starts." He indicated the wolf. "And at forty-five minutes, the rest of us start. It would not surprise me at all if the ladies decide to toy with you for a while. Cats are known for the games they play with their prey, and Karleen has been looking forward to your hunt for a few days now. Just remember: all you have to do to win is step across the county line."

Paul couldn't take his eyes off the massive wolf leaning against this guy. He'd never seen anything like it. "Do I at least get some underwear if I win?"

"Nope. You get to live. If you win, you should never set foot in Godwin County again. A poster with your picture, your crimes, and kill-on-sight authorization within Godwin County decorates every bulletin board we have. If you win and set so much as a toe across the county line again, you're a dead man. Understood?"

"What happened to Lewis? Is he dead, too?" Paul asked.

Just then, the young man's watch blared an alarm. "And that's midnight. Run. You have fifteen minutes."

Paul wanted to rage at the man, but something in the back of his mind told him the next fifteen minutes were his only hope of surviving. Giving the young man his best snarl, Paul pivoted to his left.

"This isn't over," he snarled, then took off running.

Wyatt, Gabrielle, Karleen, and those predator shifters who volunteered all watched Paul run into the night. After at most a minute, Wyatt snorted a chuckle. "Yeah, it is. You just don't know it yet."

HIS LUNGS BURNED. His legs ached. His feet throbbed.

Paul didn't know how long he'd been running, but his body screamed to stop and just let them end it. His arms bore scratches from briars and other thorns. His legs the same. His feet… well… rocks, thorns, and who knew what else had probably slashed his feet into bloody messes.

A howl washed over him, and a part of his brain gibbered in terror. The howl was closer this time. Then, a cascade of howls farther away answered the first.

Come on, Paul. Just give up. Let them end it. You've not going to win anyway. Just lie down and die.

Paul shook his head as he stopped for the briefest moment to catch his breath. No. He couldn't think like that. He couldn't just give up. He didn't know who these assholes were, but he was not about to give them the satisfaction of just lying down and letting their pets kill him. If he'd learned nothing else from his old man, it was that everybody should fight to keep living. Each of us only get one trip, and no one should be able to take it away without a fight.

Giving the night a growl of his own, Paul pushed back into a run. Every fiber of his being still ached, but he wasn't about to die if he had anything to say about it. Sure... *maybe* he could've fashioned a spear or a trap or something to take out the black cat. And *maybe* he'd get lucky and take out that ginormous wolf, too. But Paul believed people made their own luck, and he didn't see the margin in trying to fight his way free. Especially not since that scary kid had told him something about 'the rest of us' starting forty-five minutes after he did.

MINUTES LATER, Paul vaulted over a deadfall tree and attempted the same with the one right behind it, but his foot slipped on the wet moss covering the shadowed ground behind the tree trunk. He fell... *wrong*. A ghastly *CRACK!* and the sharp spike of pain told him something broke. He rolled past the edge of the trees into a clearing, perhaps a meadow, because he could see another tree-line in the distance.

Talk about the ultimate Catch-22. He could cry out and draw attention, thereby hastening his end, or he could keep quiet and try to crawl his way to freedom, probably dying in the process and almost certainly losing whatever broke if he lived.

Before he could decide, though, the giant wolf padded into view. It made eye contact with him, then regarded his broken leg. The chuff it made sounded almost disappointed. The wolf brought its gaze back to meet his for several moments before lifting its muzzle to the stars and howling.

The black cat was the first to arrive, and while the wolf was on his left, the cat arrived from his right. Like the wolf, the cat seemed to make eye contact with him, then looked at his broken leg. Again, the almost disappointed chuff.

Both the wolf and the cat lifted their heads to look in the

same direction, and it was a minute or more before Paul heard what sounded like a stampede heading his way. The piercing shriek of a raptor split the night overhead, and Paul was just in time to see an enormous shape cross the star field on silent wings and begin a lazy circle around his location.

Movement drew his attention away from the huge raptor circling overhead, and Paul screamed at the sight of a massive cat with huge, curved incisors that stopped at the wolf's side. Neither seemed to pay him any attention as the wolf proceeded to nuzzle the huge cat's shoulder as its tail set off in happy wagging. A chuff preceded the black cat's arrival on the sabertooth's right, and it joined in the nuzzling as well.

After a few moments, the sabertooth cat took a step forward, and both the wolf and the cat stopped nuzzling to stand at its side. Then, over the course of maybe three seconds, the sabertooth cat became the same young man who told Paul to run. He was just as nude as Paul, and he moved into a single-knee crouch just a few feet from where Paul lay.

"Well, this is rather unfortunate," the young man remarked. "You've given us a rather nice hunt up till now. But... I suppose 'hunt' is rather misleading as we knew where you were the whole time."

"You did?" Paul asked, frowning his confusion.

The young man pointed up just as the massive raptor whooshed by overhead. "Yep. We have air support."

"I suppose this is where you kill me, then," Paul said, his tone resigned.

The young man shrugged. "Sure, if that's really what you want."

"Huh? What kind of idiot *wants* to die?"

The young man chuckled. More movement drew Paul's attention, and he bit back another startle response as animals closed in around them. Wolves—normal size, these—bears, foxes, deer, elk, a couple lions, a couple tigers… all these and more soon surrounded Paul and the young man.

"My name is Wyatt," the young man said, "and I am the Alpha of Precious and Godwin County. In preparing our case for the warrant, we did a deep dive into your background. Who you are, what you've done, all that stuff. What we found was a man who enjoyed hunting and life in general and went out of his way to keep from being a bad guy. You don't seem like one of those so-called sportsmen who only chase trophies, and you've turned in twice your legal limit every year to the state's Hunters for the Hungry program.

"So, here's the situation. You didn't shy away from the challenge. You didn't try to cheat. You didn't just give up. In our eyes, you've earned the choice. If you choose, you're free to leave Godwin County, alive and well but still under the sentence I declared earlier; the posters are already printed. The other option is to join us, the Shifter Nation of North America; pick your breed, and if you prefer something not represented in town or the county, we'll fly one in."

Paul scanned the crowd once more. "You mean all these animals here are people?"

"Yes," Wyatt answered. "The dire wolf is Karleen Vesper; the melanistic jaguar is Gabrielle Hassan. Sheriff Clyde Wilson is one of the wolves, honestly not sure which one right now." One of the wolves lifted its right foreleg and waved 'hi.' "Okay… guess he's that one."

By this time, Paul almost tuned out Wyatt's voice. He gazed at something that had fascinated him since he was a small boy. He knew they were vicious predators, but that didn't matter. He'd always had a soft spot for grizzly bears.

"Can I choose a grizzly?" he asked, his voice strained from the pain coursing up his leg.

The lone grizzly in sight chuffed and nodded once.

"Wait," Paul held up his hand. "What about Lewis?"

Wyatt grinned. "We're letting him sweat the night in the town jail. We told him the whole town and half the county turned out to hunt you. I figure around noon tomorrow we can sit down and have the same chat with him that we're having right now. He doesn't seem to be a bad sort, just made a couple poor decisions."

"So... how does this work?"

"Well, I don't recommend what I went through to become a shifter," Wyatt remarked, and half the animals chuffed and displayed other signs of amusement. "I'll leave it up to Hank."

The grizzly in question lumbered over to stand across Paul from Wyatt. He took a couple sniffs that made Paul lose a bit of color, then lowered his massive head and bit Paul's thigh above where his leg was broken. Paul screamed and passed out.

12

The next day, we brought Paul Burkett to the town jail and released Lewis Mitchell, prior to giving him the same choice as Paul. Lewis almost passed out from sheer relief that we did not in fact maim, rend, shred, kill, or otherwise devour his longtime friend. Paul seemed like he wanted to find Lewis's reaction funny, and he probably would have... but the experience of being hunted was too fresh in his mind. After some discussion and a thought, Lewis asked about becoming an eagle shifter. One of Sheriff Clyde's deputies was an eagle and agreed to see to the matter right there.

ABOUT A WEEK after settling the matter of Lewis Mitchell and Paul Burkett, Lyssa—the feline councilor—returned to Precious. She traveled light, bearing only an attaché case and an overnight bag. She arrived in town via hired car, which promptly reversed course and left town mere seconds after she stepped onto the sidewalk.

Karleen left the diner just as she arrived and walked to meet her. Lyssa saw her approach and smiled a greeting.

"That didn't look anything like the SUVs I've seen councilors travel in," Karleen remarked as she stopped a respectful distance from Lyssa.

Lyssa shook her head and glanced back at the car as it went out of sight. "No. It certainly isn't. I've given our discussion a great deal of thought, and I'd like to visit Precious for a while and explore the possibility of a relationship with Wyatt... assuming everyone involved is still agreeable to the idea."

Karleen eyed Lyssa's overnight bag and arched an eyebrow. "Surely, *that* doesn't carry all you need for a stay measuring into *a while*."

"Oh goodness, no. I shipped my luggage before leaving Chicago, because even first-class customers lose luggage all the time."

Wait... what? Karleen blinked her confusion. "You mean you didn't fly in on one of the Council's jets?"

Lyssa shook her head. "No. I'm on three weeks' leave from my Council duties. It's the first time off I've taken in decades, and honestly, I think everyone was happy to see me take it. I can be a little fierce when it comes to work, and this will give them a break as much as me. If things don't work out here, I'll use the remaining time to visit my family in Oklahoma. I have a few things to deliver to Alpha Wyatt, and then, I'm officially on my own time."

"I think Wyatt's in the town's administration building, but I'm not sure," Karleen remarked.

"That's something I've wondered since I first came to Precious," Lyssa said. "Why don't you call it 'City Hall' or something like that?"

Karleen shrugged. "No idea. I've only been here since the kidnapping case. You'll have to ask one of the old timers."

"The Council is still working with the Magi Assembly for the next phase of that investigation," Lyssa remarked as they fell into step beside each other. "I'm not sure where that will take us."

The ladies fell into a companionable silence as they walked down the sidewalk. Just as they approached the town's administration building, its doors opened, and Wyatt stepped outside. He looked their way and smiled, then headed their way.

"Hello, ladies," Wyatt said in greeting as he gave Karleen a kiss. Then, focused on Lyssa. "You're back sooner than I expected."

Lyssa smiled her own greeting to him as she said, "Well, the Council arrived at a decision on the matter of our treaty with the United States, and I felt it was a good pause point to take some time and explore the relationship we discussed, if you and your partners are still agreeable to the idea."

Wyatt grinned. "As long as you're okay with there being no hierarchy between you three, I'm fine with it. My cat is rather firmly in favor of you."

"It was a couple days after we left before my lioness stopped sulking. She was *very* put out with me about leaving you. But before we get too far into that, I'd like to discharge the Council business so I can be one-hundred-percent on my own time."

Wyatt nodded. "That's perfectly agreeable. Should we invade Alistair's office and ask Sloane to join us?"

"That might be best," Lyssa replied.

Karleen cleared her throat. "If we're going to ask Sloane to join us, Alistair's office will be rather packed. Why don't we invade the conference room instead?"

"Excellent idea," Wyatt agreed. "Do you mind inviting Sloane while I get Alistair and text Gabrielle?"

Pivoting toward the hotel across the street, Karleen set

off. Wyatt turned back toward the door he just exited and offered his arm to Lyssa, saying, "Shall we?"

I COLLECTED ALISTAIR, and all three of us went to the conference room. We had just assumed our seats when Gabrielle, Karleen, and Sloane arrived. I sat at the head of the table, as the Alpha of Precious should, and Karleen and Gabrielle did a quick rock-paper-scissors to see who would sit at my immediate right. Lyssa watched with obvious amusement as they tied twice in a row before Gabrielle won with scissors versus Karleen's paper. Sloane sat three seats further down the table from Karleen.

Alistair assumed the seat at my immediate left as Lyssa sat to his left, and I rapped my knuckles on the table. Not sure why I did that, but it seemed appropriate if Lyssa was acting as a councilor at the moment.

"You bring word from the Council?" I asked.

Lyssa nodded and opened her attaché case. "It took some effort, but we eventually unearthed our copy of the treaty between the Shifter Nation of North America and the United States. It specified that our point of contact with the United States government was none other than the Secretary of State. The treaty contained no provisions as to the manner of our contact, should we wish to contact the government, but the Council debated the matter and ultimately voted to create a new position for the Shifter Nation. The new position is titled 'Consul,' and has the authority to act in the name of the Council for the greater good of all shifters in North America."

I had a bad feeling about where this was going, and I just had to ask, "Did the Council mean 'consul' in the diplomatic sense or the Ancient Roman sense?"

"A blend of the two, actually," Lyssa answered, her expression shifting to an almost predatory smile, "and the Council charged me with delivering the Consul's writ of authority."

Without missing a beat, she withdrew a scroll sealed with wax and a purple ribbon. She stood and walked the short distance to approach me, then extended the scroll to me.

"Wyatt Xavier Magnusson, by the authority vested in me by the Council of the Shifter Nation of North America, I hereby name you Consul of the Shifter Nation."

I felt my shoulders slump. "I didn't want to be Alpha of Precious and Godwin County. I'm only two months into that, three months being a shifter at all... and now, you're throwing *this* at me? Is the Council collectively high or something?"

Lyssa laid the scroll on the table in front of me and returned to her seat before addressing my concerns. "Wyatt, you have shown yourself to be mature, reasonable, and very level-headed. You have the strength to defend your decisions with tooth and claw if necessary, but we have no record of you ever seeking such conflict. You come to the shifter world with a fresh eye, having no prejudices or preconceptions. You also have strengthened our relationship to the Magi community. I submit to you that there is no one else who *should* carry this title and authority."

"You people are enough to drive a man to drink," I groused, heaving a sigh for flavor.

"Don't bother," Karleen countered. "It takes an entire pony keg for a shifter to feel a slight buzz."

Well, at least I'd never been one to drink. I looked from Karleen to Alistair, then Gabrielle. "What do you three think about this?"

They all looked to one another, and Alistair filled the silence. "From a 'multiple birds with one stone' viewpoint, it's a master-stroke. As Lyssa said, you're conscientious, even-handed, level-headed, and mature. Your grandfather and I have tried for years to stabilize relations between shifters and Magi, and your becoming a shifter—not to mention a primogenitor—has only buoyed our efforts. Karleen's assistance to Vicki has not gone unnoticed within the Assembly, and Connor and I have both felt a subtle shift from both sides. Yes, of course… it's only been three months, and no great changes that aren't major disasters can take place in such a short amount of time. But there have been small steps toward neutrality—for lack of a better term—from both sides. All because you have maintained your relationships with family while forging new ones with the shifters."

I turned to Gabrielle and Karleen. Both nodded toward Alistair, and Gabrielle opined, "What he said."

Talk about a fine kettle of fish. I did not need this extra complication in my life. Not at all. A small part of me still wanted to continue the 'why me' refrain, but it felt too much like whining at this point.

Yes. And I am not a kitten, the growly voice remarked. *It is only our due. The time is coming when we—the elder cousins—will step forward and assume our rightful place as leaders of the shifter world. We are too few at this time, but the day will come when I will stand with many elder cousins to form* our own *council. This 'Consul' business lays a perfect first stone of the foundation for it.*

Well, damn… that wasn't ominous at all. I was quick to respond, *I will not be some tyrant or dictator. If that's what you're expecting, we need to have this out right now.*

My cat sent me an impression of exasperation. *There is no 'we' or 'us' or 'you.' There is only me. There will ever only be me. The insistence of seeing two entities in one body is an utter fallacy. The sooner I fully internalize that, the sooner I can achieve true synthesis as the elder cousins before me achieved.*

Okay. There was a lot to unpack there, and I wasn't really

sure a meeting in the conference room was the proper time or place. I filed that statement away for later.

"What?" Gabrielle asked. "You were somewhere else for a few moments."

I wasn't sure there was any way to convey the experience in a timely manner, so I hedged. "I was just considering the matter, turning it around in my head. As far as this 'Consul' thing goes, I want to be very clear that I don't like it and never wanted it. If the Council is set on their course of establishing the position and won't consider someone like Alistair for the job—"

"Don't throw me under that bus," the man in question interjected. "I would much rather be an advisor or mentor. I am in no way qualified for such a position."

I wanted to scream at him, not the first time I felt complete and total frustration toward him. If he—a wolf of unknown years and exponentially more experience with the shifter world than me—wasn't qualified to be Consul, who in their right mind would choose me? But I didn't. I didn't say any of the angry, near-petulant thoughts that raced through my mind. Once again, the Council shanghaied me into something I didn't seek and didn't want, and they damn well better be prepared when I acted according to my conscience and *not* the ancient, moth-eaten, so-called wisdom of the ages.

"Like I was saying…" I continued. "If the Council is dead set on having me as the first Consul of the Shifter Nation, so be it. I'll do it to the best of my ability until my term ends."

Lyssa winced and looked away. That wasn't good.

"What?" I asked.

"It isn't a term appointment," Lyssa replied, her voice quiet… almost timid.

It took me a couple seconds to connect the dots, and I hoped beyond hope I was wrong. "It's a *life* appointment?"

Lyssa jerked a nod, still refusing to make eye contact with me.

"But shifters are functionally immortal! Did the councilors read a different ancient history book than I did? Because 'Consul for life' didn't work out so well for Julius Caesar."

Lyssa flinched, and I instantly felt about two inches tall. I wanted nothing more than to rage and growl and scream, but none of this was Lyssa's fault. Well... it wasn't *solely* her fault. She was just one vote in however many councilors there were. See? What more proof did they need that I had no business being Consul. I didn't even know how many councilors were on the damn Council.

I put my head in my hands and took several deep breaths. They didn't noticeably calm me, but they did give me the time to drag my emotions away from the surface. "Lyssa, I'm sorry. No matter what else happens between us, I don't want you feeling afraid of me. This is... it's so much worse than Alpha of Precious and Godwin County that I'm not sure I have the words to quantify just how much worse it is. But we have more important matters to handle. Sloane has been hunted and believed to be a criminal for too long, and I refuse to allow that situation to continue any longer than it has to. So, I will put a pin in my thoughts over this whole 'Consul' nonsense for now and revisit it once Sloane's situation is sorted."

Withdrawing my phone from a thigh pocket of my cargo pants, I unlocked it and thumbed through my contacts until I found the name I sought. I tapped the 'call' control and then switched the call to speaker.

We enjoyed the sound of the phone ringing for a couple seconds until the call connected. "Agent Hauser speaking."

"Agent Hauser, this is Wyatt Magnusson. You're on

speaker with me, Alistair, Gabrielle, Karleen, Lyssa Westridge from the Shifter Council, and Sloane Martinez."

"That… is an impressive audience. Why do I feel like I should be afraid?"

I chuckled. I couldn't help myself. "I don't know. Does your deputy director have a history of shooting the messenger?"

There was a slight pause, then, "Well, *that* doesn't fill me with happiness and joy. Why am I going to be risking my deputy director's wrath? Especially considering how many steps there are between me and him in the chain of command?"

"Because I need to speak with the United States government on behalf of the Shifter Nation of North America, and our treaty specifies the Secretary of State as our contact point. However, I don't have any contacts in the State Department."

More silence.

"How bad is this going to bite me, Wyatt? I have quite a few years until retirement and career goals I'd rather not jeopardize."

I sighed. "It shouldn't come back to bite you at all, Winnifred; I'm just looking for help to make contact with the State Department. The issue will probably come back to your desk eventually, but not in a 'bite you' situation. If it does come back to your desk, I'd imagine it would be a new case for you, but the conversation needs to start with the Secretary of State."

Silence dominated the call for several moments until we heard a heavy sigh.

"Okay," Hauser said. "Part of me quails at the idea of passing you up the chain without knowing *what* I'm passing up the chain, but at the same time, I'm intimately familiar with the concept of need-to-know. Give me a moment, and I'll give you his office number."

Another pause, though much shorter, and Hauser rattled off a phone number that several around the table were quick to write down.

"Thanks, Winnifred," I said after confirming the number. "I appreciate this."

"You're welcome, Wyatt… just try not to get me fired."

13

_____

W ashington, D.C., was one of the many places around the country that I had always wanted to visit. As I looked out across the skyline from the balcony of my hotel room, I wondered if I'd have enough time—or be in the mood—to see a few sights around the city after the conversation with the Secretary of State.

The Shifter Nation of North America did not exactly have 'normalized' relations with the United States government. Whether it was in spite of—or because of—the fact that most shifters within the USA considered themselves American citizens was anyone's guess. The last time the Shifter Nation had formal relations or communications with the United States government, the country's executive branch still had a War Department.

I couldn't help but feel the issue of correcting Sloane's situation was going to be a tough row to hoe. I didn't even know if the current Secretary of State *knew* she was the point of contact for the Shifter Nation, let alone knew that shifters existed. Back when I first became a shifter, either Gabrielle or Alistair told me that every branch of the US military except the Air Force had shifter-only units, which implied the government was aware of us.

But to be honest, that only raised more questions in my mind. I mean... if the government knew about shifters to the point that most of the major military branches all had shifter-only units, why was the idea of Sloane being an avian shifter so important to that black ops group? Were they somehow cut off from the government as a whole for however long the government had organized shifter-only units? Or were those units compartmentalized within the military to the point that very few people knew about them?

The situation was thoroughly frustrating. I felt like I was supposed to draw a map of a landmass from orbit... with the entire planet shrouded in fog.

Slender arms wrapped around me as Gabrielle said, "Hey... are you okay? You've kinda turned into the strong, silent type lately. Is it the 'Consul' thing?"

Heh... if only. "Not exclusively. I don't like not knowing what kind of situation I'm walking into, but I don't know of any way to get the information I need without walking into the situation. Plus, I have no training in diplomacy or statesmanship or anything like that, and I'll be face-to-face with people who make a career of it. I would say the Council threw me to the wolves, but I'm not afraid of any wolf except Karleen."

"Damn right," the woman in question opined, mere heartbeats before she wrapped her arms around me.

"I guess my main concern is making some huge mistake or embarrassing the shifters. I don't want to be the guy who caused a war between the shifters and the United States."

Gabrielle tiptoed to kiss my cheek. Karleen apparently didn't want to be left out and kissed my other cheek.

"Wyatt, you're letting your fears run away with you," Gabrielle remarked as she and Karleen rubbed my back and chest. "Yes, it will be apparent to the Secretary of State *right now* that you're new to all this, but forty years from now when we're back here again over something, the Secretary of State then won't have any idea you were nervous now. That is one of the major advantages shifters have over humans or even Magi. We don't die from old age... or even disease. It gives us the potential to establish a level of continuity in government unheard of in the human world. Just look how the pendulum of American politics swings from one extreme to the other; the two parties care far more about achieving their goals or denying the other party their goals than serving the American people. I know Alphas who have led their territories for longer than the United States has *existed* as a country. I'm not saying shifters are perfect or better than humans, just that we have the opportunity to create greater stability. Keep that in mind when you're meeting with the deputy director tomorrow, and again whenever he can get you in with the Secretary of State."

Karleen poked me in the ribs and added her two cents, "What she said."

I pulled my arms free of them so I could gather them close and tried kissing both of them at the same time. I'm not sure how successful I was, but they seemed to appreciate the thought.

"I have no idea what I did to deserve you two." I then gave each a kiss of their own.

"We feel the same way," Karleen replied.

I FOUGHT a yawn as we followed our escort to meet with the Deputy Director of the Paranormal Branch. We must've made for quite a sight, because almost everyone stopped to watch us pass. Or maybe it was just the gorgeous women walking with me.

Vicki walked on my left while Gabrielle enjoyed pride of place on my right. Karleen and Lyssa followed us. I wasn't sure why Vicki had asked to come with us and present the Magi's issue after we discussed the situation with Sloane, but I saw no problem with that. If nothing else, it would present a united front to the Secretary of State. I hoped we didn't need that, but between the five of us, I couldn't imagine anything we couldn't handle.

Our escort delivered us to a door with no placard and led us inside. He introduced us to the receptionist and wasted no time in vacating the area. The receptionist was a young man who greeted us with an open smile and quickly notified the deputy director we had arrived. There wasn't even time to sit before the receptionist ushered us into his office.

A man on the upper end of middle age stood as we entered and walked around what looked to be a handmade oak desk. Pictures of the man and various public figures I recognized lined one wall, while family photos decorated another.

"Alpha Wyatt," he said as he extended his hand, "it's a pleasure to meet you at last. I'm Lowell Nathanson, Deputy Director of the Paranormal Branch of my agency."

"Sir, this is my sister Vicki, who has accompanied us on Magi business, since the Secretary of State is the point of contact for their treaty as well. These ladies are Gabrielle Hassan, Karleen Vesper, and Lyssa Westridge. Lyssa is one of the feline representatives to the Shifter Council."

Nathanson shook hands with each in turn as I introduced them. When he reached Lyssa, she was quick to say, "Please, do not consider my presence as anything other than an advisor. The Council has invested Alpha Wyatt as the first Consul of the Shifter Nation, and as such, he has our complete trust to handle any and all matters pertaining to our treaty."

"Consul of the Shifter Nation, you say? Is that in the diplomatic or Roman tradition?"

Lyssa's smile went so far beyond predatory that I feared she might be picturing the deputy director with a side of ketchup and mustard, or perhaps steak sauce. "Why, both, of course."

That rattled the deputy director. He did an admirable job of hiding it, but four of his five guests could hear his heartbeat. No matter what a person says or shows through an expression, the heartbeat never lies.

"I see. He must be something special indeed to go from a new shifter to Alpha of Godwin County to Consul of the Shifter Nation in the span of three months. Please, let's be seated."

"You have *no idea* how special he is," Lyssa replied, sounding entirely too much like a purr to me.

We all assumed our seats. Vicki and I sat in the two guest chairs I suspected were his regular guest chairs as the ladies picked their seats from the three chairs around mine.

As soon as we all had seats, Nathanson began, "I have already contacted the Secretary of State and arranged a meeting. Since no one likes surprised predators close at hand, I feel I should inform you that she asked me to attend the meeting as well, as I have more immediate experience with you and shifters in general. I gave serious consideration to calling either Agent Hauser or Agent Burke to D.C. as they have even more direct and recent experience with shifters, but the Secretary felt a teleconference would suffice." Nathanson paused for a moment, then grimaced. "I should also warn you that, government politics being what they are, the Attorney General—being my cabinet-level supervisor— will also attend the meeting."

"You are not enthused about that," I remarked, stating the obvious. "Why?"

Nathanson looked toward his wall of family photos for several moments in silence before turning back to us. "Because he has stated at multiple points in the past that anything paranormal is a bunch of 'cockamamie folderol' and having a Paranormal Branch of this agency—especially at our funding level—is beyond absurd."

"So he doesn't even believe Magi exist?" Vicki asked.

Nathanson snorted a chuckle. "No. Shortly after he took office, someone came to give him a briefing on the true state of the world… to include all the different groups of magic-users, shifters, and everyone else… and he promptly ran the poor soul out of his office. He said something to the effect of having no time for a such a fraud and pack of lies perpetrated on the federal government. To be quite honest, I'm just as glad he doesn't believe in Magi, because I'm not confident that he wouldn't come down on the 'suffer not a witch to live' side of the matter."

Vicki sighed. "Oh, dear… one of *those*."

"Yes," Nathanson agreed. "I'm afraid so."

"And there's no way to keep him out of the meeting?" I asked.

Nathanson shook his head. "Not really. I could pass a request to the Secretary of State that he be excluded based on his statements and conduct in the past, but I'd rather not do that, since he's a 'shoot the messenger' type. Especially since he'd have no way of venting his spleen on any of you. Matter of fact, I probably shouldn't have said anything at all, but like I said, I *know* who we're dealing with. I wanted no part of being in the same room with surprised predators who might possibly feel threatened. That just doesn't seem like a wise idea to me."

I fought the urge to laugh. "I may be new at this, but even

I'm aware it wouldn't be diplomatic to eat the Attorney General, no matter the level of provocation. Out of everyone who will be in that room, you have no reason to fear *us*."

"I appreciate that. In regards to the meeting, the Secretary has cleared her afternoon schedule tomorrow and has offered the use of a car and escort. If you accept the offer, don't worry that you'll be forced to ride with the Attorney General. The Director and I will have that... privilege."

Never one to make unilateral decisions, I looked to Vicki, who nodded. Then turned to my ladies, who nodded as well. I returned my focus to the deputy director. "Please, express our acceptance of—and appreciation for—the car and escort."

"I will be happy to do so. Where should I have them sent?"

Gabrielle was quick to offer up the name of our hotel, and Nathanson nodded his recognition. From there, the meeting became more of a general conversation for a short time until it was politic for us to depart. I personally didn't understand all the nuances of it, but the ladies seemed aware and comfortable with it. Maybe I'd pick up on it with time and experience, or maybe not.

WE SPENT the next morning in preparation for the meeting. Vicki spun us up suits and dresses... well, *suit* and dresses... and we went through everything multiple times. None of us wanted to get anything wrong.

At the appointed time, we trooped downstairs to meet the car that would take us to the State Department. Two people in suits greeted us as we stepped off the elevator, introducing themselves and leading us outside. Two blacked-out SUVs framed our conveyance as it sat in front of our hotel's entrance. The car was not *quite* a limousine, at least it wasn't a stretch, and I tried not to gape at the thickness of the doors when the gentleman stepped forward and opened it for us. I gestured for the ladies to precede me, then joined them. The gentleman closed the door and walked back to the chase SUV as the lady who met us opened the front passenger door of our car and slid inside.

Our shifter hearing was such that—even through the privacy partition—we heard the woman inform everyone that we were ready to go. Like a well-oiled machine, the drivers put us in motion, and I watched the streets roll by as we left the hotel.

"WHAT ARE the chances that we'll be able to leave the hotel now and not attract all kinds of attention?" I asked a few minutes into the drive.

My traveling companions offered a round of chuckles in reply.

"It would be one thing to be picked up in an official State Department vehicle, but to be dropped off by one as well?" Lyssa remarked. "If you were hoping to be just another face in the hotel after this, I'm afraid your hopes will be dashed."

"Any luck getting one of those service-animal vests for my feline form? Maybe we could tour the sights that way."

All of the ladies—even my sister—erupted in full-throated laughter, which was my intention. The idea of a Smilodon walking around the National Mall on a leash and wearing one of those vests was just too absurd. Vicki's expression as she regained her composure told me I gave her an idea for a future gift, but that was okay. She hadn't pranked me in a while and was probably experiencing withdrawal symptoms to some extent.

"What are the odds they wired the passenger area for

sound?" Vicki asked, and Karleen, Gabrielle, and Lyssa promptly shook their heads 'no.'

Karleen said, "The only electronics I can hear are beyond the privacy partition, and even an unpowered microphone creates a tiny electrical hum that we can hear as it generates the electrical pulses. Now, there's nothing saying they don't have a laser mic pointed at the privacy partition, assuming the partition isn't so thick it completely deadens sound vibrations."

Conversation moved on to other topics, including the places everyone wanted to visit in the city. It wasn't until a lull developed that I glanced outside and felt like the bottom dropped out of my stomach.

Our little three-vehicle motorcade had turned into the White House.

"Uhm… I thought we were meeting with the Secretary of State," I said, interrupting the ladies' discussion.

Lyssa nodded. "That's the plan. Why?"

Her back was to our direction of travel, so she couldn't see where we were headed. Karleen and Gabrielle did, though, and both muttered variations on the theme of "Oh, shit."

Just as Lyssa and Vicki spun to look out the partition, it came down, and the agent in the passenger seat leaned into view, saying, "Apologies for the surprise. Your visit has been reclassified as an official working visit, and the President requested that we include her in the meeting."

The ladies all looked to me, silently waiting for my response to guide theirs. In the end, I simply shrugged. "Oh, well… at least you didn't tell us up front so we sweated meeting the President for the ride over. I suppose that's something of a kindness. Deputy Director Nathanson and his party are already aware?"

"Yes, sir," the woman replied. "In fact, they arrived just a few minutes ago with the Secretary of State."

I felt a swell of gratitude that no one considered this a full state visit. I had no wish for all that pomp and pageantry.

"Say… are you allowed to tell us *why* the visit was reclassified?"

The agent pursed her lips and looked out the windshield for a couple seconds before turning back to us. "I probably shouldn't, but since it's been almost eighty years since the Magi Assembly and the Shifter Nation communicated with the government, the Secretary of State brought the matter to the President's attention. The President promptly expressed interest in meeting you, which led to the reclassification."

I smelled a rat. "I would think such a dramatic shuffling of the President's schedule would take place as far in advance as possible. Had the meeting already been reclassified when we spoke with Deputy Director Nathanson?"

The agent adopted an expression of such pure, uncontrived innocence that I felt Vicki should take notes. "I'm sure I couldn't say, sir."

The more I thought about it, though, I had a really difficult time feeling offended. I mean, sure… it was unlikely they would've sandbagged a representative of a foreign *human* country like this, but at the same time, we weren't human. I wasn't sure even President Roosevelt met Magi or shifters during the war era, so this was probably something of a singular experience for President Williams.

A random thought popped to the forefront of my mind. If I was stuck with this 'Consul' nonsense, how many presidents would it take before I considered meeting one to be routine… or even worse, blasé?

The vehicle slowed to a stop, and the agent in the passenger seat exited. An agent approached my door from the chase car and opened it. I stepped outside and held my hand for each of my fellow passengers in turn. When I turned toward the building, it took all my willpower not to freeze like a deer in headlights. Standing in the vestibule— just past the security checkpoint--was Olivia Williams, President of the United States.

Olivia Williams was a first-term president out of Oregon, and she was not only the first woman to be elected to the office but also the first *Hispanic* woman. As much as the conservative rank and file would have loved to stand up in wholesale opposition to her policies and platform, the overwhelming landslide victory she enjoyed made doing so a very risky political proposition, which led to something of a cautious detente between the White House and Capitol Hill uncommon in recent years.

THE FACT that I had zero idea what to do had to be writ large across my entire posture, expression, and demeanor. I have no idea how it felt for foreign dignitaries with decades of experience to approach the White House, let alone the President... but for me—someone who wasn't even twenty-five—it was thoroughly intimidating.

Before the moment could become too awkward, the growly voice came to my rescue.

Remember that I am an heir to power and majesty older than humans' written language. Yes, I personally may be few years beyond a kitten, but my ancestors and younger cousins once ruled *this world.*

With that in mind, I crossed the distance between us and used my enthusiasm for the meeting—buried though it was beneath my anxiety—to adopt a genuine, honest smile as I said, "Hello, Madam President. I'm Wyatt Magnusson."

She returned my smile with one of her own and lifted her hand as she replied, "I'm Olivia Williams, Mister Magnusson."

"Please, 'Mister Magnusson' is my grandfather. I would appreciate it if you would call me Wyatt. May I introduce my associates?"

Williams answered with a gracious nod. "Please do."

"This is my sister, Vicki; she's representing the Magi Assembly. These ladies are Karleen Vesper, Gabrielle Hassan, and Lyssa Westridge."

"It's a pleasure to meet you all," Williams said as she turned toward the entrance. "Protocol said that someone else should have met you, but I chose to pull rank. I've never met a Magi or shifter before, that I know of, and couldn't resist being one of the first to greet you. The others are waiting for us inside."

She led us into the White House as she talked. Her entire demeanor suggested an almost-child-like fascination with us, and she didn't seem to prefer Magi over shifters or vice versa. A short distance inside, she stopped, then led us into an empty office before turning to us. The agents serving as the President's close protection closed the door behind us.

"Please forgive me, but I just have to ask. What's it like?"

We all glanced at each other. I asked, "What's what like, ma'am?"

"Being a Magi or being a shifter. Either. Both."

"For me," Vicki said, "being a Magi is almost equal parts

duty, responsibility, and awe. Yes, being able to alter reality according to my will is incredible, but my position within the Magi is almost akin to the heir of the reigning monarch in the UK. Not quite a direct comparison, because fifteen families make up the core of the Magi Assembly, but certainly close."

Vicki turned to us, and Lyssa stepped forward. "As for being a shifter, I'm not sure I can convey what it's like to you. Suppose someone asked you what it's like to be a woman. Not the first woman to be President. Or a woman in government, but just what it's like to be female in general. Except for Wyatt, we're born shifters; it's all we've known."

Williams nodded her understanding, then settled her attention on me. "So, if I may be so bold, how would *you* describe it?"

"Dropped in an ice bath while you're fast asleep," I answered without hesitation. "It was that much of a shock. A part of me is now a massive predator that hasn't walked the land in thousands of years. I'm so much stronger than I was as a human. More durable. A little faster, but Smilodons aren't really built for speed. I have yet to exhaust my endurance, and all shifters heal at an unbelievable rate. I took a blast from a twelve-gauge shotgun straight in my side and pretty much shrugged it off."

"What was the load?" one of the agents asked.

I turned to look at the agent and shrugged. "I'm not sure, to be honest. There wasn't really a size gauge handy to measure bloody pellets with, but I'd say it was either double- or triple-aught buckshot."

Talk about making a couple agents more tense...

"But that's not uncommon for shifters. Gabrielle, here, took a blast from a shotgun, too."

"It was more a glancing shot," Gabrielle was quick to clarify.

Williams shook her head, amazement plain in her expression. "I cannot imagine what it would be like to shrug off a shotgun blast. That's… incredible. But I've kept the others waiting long enough. We should be on our way."

A SHORT WALK delivered us to a conference room where the directors, Secretary of State, and the Attorney General waited. Everyone stood when the President entered, though the Secretary of State bore hints of a frown.

"Yes, Lucy, I know," the President said, acknowledging the 'affronted schoolmarm' expression that lurked near the surface before turning back to us. "I would normally save my friend for last, but that would disrespect the office she holds, so allow me to introduce Lucy Perez, Secretary of State."

The President then went on to introduce the Attorney General, Lowell Nathanson's boss, and Nathanson himself. Yes, it violated uncounted rules of protocol for the President to handle the introductions and conduct us to the conference room, but she still hadn't lost the child-like enthusiasm for meeting Magi and shifters.

I introduced everyone in my group, but before we moved toward seats, the Secretary of State sandbagged me yet again.

"And do you have any titles we should know?" Lucy asked.

If it hadn't been for the perpetual scowl gracing the Attorney General's visage, I probably would've forgotten we were in a conference room of the White House. The President and the Secretary of State were *that* personable and welcoming.

I tried not to sigh as I answered, "I am Alpha of Precious and Godwin County…" someone tapped my heel "…and Consul of the Shifter Nation of North America. Vicki, do you have anything to confess?"

Amusement colored the expressions of both the President and the Secretary of State at my phrasing as Vicki stepped to my side. "In formal situations, I am announced as Heiress of Clan Magnusson, Heiress to the House of Merlin, and Bearer of *Requiem*, the Black Staff of Ruin."

Yep. Nice to see I wasn't the only one who could make a protection detail tense...

The President moved to a seat and gestured for all of us to follow. I had the amazing luck to find myself sitting across the table from the federal sourpuss, Mister Attorney General himself.

"Now, what brings you to contact the government?" the President asked.

I cleared my throat, mildly unsure of how to proceed. Ah, well... like the man said, 'begin at the beginning.'

"Madam President, you are probably not aware of a farm that suffered a double homicide and arson in Nebraska. An elderly couple by the name of Higgins owned the place, and while the authorities now pursue their then-farmhand—one Sloane Martinez—the perpetrators were in fact members of a government black ops group out of a base in the northern edge of the Grand Tetons."

"And just how do you know all of this?" the Attorney General interjected, his tone harsh and argumentative.

Oh, boy... here goes. "For one thing, we have Miss Martinez who explained what happened, and secondly, we... *interviewed*... the black ops team that began accosting people in Precious when they came looking for her. The statements we recorded from the black ops team matched Miss Martinez's account."

The Attorney General glared at me. "You expect us to believe that you captured American black ops personnel who then *volunteered* all sorts of information about their mission and base location? That just proves you're lying."

I sighed and shook my head. "Shifter senses are sufficiently acute to pick out when a person's heartbeat changes in the course of lying. Beyond that, well... Vicki?"

Vicki recited a series of words in a language long since dead, and the Attorney General's hostile expression faded into vapid adoration. Vicki said, "Name one file you've read in the past two weeks that is classified as Top Secret - SCI. Just the name of the file, if you please."

"Operation Autumn Thunder, Mistress." The man's expression of vapid adoration never wavered. "Are you sure that's all I can do for you? Anything you want, I'll do."

Every other government functionary—from the President down to the sole protection agent in the room—gaped at the Attorney General.

An impish grin curled Vicki's lips as she asked, "Anything? Is there no limit to what you'd do for me?"

"Oh, no, Mistress. No limit at all. If you asked it of me, I'd steal that man's firearm and shoot the President. It's been a few years since I was active duty, but I still exercise and practice. I'm confident I could take him."

Vicki traced a gesture with her hand as she spoke another series of words. The Attorney General's expression of vapid adoration faded and tried to re-settle into his former 'hostile bulldog.' But a full and complete memory of what he'd just said settled in his mind. He went white as a snowbank at a ski resort.

"And *that* is why you should always honor the treaty with the Magi," I remarked. I fished a couple memory cards out of my pocket and passed them to the President. "Those contain unedited recordings of our discussion with the black ops team. The Shifter Council empowered me to speak on behalf of all shifters and ask that this matter be dealt with and *soon*. Sloane is a shifter and, as such, covered by our treaty with the United States. Even if she were guilty of the murders or arson—which she isn't—she would be *our* responsibility. We would appreciate it if you would police your people likewise."

By now, the Attorney General shook off whatever shock rendered him speechless, and he shot to his feet, knocking his chair over to strike the floor with a heavy *BAM*!

"Madam President, that... that witch spelled me. She *made* me say those things. I want her arrested!"

"My sister is Magi, not a witch," I countered, calm as could be. Though I did fight a smile. "That was a simple charm spell, and as I understand it, it could not make you do anything you find truly reprehensible."

The President sent an arched eyebrow down the table to Vicki. "Is that true?"

"More or less," Vicki replied. "Brother dear has never studied the Magi arts, so his understanding is a little imprecise. But he is essentially correct. Would you permit another demonstration?"

The President took a deep breath and slowly released it as a heavy sigh. "I probably should say no, but if we don't settle this, it will linger as a deep-seated doubt and fester. Proceed."

Vicki repeated her gesture and words, and the Secretary of State developed an expression of vapid adoration. She gazed longingly at Vicki as she said, "Please, Mistress; tell me how I can make you happy."

"Kill the President at the head of the table," Vicki replied without missing a beat, and in the corner of my eye, I saw the protection agent tense.

The Secretary of State looked from Vicki to the President and back several times. During which, her breathing became labored, her expression shifted to extreme torment, and tears flowed from her eyes like Niagara Falls.

"Please, Mistress, not that. Please not that. She's my oldest friend. I love her like family."

Vicki repeated the gesture and phrase to cancel the spell, then gestured toward the Secretary of State like a gameshow hostess revealing a prize. At that point, everyone in the room associated with the federal government swiveled to look at the Attorney General.

The old warhorse snarled and seemed like he wanted to spit at the President. "You think just because you sashayed away with eighty-percent of the vote it gives you some kind of mandate? I didn't take this stupid job because you asked; I took it to collect evidence of your failures... evidence that I would make sure the people see when the time is right. Aw, hell with it. Damn you anyway!"

With another snarl, the man surged out of his chair and thrust his hand at the President. If the room had only contained humans, he might have succeeded in stabbing her with the little spring-assist pen knife in his hand.

My hand closed around his wrist while the point of the blade was still a solid six inches from the President. He jerked, pushing and pulling, but could not break my hold. By now, the protection agent had his sidearm out and pointed at the Attorney General, as he hissed code words into a mic in his suit jacket's sleeve; then, with an alert sent, he shifted into a proper, two-handed grip on the pistol.

"Sir," I said, "I have complete control of his arm. Would you like him divested of the knife?"

Six more protection agents flooded into the room. Four pulled the President away from the table and out of the room while the others stood with their sidearms drawn and at the low ready position.

The original protection agent in the room nodded, asking, "Can you do that without hurting yourself?"

"Sure." I clenched the hand that held the Attorney General's wrist. At first, it sounded like gravel grinding together, and the AG grimaced. Then he gritted his teeth but still refused to drop the pocketknife. His expression revealed a steadily increasing level of pain, until a ghastly *CRACK!* echoed throughout the room. The AG went white as a sheet. His knife-hand went limp, and his knees buckled. The pocketknife clattered on the tabletop.

The agents swarmed the soon-to-be-former Attorney General as the man collapsed to the floor. Once they had him secured, one of the agents sounded an 'all clear' while the original agent stared at me.

"Did… did you crush his wrist?"

I nodded.

"Single-handedly?"

I nodded again.

The agent took a deep breath and released it slowly while he shook his head. "Thank heavens you're one of the good guys."

Another agent held the pocketknife up in a gloved hand as she examined it closely. Then, said. "Look at this. It looks one-hundred-percent ceramic, but our scanners should've caught it."

An agent walked in who must've been a supervisor, because everyone tensed. She arrived just in time to hear the comment about the knife. "Make a note on the evidence bag that it goes to R&D once the case is over. If he got it through the scanners without being caught, we need to improve the scanners. If someone passed it because he was the AG, we need to know that, too."

She crossed the room and stopped in front of me. I stood to greet her as she said, "Gloria Miller. I'm in charge of the President's protection detail. What I've heard so far says we have you to thank."

"No thanks necessary, ma'am. I just did what needed done."

Yet another agent entered the room and approached

Vasquez. "Ma'am, the President is insisting to return to the meeting. We've tried explaining—"

Gloria held up a hand and gave me an appraising look. "How near of a thing was it that he's still alive?"

"If I would've had a change of clothes and a way to keep the blood off the floor, he'd probably be dead."

Gloria nodded, then turned to the agent. "Let's move the meeting somewhere else, because this is technically now a crime scene. Otherwise, I'm okay with the President returning to the meeting. I think the only way she'd be safer is if we wrapped the 82nd Airborne around her."

The agent nodded once and left.

Gloria looked to the Secretary of State, seeming to notice her tear stains for the first time. "Ma'am, are you well? Do you need medical attention?"

Lucy shook her head and took a breath. "No, Agent, but thank you. I volunteered for a demonstration, and it rattled me a bit. No harm."

Gloria turned her attention back to me. "Why would a change of clothes hold you back?"

"Are you aware of shifters, ma'am?" I asked.

"Ah, yes," Gloria remarked. "May I ask what breed?"

"Smilodon."

It took maybe five seconds for confusion to dominate Gloria's expression. "I'm not familiar with…"

"Sabertooth cat. According to Doc back in Precious, I'm about twenty to thirty percent larger than the largest, complete *Smilodon populator* fossil recovered to date."

I noticed Gloria's jaw go a little slack. "How big?"

"In my fur, I'm about a thousand pounds with three-inch claws—plus or minus—and my curved incisors are somewhere between four and six inches long. Honestly, ma'am, I think they're still growing. When Doc measured me in my fur, my claws were only two inches long."

Several agents stopped what they were doing to stare at me by the time I stopped speaking.

"I see what you meant about keeping blood off the carpet," Gloria remarked.

One of the conference room doors opened to admit an agent and a woman about my age. The woman walked straight to me and spoke to me while addressing all of the meeting's participants.

"Ladies and sirs, I am Sarah Givens, the President's personal assistant. She invites you to resume the meeting in the Oval Office, and Agent Harald and I can escort you there."

I scanned my group, who all responded in the affirmative. The Secretary of State, the Director, and Deputy Director Nathanson did likewise. Sarah beamed a smile as she turned and led us out of the conference room.

15

_____

S arah led us down the hall and into the West Wing. We passed through a series of hallways until we arrived at our destination. If I had felt intimidated at the thought of meeting the President, meeting the President in the Oval Office only added to it. The fact that I had just saved her from harm, maybe even saved her life, did nothing to lessen the intimidation factor.

When Sarah opened the door, we found the President leaning against the Resolute Desk. She righted herself as we entered and walked straight to me.

"Thank you," she said. "I… that knife…"

"Please, ma'am, don't give the matter any further thought. I'm glad we were there when he finally felt cornered. How many meetings are there when it's just you, him, and other Cabinet-level officials?"

"Too many to bear thinking on," the President replied, then gestured to the sitting area. "Please, everyone, be seated and comfortable."

We chose our seats but waited for the President to sit

first. I noticed a couple meaningful looks pass between the President and Secretary of State, and I suspected hugs would be exchanged once they were alone and could be just two women who'd been friends since elementary school.

"So, as I recall," the President said, "you wanted us to look into the black ops organization that's hunting one of your shifters. I have no problem with that, even if it were not part of our obligations under the treaty. Did they ever explain why they were hunting her?"

I couldn't keep from sharing a glance with my ladies before turning back to the President. "They collected numerous reports of a woman who could turn into a giant bird, ma'am. They wanted to collect her for 'study.'"

The President blanched. "Oh, my. Even if those rumors were true, that's horrible. I'm glad you brought this to our attention."

I wanted to tell her they weren't rumors, but it was Sloane's choice whether she be included in the shifter database. I didn't know if Doc had included me in there yet, but if this 'Consul' nonsense was going to stick, he might as well. It might make future discussions easier if people knew they sat across a table from a thousand-pound sabertooth cat.

"I also understand that Miss Magnusson brings a matter of Magi concern, but before we get to that, I would like to see greater contact and communication between shifters and the government. Would you accept a consular office in Precious?"

Oh, shit... this was getting way, way out of hand. "Ma'am, with all due respect, I'm not sure Precious is the right choice. The Shifter Council meets in Chicago, and I would think they would be the natural and best focus for a consular office."

"Please forgive my interruption," Lyssa interjected, "as

Wyatt introduced me earlier, I am one of the feline representatives on the Shifter Council. As such, I was both a witness to and a participant in the discussion that established the position of Consul of the Shifter Nation, so I feel it incumbent upon me to clarify a misunderstanding. The Council of the Shifter Nation of North America intended the position of Consul to be on par with other heads of state such as yourself, so Precious is very much the place to establish a consular office if you feel such is needed or desired."

Well, damn. She threw me under the bus... again.

The President looked from me to Lyssa several times. Her expression soon betrayed her curiosity, and I wondered if Lyssa would yet again speak up. This time, though, the lioness seemed to think silence was the better part of valor.

I turned to the Secretary of State. "If you are directed by the President to establish a consular office in Precious, I recommend you contact Alistair Cooper. He is essentially my right hand in managing the town, and I suspect I'll lean on him even more in the future once this 'Consul' nonsense fleshes out into a full-time headache."

And just like that, the light of understanding flared in the President's mind. At least she *chose* her fate. The Shifter Council pretty much drafted me. The Secretary of State and the President shared a quick glance before the President cleared her throat and looked to Vicki, asking, "And what matter did the Magi Assembly wish to address?"

Vicki produced a manila envelope and laid it on the coffee table between her and the President. "That envelope contains memory cards with a recording of a meeting I was summoned to by agents of the federal government. A second memory card contains pictures of the people we spoke with and interacted with, as well as PDFs of all email communications... including the email that delivered the coordinates to which I was to portal for the meeting. If I had not asked

Karleen to accompany me, I would now be detained in some government black site as an enemy combatant with no due process or notification of my family, because I refused to surrender the Magi formulae for -bane weapons and ammunition."

The President and the Secretary of State shot each other a confused look before Lucy asked, "I'm sorry, but would you mind explaining what 'bane' means in this context?"

"Sorry. That is kind of a Magi thing. So... for centuries, Magi have developed and maintained formulae to create imbued items, basically embed magic into items to achieve a desired effect. I have a ring of elemental protection right now; I'm never too hot or too cold. As long as I wear it, I won't suffer heat exhaustion or frostbite. We have many, many formulae for imbued items, but the recent unpleasantness in the Pacific Northwest brought -bane weapons and ammunition to everyone's attention. Everyone knows the so-called werewolves have a vulnerability to silver, right?"

Heads nodded around the room, even the protection agents.

"Wrong. I could shoot my brother with a silver bullet, and it wouldn't do any more damage to him than a hollow-point or armor-piercing bullet in the same caliber... which is almost none. In fact, given how soft silver is, it would probably do *less* damage than regular bullets. Shifters are damned hard to kill... *unless* you use a shifter-bane weapon or shifter-bane ammunition. Same thing with the intelligent undead. Holy water just makes them wet, and my grandfather witnessed a pope trying to hold a vampire at bay with a crucifix. The vampire ate him before the pope made it ten words into his chant."

"Which pope was that?" the President gasped.

Vicki looked at me, and I could see the gears turning. Then, she turned back to the others. "Uhm... Damasus II, I think? Maybe? It might have been Pius III. Grandpa said he was young at the time, and it was before he met Grams. But getting back to the -bane weapons, the Magi Assembly has no intention of releasing the formula for them in any way, shape, or form. Further, the guy in the meeting assured me that his people already have a Magi to do the work; they just needed the formulae. The Magi Assembly wants independent verification that—if this Magi exists—he or she is not being held against his or her will, like these people attempted with me. Much like the Shifter Nation, we agreed to the co-mingling of Magi among the American citizenry with certain provisions, but if the government prefers a more distant relationship, the Assembly is willing to go that route."

"It seems we have some work to do," the President remarked, "not to mention relationship repair."

I looked to each of the government people before settling on the President. "I would think a month is more than sufficient to expect a preliminary investigation report... on both of these issues."

The Director and Deputy Director Nathanson gaped at me. When he spoke, the Director's voice was almost a squeak. "A month? There's no way you can expect us to deliver a report in a month."

"With all due respect, sir, you haven't seen the depth and breadth of the evidence we're handing you," I countered. "We'll retain custody of the black ops team, but your people are more than welcome to visit Precious to interview them. I honestly don't care what you do with the black ops group. I just want Sloane's name and record cleared, so she doesn't have warrants plaguing her, and I want this group to stop hunting shifters. Personally, if they had built their base inside one of the shifter enclaves, I would never have brought the matter to your attention; they'd be dead now. But as I feel very confident that the base is within United States territory, I do not want to endanger our relationship."

The Director turned to Nathanson. "What are your thoughts? Since both of these issues fall squarely inside your side of the house, your people will take point on them."

Nathanson leaned forward and rested his elbows on his knees as he stared at the carpet. When he resumed a sitting posture, he answered, "We should put a team together under Special Agents Hauser and Burke. Hauser earned SAiC not long before that kerfuffle with the child trafficking operation, and both agents have experience and a good rapport with both the shifters and the Magi. They're still technically liaising with the shifters and Magi on the child trafficking thing, but I haven't heard any new developments lately."

"The entire operation has gone to ground… *hard*," Vicki offered. "We have Magi who specialize in fugitive location and retrieval working the case alongside shifters with similar expertise, but it's been a hard slog. We have cut off the one point of access we know where they obtained charms from a hedge wizard, but that hasn't shaken anything loose as of yet. How are the abduction rates? Have they remained steady, increased, or dropped?"

"Ah… honestly, I'd have to call for that information," Nathanson replied. "It's not something that normally crosses my desk."

"Since Hauser and Burke are already liaising with the shifters and Magi," the Director said, "and since they seem to be in something of a holding pattern at the moment, I see no reason they can't assemble a team to investigate these two matters." The Director made eye contact with the President. "Ma'am, with your permission, I'll direct Deputy Director Nathanson to implement that tasking with orders that Hauser and Burke report both to us and the Magi and shifters."

The President nodded once. "Yes. That sounds like an excellent idea to me, and Director, please copy me and the Secretary of State on all reports associated with both investigations."

"Of course, ma'am."

"I don't suppose you're interested in being Attorney General?" the President asked, a slight smile curling her lips.

The Director swallowed hard. "Uhm, ma'am, I'm happy to serve in whatever office or capacity you need, but I am rather happy where I am."

"Ah, well," the President replied, "like my undergraduate Composition professor told me, nobody's perfect." Amused expressions circled through the group. "Do we have any other official business?"

Everyone looked to one another. I said, "I think we've discussed all the shifter-related business I came to discuss. Vicki?"

"We've addressed all the Magi business."

Neither the Director, Deputy Director Nathanson, nor the Secretary of State had any business.

"Very well, then," the President said. She stood, and we followed suit. "Director Ames, Deputy Director Nathanson... thank you both for coming today. Lucy, do you have time to discuss the consular office further?"

"Of course, ma'am," the Secretary of State replied.

The Director and Nathanson thanked the President for her time and bowed out of the Oval Office. As soon as the door latched, the President turned back to us, her expression once more akin to child-like delight as she asked, "How rude would it be if I asked to see your Smilodon?"

I couldn't stop myself from grinning. "Well, I don't consider it rude, myself, but I don't know how born shifters see it."

Gabrielle and Karleen leaned into me from either side as

Gabrielle said, "Oh, we never mind any reason to get your fur on."

I pointed to the door over my shoulder. "What's through that door? I could shift right now, but I'd destroy my clothes. Vicki could spin me a new set, because she created these, but doing so might alarm your protection detail unnecessarily."

"That door connects to a private dining room," the President answered. "I don't mind passing word to the staff that the room's off limits for a time, but I'd really like to see you shift if you don't mind. Frankly, I've been fascinated with shifters ever since I read the brief... something like a week after my inauguration."

"Mind spinning me up some new threads, sis?"

Vicki grinned. "Not at all, brother dear."

I stood and moved away from the sitting area. I stood in an open space that allowed access through a couple doors and tried to eyeball the dimensions. The space looked wide and long enough. I turned my attention to my audience, asking, "Ready?"

The President and Secretary of State both nodded, their expressions eager.

I touched that part of my mind that was no longer human and willed the shift.

OLIVIA WILLIAMS almost couldn't believe she had a shifter in the Oval Office who was going to shift for her. It took all her willpower not to squee like a teenage fangirl, despite being in her mid-40s. Ever since she read the brief and sat through the initiation that humans were not alone on the planet, she wanted nothing more than to meet a shifter. And now...?

Wyatt's clothing exploded. Strips of fabric and shoe leather flew *everywhere*. Where a handsome young man stood just moments before, a massive cat unseen on Earth in thousands of years now stood. His shoulders were taller than the back of the sofa, and she could see his coloration was very similar to modern African lions. Unlike the modern lion, though, Wyatt had tiger stripes a deeper tawny color than his coat. Wyatt padded around the sofa, and Olivia decided he had underestimated the length of his incisors; they were closer to eight inches long. He stopped about two feet away from the President and sat on his haunches, then lifted one forepaw. She could actually see the tendons and muscles flex in his paw to extend five claws that glistened in the light. She stood and leaned closer for a better look, marveling at the claws' size. She reached a finger toward his right incisor.

Wyatt pulled back at the same time one of Wyatt's associates said, "Stop!"

Olivia froze and turned toward the woman who spoke. "What's wrong?"

"Shifter blood and saliva—either one—are almost guaranteed to turn a regular human into a shifter," the woman Wyatt had introduced as Gabrielle explained, "and since Wyatt is a primogenitor, there's no telling what breed of shifter you'd become."

"Oh," Olivia said. "May I pet him at least?"

Wyatt bobbed his head in a nod at the same Gabrielle answered, "Sure. We love the texture of his fur."

Olivia placed her hand on Wyatt's head between his ears and stepped closer as Wyatt stood so she could slide her hand along his spine. She glanced at Agent Harald and saw he looked a little wild around his eyes. When she brought her hand back to scratch Wyatt's head between his ears and Wyatt gave a huge, contented yawn, poor Agent Harald looked ready to have a coronary.

"Be careful about scratching him, too," Karleen opined. "If

you hit the proper spot, you'll put him right to sleep, and good luck moving him for a couple hours."

"Having a sleeping Smilodon in my office wouldn't be so bad, would it?"

Karleen scoffed. "You say that now, but you haven't seen him shed."

16

Nadine Givens exited the passenger side of her family's SUV and took in the small-town ambiance. In so many ways, Precious reminded her of the mining town where she and her siblings grew up. A town long since abandoned as economic realities evolved.

The convoy of five SUVs bearing her immediate family drew more than the occasional long look from passers-by, and Nadine popped a piece of her mother's home-made peppermint candy into her mouth. Since her childhood, peppermint had been her go-to weapon in the fight when her nerves became unsettled.

Nadine felt that even peppermint might not be up to the task this time around, though. No... this time, the peppermint candy faced its most fearsome foe yet. Not bills. Not a child's health scare. Not a disagreement with her mate. Oh, no. Those were easy compared to this. The source of her unsettled nerves now was none other than her baby sister, Karleen.

Walt, her mate and husband and father of her children, walked around the front of their SUV and stopped at her side. "So, tell me again why moving the family get-together to Precious without even asking Karleen or the local Alpha was a good idea?"

Nadine closed her eyes, counted to five, and huffed a sigh. "Walt, if we don't take some drastic action, we're going to *lose* her... possibly forever. You weren't there the day I told her about Rick's newest and how the kids always ask about Aunt Karleen. Our absence in her life is a hole in her heart, and it doesn't have to be that way. That's not how wolves live. Family is our bedrock. I don't know how she made it sixty-odd years by herself alone; I would've thought that would drive any wolf shifter insane."

Walt didn't *quite* grimace, then shrugged. "Well, I hope she spares you for the children's sake at least. Goodness knows, she's never met *me*. I'll go to the hotel and ask them about any vacancies they have."

As with every other time the family traveled together, getting everyone and all the luggage out of the vehicles and into the hotel was just slightly less complex than the invasion of Normandy. Fortunately, Precious's sole hotel had sufficient vacancies, because the Vesper clan took up an entire floor between rooms for children, parents, and grandparents. The wolf shifter working the front desk—a sweetheart named Melody—made the process as easy and straightforward as possible. She even recommended the local diner.

I leaned back against my seat after clearing my plate. Visiting the capital was nice enough, and if I'm being honest, it was great meeting the President. But there's nothing like home, including Gladys's diner. Gabrielle told me one time that we weren't the only shifter family that used the diner as their sole source of food. As much as shifters had to eat just to 'break even,' most families would've had to have at least one person almost live in the kitchen full time. Plus, when comparing Gladys's prices versus a grocery bill plus time spent cooking or preparing meals, there wasn't that much difference in the dollar amount. It might have been different if the cost of living had been higher or if it was a more urban area, but it was the rare shifter or group of shifters who chose urban life full-time over one of the shifter territories across the country.

"Thank you for inviting me to dinner," Lyssa said as she pushed her empty plates toward the center of the table. "I wasn't sure you'd be interested in exploring a relationship after... well... D.C."

I gave her my best mock glare. "You mean where you threw me under the bus by telling the President I—as Consul of the Shifter Nation—was pretty much our head of state? Oh... or what about how you never mentioned that when you dropped the job in my lap?"

Lyssa met my mock glare with a demeanor of insouciant innocence as she replied, "Sure... why not?"

She must've taken lessons from Vicki.

"Are you ticklish?" I asked.

Lyssa blinked at the non-sequitur. "Huh? What does that have to do with anything?"

"Well, I have to get my revenge somehow, and the other ladies and I have evolved the tickle fight into an art form."

Her nonchalant expression returned as she answered, "Well, wouldn't answering your question betray any tactical advantage I might have?"

"I guess I'll just have to find out for myself... later."

Lyssa's expression shifted into a heated look. "Oh, please do."

The conversation moved to other topics as we sipped our drinks and one of Gladys's servers retrieved our dishes and asked about refills. That was another nice thing about the diner; none of the staff ever gave the impression a customer needed to hurry up and vacate after the meal.

"We should track down Sloane and let her know about the progress we made," I remarked. "I'm sort of surprised Hauser hasn't called already about the cases, but I suppose one day is probably too soon."

Karleen grinned around her drink's straw. "Humans don't move as fast as we do, Wyatt. With us, decision leads directly to action, but—"

She stopped speaking mid-sentence as her expression became one of shock mingled with disbelief. I looked around but didn't see anything sufficiently odd for such a reaction.

Gabrielle reached out to her, placing a hand on her wrist and asking, "What's wrong?"

After several more seconds of immobile silence and her disbelief transitioning toward anger, Karleen said, "What the hell are *they* doing here? I thought I made my point clear enough."

I followed Karleen's glare as best I could, and the only thing that stood out in her possible sight line was a group of people on the sidewalk across the street. They looked like a family, and what's more, they weren't from Precious.

While most Alphas have rather relaxed rules about other shifters visiting their territory, a few reactionaries still existed who would treat this family's unannounced arrival as nothing short of an invasion. I was not one of those reactionaries, but even the most progressive Alpha appreciated a quick meet-and-greet along the lines of "Hi, we're just passing through and needed to stop for the night."

I turned my gaze from the group as they started crossing

the street to regard Karleen. "Is there a problem? Do you know them?"

It's a wonder Karleen's teeth hadn't turned to powder; she clenched her jaw *that* hard. About the time the first of the group set foot on the sidewalk in front of the diner, she bit out, "They're my family."

Oh, boy…

From their expressions, Lyssa and Gabrielle—like me—watched with a certain fascination as the woman leading the group grasped the door handle and pulled it open. The bell overhead rung as she entered the diner, and I knew the moment her eyes adjusted. She froze mid-step as she stared at our table, gaping at the sight of Karleen, blocking the door and creating a pile-up behind her.

Oblivious to the awkward moment filling the space between the woman and Karleen, Gladys flounced over to greet them. "Come on in and find yourselves a table. Don't worry; we only bite if you ask nicely first."

The woman blocking the door looked like a fish flopping on the shore as she worked her jaw without making any sounds. Gladys finally realized something was going on, and she turned to look in the direction the newcomer stared, her eyes falling on our table. Her puzzled expression immediately shifted back to a beaming, welcoming smile as she swung back to the woman.

"Oh, now don't you worry none; that's just our local Alpha. He's a friendly, laid-back sort. Come on, come on. We have all kinds of tables. We can even push two or three together if one isn't enough room."

Karleen stood and made her way to the door. Before she reached a comfortable distance for confronting the woman I felt safe in naming a close relative, a young girl squeezed through the door and beamed up at Karleen.

"Momma," the girl asked, her voice laden with eagerness and hope, "is that Aunt Karleen?"

Now, Karleen froze. But the moment didn't last. Those piled up just outside heard the youngster's question and almost pushed the woman further into the diner. A couple who didn't look too much older than Karleen pulled her into a tight hug between them, the woman in the couple making noises about how long it had been since she'd seen Karleen.

Gladys herded the group into the corner opposite us and waved down a couple servers to help her put a few tables together. Once everyone was certain there was no imminent danger, the diner's other patrons went back to their meals or conversations.

Minutes passed, and two servers delivered their drink orders. When the servers left to put in the family's food order, Karleen stood and walked back to our table. She stopped between my and Lyssa's seats, and the nervous wringing of her hands was impossible to miss.

"They're my family. I… I haven't spoken to anyone but my sister since I left home. May I introduce you to them?" Karleen asked, her voice far more cautious than I'd ever heard it.

Talk about being caught off guard. Gabrielle and I shared a look, and she said, "Don't you want to spend the evening with them first? I mean, if it's been that long…"

Gabrielle's voice trailed off when Karleen shook her head 'no,' then said, "You don't understand. Nadine convinced the family to bring their get-together here, just to meet me and… well… us."

"You sure they'll be okay with what we have with Wyatt?" Gabrielle asked. "Even though it's not unheard of, it's still not that common."

Karleen snorted. "If they have a problem with it, they can

get glad in the same pants they got mad in. I'm not apologizing for or hiding what we have."

Gabrielle and I shared a look that ultimately resulted in me shrugging. "Might as well get it over with, then. No sense in delaying."

When Gabrielle and I stood, Karleen tapped Lyssa's shoulder. "You should come, too. You're here to explore the possibility of a relationship with us, and this is part of 'us.'"

Lyssa turned to meet Karleen's eyes with her own and offered a smile of thanks as she stood. "I appreciate that."

NADINE DIDN'T KNOW what to expect when Karleen said she was going to get her family, and her worries only increased while her sister stood at the other table and talked with the people sitting there. When they all came back, though, the first thing she noticed was how much stronger the aura of a dominant alpha shifter became. It was like there was two of Karleen standing there, and that's when Nadine *knew*. The young man who looked 20-something to everyone else's thirty-something was the feline primogenitor.

"This is Gabrielle Hassan," Karleen said. "You may have heard shifters talking about the Huntress? Well, this is her." Nadine enjoyed watching her brothers sit a little straighter in their seats upon hearing that. "This is Lyssa Westridge; she's visiting to explore the possibility of a relationship with us, and she's also one of the feline councilors." Even Nadine sat a little straighter at *that* piece of information. "And this is our mate, Wyatt Magnusson, the Alpha of Precious and Godwin County."

The aura of a supremely powerful alpha shifter became a more elongated oval as the young man Karleen introduced stepped around Gabrielle and Lyssa to approach the table.

Nadine watched her brothers for any signs they intended stupidity, and she forced her expression to remain neutral when she saw how intimidated they were. She watched 'the boys' measure themselves against the sheer presence Wyatt exuded and fought to keep a straight face when their silent mannerisms reminded her of when they tried standing up to their father after entering adolescence.

A silence descended on the table at Wyatt's introduction, but he stepped into it with an easy smile and gracious demeanor, saying, "It's a pleasure to meet you and, please, be welcome in our cozy little town. Karleen, you should sit with your family and get to know each other again. If you're up for it, we'll have a big picnic tomorrow."

Nadine smiled at the invitation. Regardless of how young he seemed, Alpha Wyatt handled the situation very well. Yes, the family would very much appreciate catching up with their long-lost relative, and he seemed to understand that should happen *before* any potential inclusion of Karleen's own family.

"Are you sure?" Karleen asked, and Nadine couldn't believe how cautious and nervous her brash, confident, always-in-control sister sounded.

Wyatt simply nodded. "Take all the time you need, and the picnic can wait a day or two if that's better."

I WATCHED the hopeful smile that fought to break loose from Karleen's iron self-control, and I felt a swell of warmth and happiness for her. We'd never really talked about her family, but the few times she had talked around the topic, I could tell how much Karleen's estrangement bothered her. I reiterated my welcome to her family and pulled Lyssa and Gabrielle with me as we bid them good evening.

My next stop was the payment counter where Gladys looked on. The challenge? Pitching my voice low enough that neither Karleen nor any of her family heard what I was about to say.

"Our check, please," then almost whispered, "and *their* food is on me as long as they're in town."

Gladys almost beamed. "You are a good man, Alpha Wyatt, and I am damn glad you moved to Precious."

I passed Gladys a fifty to cover our meals and a healthy tip for the server, and Gladys promised to give me the bills after their visit. We turned and waved at Karleen and her family as we left the diner.

AS SOON AS we walked beyond the windows of the diner, Gabrielle pulled me into a tight hug. "I *love* you, Wyatt. That was such a good thing you did for Karleen."

I couldn't keep from giving Gabrielle a quick kiss. "Love you, too, and I know how much she needed this. I'm glad they came here."

The sight of the hotel prompted a thought, and I led the ladies across the street and into the lobby.

Melody beamed at us as we stepped through the doors, chirping, "Hi! What I can I do for you?"

"Do you have a large group of new guests per chance? The Vesper family et al?"

"Why, yes, we do, Alpha Wyatt," Melody replied, her expression full of contrived surprise. "However did you know?"

I smiled at Melody's antics, then said, "They're officially guests of the Alpha. Send their hotel bill to me when they check out."

"Message received, Alpha sir. Their money's no good here."

"Thank you, Melody. Have a nice evening."

We turned and exited the hotel, and we resumed our journey to the Alpha's house. A short distance down the street from the hotel, Lyssa asked. "So, what's our plan for the rest of the evening?"

I replied with my best confident smile. "Well, Gabrielle and I could teach you how to play 'Catch the Cat.'"

17

Winnifred Hauser left Burke with her preparations to interview Leah Brenner and headed for the room where Mitchell Cavendish waited. She nodded in passing to one of her fellow agents as she approached her destination and fought hard to keep a straight face. Yes, every person in this field office was a 'fellow' agent, but she and Burke were the only agents from Paranormal Branch on the floor, possibly the only Paranormal Branch agents in the entire zip code. Her section of the agency didn't exactly advertise and often recruited through either obscure psychological evaluations or when a regular agent had an 'Oh, shit… the supernatural is *real*' moment. That was how Hauser herself joined, but this was not the time for reminiscing. Hauser rolled her shoulders and her head while she pushed those memories aside and focused on the interview with Mitchell Cavendish.

One deep breath slowly exhaled, and time to go…

MITCHELL CAVENDISH LOOKED up as the door opened to admit a thirty-something woman in a navy pantsuit. She wore her honey blond hair in an attractive up-do, and Mitchell admitted to himself that he'd probably hit on her if they met somewhere else. She placed a folder on the table in front of her seat and unbuttoned her blazer before pulling the chair back and sitting.

"Mister Cavendish," she said, "I am Special Agent Winnifred Hauser, and we are here today to discuss your sins... at least a few specific sins. I'm not sure we have sufficient time to discuss *all* of them."

She paused, but if she expected him to volunteer something or speak to fill the silence, she didn't know him as well as she thought. So far, this little escapade was tame compared to SERE school. He'd wait her out.

The pause ended up so brief that Cavendish wondered if it was a test. "Mister Cavendish, I refer to the events on the 30th floor of a Midtown high-rise, here in Manhattan. Specifically, the events where you and your associate Leah Brenner attempted to hold one Victoria Magnusson against her will."

Shit. How had these guys ended up with that? Knowledge of the supernatural still required SCI clearance in most cases.

"The Magi Assembly lodged a formal complaint with the Secretary of State."

Seriously? She expected him to cough up classified info because some people wrote a harsh letter to the Secretary of State? That's not how things worked.

"I see your reticence to cooperate, Mister Cavendish. That's fair. You don't know me or my clearance. The thing is, your boss already hung you and your associate out to dry. The President called the Director of the CIA to the Oval Office and had a long, pointed conversation about why one of that agency's black operations summoned and threatened Miss Magnusson, including your claim that you have a Magi.

Especially considering the CIA is not authorized to conduct operations inside United States territory. The Director and the next three levels down disavowed all knowledge of your activities. Here, let me show you."

Hauser pulled a mobile device from her blazer pocket and fiddled with it for a few moments before placing it on the tabletop and tapping the screen. The device began playing a recording that started with the President greeting the Director of the CIA, and it wasn't long before the President got to the heart of the matter. The longer Cavendish listened to his director's passionate assertion that he knew nothing of Mitchell Cavendish's actions or any Magi being held, the more Cavendish realized his career quite probably was over.

As soon as the recording ended, Hauser gave him a bright smile. "So, tell me about your captive Magi, Mister Cavendish, or would you prefer I recommend to the President we turn you over to the Magi Assembly? I hear they have rather painful methods for rooting through criminals' minds."

WINNIFRED HAUSER EXITED the interview room and soon found Agent Burke leaning against one of the desk's they were given while they worked in the Manhattan field office. Regardless of what else Hauser might say of the woman, Edwina Burke had one hell of a poker face.

"Well?" Hauser asked as she dropped her folder and mobile onto her desk.

Burke shrugged and maintained her non-expression. "Brenner basically told me where to go and what to do when I arrived. Pretty much dared me to do my worst. How about you?"

"Yeah… I struck out with Cavendish, too. I even played the recording where their bosses sold him out to dry."

"They're calling our bluff about turning them over to the Magi," Burke agreed. "I say let's show 'em it's not a bluff."

Hauser nodded her agreement. "As much as I hate to admit it, we probably don't have the information or the tools to break either Cavendish or Brenner. Have you looked at their jackets?"

"A couple of very scary people on paper. I'm not sure I'd want to meet either one in a dark alley if they were of malicious intent."

A thought forced its way to the forefront of Hauser's mind, and she chuckled. "We could always call Wyatt and tell him these two threatened Vicki."

Burke rolled her eyes. "I thought we wanted information and not a bloody mess."

"Fine," Hauser replied, dragging the word into a tired sigh that would've impressed even the most jaded teenager. She retrieved her actual mobile and dialed a number.

"Nathanson, here," the deputy director said upon accepting the call.

"Sir, this is Special Agent Winnifred Hauser. Burke and I are not confident we will break either Cavendish or Brenner, and we found no records in their offices about any captive Magi. What are your thoughts on turning them over to the Assembly?"

Silence ensued for several moments.

"I'm wrestling with my knee-jerk reaction that we do not give up our people, Hauser. Even if their chain of command is swearing on a warehouse of Bibles that Cavendish and Brenner aren't theirs, despite the employment records we have. You should have seen the looks on their faces when the President laid those records in front of them. They were priceless. How long until you have to cut them loose?"

Hauser grinned, even though Nathanson couldn't see it. "Sir, we're only five hours into the forty-eight we're allowed to hold them before we have to charge 'em or kick 'em out."

"Fair enough. I will call you back as soon as I have something."

NINETY MINUTES PASSED, during which Hauser and Burke worked their other new case... the matter of Sloane Martinez. It looked like they would have to visit the small town in Nebraska, because the local officers seemed reluctant to listen when Hauser called. She no sooner ended that call when her mobile rang.

"Hauser," she said after accepting the call.

"This is Deputy Director Nathanson. There's an AUSA en route with extradition paperwork. We're giving them to the Magi, with the condition they copy us on whatever information they acquire."

Before Nathanson finished speaking, Vicki Magnusson and four other people she didn't know appeared about ten feet away. Every agent in view turned to stare.

"Sir, the Magi just arrived. I should probably get them checked in before the building goes on lockdown."

Hauser heard a heavy sigh. "Yes, please do. Nathanson out."

"You know, Vicki," Hauser said as she crossed the space to greet Wyatt's sister, "most people use the front door."

Vicki replied with a shrug and an impish grin. "Most people don't have a way past the pointless authority games... or infinitely more patience for them. So, my grandfather tells me you're giving us Cavendish and Brenner?"

"Yes, but we don't have that paperwork yet. The AUSA hasn't arrived. You may have your hands full with them. They each have top marks from their SERE instructors."

Vicki just smiled. It wasn't friendly. "Let's see how they handle a good charm spell."

∿

I SAW them approaching where I sat chatting with Lyssa... two of Karleen's brothers. I should have remembered their names, but that was last night. And... well... I hadn't paid that much attention when Karleen introduced us. I knew they were the oldest two, and the youngest son was Rich? Rick? Ric-something...

Whoops.

Lyssa and I continued conversing, and I told a couple stories on myself that brought out a beautiful laugh. Yeah, if I was going to be honest, she was growing on me. Lyssa Westridge was intelligent, well-spoken, well-read, and a complete joy in person.

"So, you're the guy that embarrassed Thomas Carlyle?" Not-Rich-One asked as they stopped at the picnic table where Lyssa and I sat. "And you think you're man enough to mate our little sister?"

They didn't see the lioness roll her eyes at their unwelcome intrusion into our afternoon.

"Listen, guys, we're not having this discussion," I said. "The last time I tried having a friendly, no stress discussion about that situation and its fallout—for lack of a better term—I ended up Alpha of Precious and Godwin County. I feel like any conversation I permit between the three of us on this topic will end up in our arena, and I really don't want to kill Karleen's brothers... especially when you both have kids."

"Get a load of this kid," Not-Rich-Two scoffed. "He thinks he can take us both."

Not-Rich-One gave me a patient look any parent would recognize. "Kid, you're what... twenty? Twenty-five? Either of us have sixty years on you. We don't care about whatever fiction the Council threw together to make you Alpha here, and we're damned sure not interested in being Alpha here... either one of us. So, why don't you cut the attitude and explain yourself before we have to spank you like the unruly child you're being?"

Well, so much for being nice...

Lyssa just closed her eyes, shaking her head as she spoke, "I feel like I should go find your families to knock some sense into the both of you. Jason McCourtney's remaining Betas *fled* after Wyatt ripped off the first challenger's head, and neither of you are even enforcers in your respective packs. You should leave right now, before this escalates to the point that you find out just who gets spanked. And I promise you both... it *won't* be Wyatt."

Both Not-Rich-One and Not-Rich-Two scoffed. Not-Rich-Two said, "So, *Alpha* Wyatt, are you going to hide behind a woman? Sure... she's a lioness and a councilor, but someone man enough to embarrass Thomas Carlyle and evict him from his seat on the Council ought to be man enough to defend himself."

Okay. I was beyond done with this. I stood and stepped away from the picnic table to face the brothers square on. Lyssa looked like she wanted to say something, but she just grimaced and shook her head again.

"Are there precedents for settling disagreements somehow that *can't* be ruled an undeclared dominance fight when one of the parties is an Alpha?" I asked Lyssa.

She replied, "Normally, the Betas or enforcers handle unruly guests who abuse the Alpha's hospitality."

"Jack! Will!" Karleen shouted as she approached at not quite a jog. "What do you think you're doing? We *talked* about this."

"And there's one of my Betas now," Wyatt remarked and fought the urge to grin. "Should I leave this in her hands?"

Now, the smug superiority the brothers displayed vanished from their expressions. Not-Rich-One—apparently either Jack or Will—asked, "Karleen is one of your Betas?"

I just nodded and crossed my arms over my chest as Karleen arrived with her parents in tow.

"What are you idiots doing?" Karleen demanded, her clenched fists resting on her hips as she stopped to stand at my side. "I *told* you last night not to mess with Wyatt, and what do you do the first minute my back's turned? Shove your heads up your asses and do the one thing—*the one thing*—that just might get you killed. Do you *want* your kids to watch a sabertooth cat rip your heads off or eviscerate you and write his name in the dirt with your guts? Get this through your heads. He is not some random feline shifter. He's a primogenitor... like *me*. Do you *want* to fight me? I thought you learned *that* lesson before I was out of ninth grade."

The one saving grace in all of this was that these guys' wives kept their children far enough away that it was unlikely they'd hear the aunt they just met read their fathers the riot act. No one wants to receive a beat-down—verbal or otherwise—in front of his or her children.

"Can I leave this with you?" I asked Karleen.

Karleen nodded without breaking her glare. "You bet. If they piss me off, I'll just have Gabrielle handle it."

Now, the brothers frowned. Not-Rich-Two asked, "Who's Gabrielle?"

"She's not one of my Betas," I answered. "But you've probably heard of her professional moniker. The Huntress."

Even the brothers blanched at that. Yep. I could absolutely leave this mess with Karleen.

I turned to Lyssa and offered her my hand. "I do believe

our pleasant conversation has been rather proficiently spoiled. Shall we re-locate to a friendlier venue?"

Lyssa smiled as she took my hand and stood. "Why, yes, kind sir. We shall."

I expected Karleen would tell me how she handled the situation. Once she calmed down enough to keep from going back to the hotel and spanking her brothers again just because of the memory. She was fiery like that.

A fter spending a pleasant afternoon with Lyssa, I walked her back to the hotel, where we parted ways with a quick, chaste kiss. I then crossed the street to the town's administration building to see if anything waited for me in my Alpha persona. As I did so, I reflected on how much I had enjoyed Lyssa's company. My relationship with Karleen and Gabrielle felt like it kind of fell together. But Lyssa and I... that felt more like a conscious choice.

Nothing that required my immediate attention waited for me in my office at the admin building, so I backtracked out of the building. I was a few hours past the official closing time, but miracles of miracles, the Alpha had a key to the place. I made sure I left the door locked and ambled toward the house.

It was a pleasant evening for a walk, and I spent the time reflecting on my afternoon with Lyssa. No matter how I looked at the situation, Lyssa becoming my next mate seemed almost inevitable at this point. I wasn't sure how I felt about that. I had never been one of those guys who was into the idea of multiple partners. But Gabrielle and Karleen were *very* different, and I'm not sure I could choose if someone told me I had to give up one of them. I'm not sure they'd want me to choose, either.

As I approached the Alpha's house, half the sun hid behind the mountaintops to the west, and I noticed Karleen arriving, too. She did not look happy.

"Hi," I said. "Are you okay?"

Karleen snorted her displeasure. "Hell no, I'm not okay. I tried talking sense into my brothers *again*, and my parents even offered a few pieces of wisdom. But it all came to naught. Jack popped off about how I must be a closet pedophile for taking up with someone so much younger than me, regardless of the fact we're both shifters, and I had him on the ground with my hand around his throat before I realized what was happening."

Oh, crap… *that's* not good. "What happened?"

"I didn't kill him. I *wanted* to, but I didn't. It did take my sister, my youngest brother Rick, and my parents to pull me off him. Nadine said my eyes went full wolf." Karleen clenched her hands into fists and growled. "Seriously… what is their problem? Attacking either one of us is a death sentence to them. I don't even know how many regular shifters it would take to bring down one of us."

I cannot let this stand, the growly voice opined. *Family or no, he has slandered my mate's very* person, *not just her honor. I cannot allow it to pass.*

"Karleen," I began. Then, trailed off because I didn't know how to say it.

She unclenched her fists and nodded, then spoke in a quiet, sad voice. "I know, Wyatt. You can't let it stand. I debated not telling you, but you'd find out eventually. I didn't want you heading off to wherever he lives when you heard about it."

"I don't think you should come with me."

Karleen shook her head, still not meeting my eyes. "No. I know you have to respond, but I don't want to watch. No matter what else there is between me and them, they're still my family. I don't know what... he didn't used to be like this."

I turned to go, then stopped and turned back to her. "Which one was Jack? The one standing closest to the picnic table?"

Karleen chuckled. "No, that was Will. Jack stood farthest from the picnic table."

Okay. I was looking for Not-Rich-Two, then.

With a quick nod, I resumed my trek to the town's hotel. By the time I reached the entrance, I seethed at the wolf's abuse of his own blood sister. I hit the doors of the hotel like the V Corps hit Omaha Beach. The doors slammed against their stops with such force the collision sounded like miniature thunderclaps. Melody and the young man standing with her at the front desk whipped around, and the color drained from their faces when they saw me.

"I'm looking for the Vesper clan, and tell George to send the bill for any damages to me."

"They're not here," Melody replied. "They walked over to the diner about ten minutes ago."

"Fair enough," I said and pivoted on my heel.

MY ENTRANCE at Gladys's diner was more restrained. The doors and entire street-facing wall were glass, and I had no wish to shatter any of it. The moment I stepped inside the diner, every conversation in the place ceased. If this had been one of those old Westerns, crickets would have chirped somewhere behind me, and they would've sounded deafening.

Karleen's family sat around three tables pushed together about a third of the way into the dining room. From the male faces I saw, I decided Not-Rich-Two sat with his back to me. I strode across the room and reached across with my right hand to grip the back of his neck as close to a vise as I could manage.

"We need to talk," I said and turned back to the door. Then started walking. My fingers dug into his neck as I pulled, and my strength was sufficient to pull him backward out of his seat. The man's heated invectives filled the diner to the accompaniment of his chair clattering against the floor.

Two of the diner's customers closest the doors hurried to hold them open for me, and as soon as Not-Rich-Two and I cleared the sidewalk, I gave him my best underhand toss and sent him on a low arc into the street.

"Who the hell do you think you are?" Not-Rich-Two growled as he moved to stand.

"I think I am the Alpha of Precious and Godwin County," I replied as I stalked closer to him. "I think I am the feline primogenitor. I think I am Karleen's chosen mate. And I think I am fed up with your poor attitude. I no longer care what your problem is. I no longer care about trying to be nice to the family of one of the women I love. And I no longer care whether you leave this town alive. You've been spoiling for a fight since you rolled into town, and it's about time you had one."

With a growl, Not-Rich-Two charged me, hunched over like he meant to tackle me. A little less than two months ago, he probably would have kicked my butt. But that was two months ago. I stepped into his charge and delivered a vicious uppercut right to his nose. I heard bone snap as his head flew up, and I put my shoulder and back into a left hook that caught him square on his right zygomatic bone. I felt bone crack under my fist there, too.

This whole time, his hips and legs continued their forward momentum, and the arrival of my second strike arrested his forward motion enough that his feet left the pavement and he started to roll in mid-air. Gravity soon overcame his force and mine, and Not-Rich-Two hit the pavement on his right side in a bone-jarring crash. The roll continued until he lay on his back.

I had yet to deal any harm that he wouldn't heal in a matter of hours with shifter healing—if not minutes, but at the same time, I couldn't bring myself to keep beating on him. It was beyond obvious to me that he underestimated the challenge I presented, and he was now far enough behind in the fight that I didn't see how he could pull himself together to present a threat before I had the time to do whatever I chose. I crossed the short distance to where he lay and saw blood running out both nostrils and back across his cheeks to drip and pool on the pavement under him. Upon closer inspection, I saw his right pupil was at least twice the size of his left as well.

"I'm... going to... kill you," he gasped between hacking coughs that painted his lips with his own blood.

"Maybe so," I replied, "but not today."

I crouched and lifted his right foot off the pavement and put my back into pressing down on his knee. When the joint gave way with a savage cracking pop accompanied by a scream, I repeated the action with his left leg.

I need a claw, I sent to that part of my mind that was no longer human, and my right forearm and hand shifted into the foreleg and paw of my Smilodon. I flexed the appropriate muscle to extend the claw that would've been the fingernail on my index finger and leaned over my former opponent's head. With careful precision, I carved 'Precious' into his forehead and stepped back to survey my handiwork.

The blood had mostly stopped flowing out of his nostrils, but the fresh wound on his forehead bled like a river... as most head wounds do. And since that wound came from a shifter's natural weapons—my claw, in this case—he'd heal at a rate similar to plain humans. He might even end up with a scar. I nodded my satisfaction at the state of affairs and turned back to the diner.

And found half the diner crowd piled up against the windows watching. Not surprised, really.

They parted like the Red Sea before Moses as I re-entered the diner and walked up to the table where Karleen's family sat. They all sent apprehensive expressions my way.

"I cannot abide his treatment of Karleen, and what's more, I can't say I'm all that fond of his family not doing a better job of reining him in. You have one hour. Get your trash off my street, and get out of my territory. None of you are welcome in Godwin County any longer, and if I see the rabid mutt bleeding on my street within the next year, I'll kill him. Do you understand?"

Not-Rich-One shot to his feet, his hands clenched into fists and his face a thundercloud.

Before he finished drawing breath to speak, I said, "Fido outside never laid a hand on me. You think you can do any better?"

Then, I made my insult plain by taking my eyes off the entire group to look at my watch and said, "Okay. You now have fifty-seven minutes. Gladys, these people are no longer guests of the Alpha; give them the bills for all the food they've eaten while in town. Call Sheriff Clyde if they give you any problems."

I turned and left the diner, half expecting to hear Not-Rich-One charge my back. He didn't, so maybe he had more sense than his brother.

As I stepped onto the sidewalk again, Not-Rich-Two shouted at me in a voice that sounded like a high-volume groan. "You're a dead man; you hear me? I'm gonna kill you!"

I stopped, considered the situation, and walked over to

him. He looked like his shifter healing worked to put his bones back in their proper places, but his forehead still bled like a burst dam. His right pupil was still outsized, too, so it didn't seem like his healing had sorted out the concussion yet.

I shook my head. "I can't say as I care what you think. I just gave your family an hour to get out of Godwin County and live. You're welcome to do what you want, but if I see you again within a year, you're a dead man. Give that some thought."

I turned and left him. On my way home, I stopped at the hotel and repeated my spiel about the Vesper clan no longer being guests of the Alpha. Melody told me she was staying to handle the front desk until they left, because the evening guy was new. About that time, Lyssa sauntered out of the stair-well with a newspaper under her arm. She gave me a wink and blew me a kiss as she walked to one of the lobby chairs that faced the front desk and sat, then unfolded the newspaper.

Well, that was that, then. If Lyssa was going to be silent but available backup for Melody, I almost felt sorry for anyone who caused a problem. Lioness versus wolf? Yeah, the only way the Vesper clan was winning that fight is if all of them joined in at the same time, and I suspected Lyssa could hold her own until reinforcements arrived. One on one, Lyssa would paint the lobby with Not-Rich-One's blood and write her name in his guts if he refused to see reason.

Nothing left to do 'in town,' I headed home.

THE VESPER CLAN made it out of Godwin County within the allotted time, or so Sheriff Clyde told me. Whether that was due to their own industriousness or the fact they had a rather impressive escort was not for me to say or speculate. Sheriff Clyde told me that—aside from himself and a deputy —Buddy Carrington and his posse, Burt—one of the town's two tiger shifters, Grant's lion pride, Sloane in her avian form, and several other raptors all followed the Vespers at a respectful distance until they crossed the county line.

Well, as long as they were gone, that was the important part.

Both Gabrielle and I tried engaging with Karleen about the situation, but beyond a whispered 'thanks' when I mentioned I didn't kill her brother, she showed no interest in discussing the matter. In the end, I chose to let quiet dire wolves lie. There was no point in trying to *make* her talk about it, especially if my goal was to help her work through it.

Sunlight dappled Karleen's coat as she ran full-out through the forest. The tree canopy hid a cloudless sky, and a light breeze rustled the branches and limbs around her as she ran. The forest's panoply of scents delighted and intrigued her, and she fought the urge to pick up the trail of one of the many animals she smelled and hunt it. Just for sport. She wasn't too hungry yet.

Her explorations around Precious had revealed a cliff overlooking a large meadow that served as a kind of buffer between the western and eastern ranges, and that cliff was her destination. The trees began to thin, and she slowed her run, lest she burst out of the forest and dive right off the cliff because she couldn't stop. She learned *that* lesson very well, not too many years after leaving home; it was unwise to sprint full-out through terrain that one does not know.

As Karleen stepped onto the rocky shelf and the sun warmed her body, she scanned the meadow far below. A few animals—deer and such—roamed the field, but without attracting their attention, there was no way to know if they were shifters. And Karleen wasn't in the mood to socialize.

I should have killed him for his offense, brother or no, her growly voice—as Wyatt called it—opined as she settled herself on the cliff.

Karleen chuffed, the wolf version of a resigned sigh. *I suppose I should have, but what would that have done to the family?*

The family should know better. If one is sharing a meal with a dragon, one should take steps not to piss off the dragon.

So I'm a dragon now? Karleen shot back, adding a mental snort.

No, but compared to the family, I might as well be. I do not think I would lose even if the entire family attacked me... and definitely not if Wyatt *was there.*

I guess that depends on how one defines 'lose.' I love my sister and my parents. I don't want to fight them... or fight with *them.* Karleen chuffed another resigned sigh. *It felt good to be part of the family again.*

I still am a part of the family. My brother's conduct is not my *fault.*

Karleen lifted her head from her paws and scanned the meadow once more. Nothing piqued her interest. *Was Jack right, though? Is Wyatt too young for me?*

The part of Karleen that had never been human sent her the impression of a growling wolf. *There was nothing* right *about that poor example of life. Am I happy with Wyatt and Gabrielle?*

Yeah... I really am. I wouldn't trade what we have for anything.

It does not matter what anyone else thinks. Only what they do. And if someone is offensive or dishonorable, I should explain *their error. With teeth and claws if necessary.*

So, I should have handled the situation with Jack?

This time, the non-human part of her didn't immediately respond, and Karleen had the impression of extensive thought.

No, I think I handled that particular matter exactly as it should have been. Yes, he and they are my family, but they were also guests of the Alpha. That escalated matters such that it was Wyatt's place to handle it.

Karleen sent an impression of her agreement to the growly voice.

Good. Am I finished moping? A truck from a farm sat behind the diner as I left, and I smelled bison.

Karleen chuffed a laugh and let her tongue loll out the side of her muzzle in a canine grin. A couple bison steaks did sound nice...

I FINISHED my last set of burpees and leaned against the wall. I *hated* burpees and always saved them for last on the days they popped into my exercise queue. Granted, my shifter metabolism went a long way to keeping me fit, but I'd discovered that exercising helped clear my mind and get me ready to face the day. A part of me felt like I should go to one of the bigger cities and join a gym, just to enjoy the looks on everyone's faces as I bench-pressed five hundred pounds or something like that, but I also remembered the treadmills when Doc did his shifter assessment. I think he kept the most extreme U-shaped one as a souvenir. And then, there was Gabrielle's warning that shifters could turn humans with saliva or sweat. From what she said, turning people with sweat didn't happen very often, but it *had* happened.

Nah... probably ought to leave the human gyms alone.

I left the exercise room, headed for the shower in the master suite. Gabrielle sat at the small dinette tucked into a corner of the kitchen, and she froze—fork halfway to her mouth—and watched me until I went out of sight. I saw her take several deep breaths as I passed.

I wasn't more than a few steps down the hall that led to the master suite when I heard Gabrielle shout after me, "Walking around the house like that will make a girl hungry for more than just breakfast!"

I couldn't stop the grin that took over my face. I didn't notice the expressions of raw desire from the women around town as much anymore, but when I did, it still felt a little weird. As far as Gabrielle and Karleen—and Lyssa—were concerned, though, I rather liked it.

"Well, don't make threats if you won't follow through with them," I shouted back and kept right on walking.

She caught up with me just as I reached the shower.

WE WERE TOWELING off from the *extended* shower when the doorbell rang. I threw on a robe and padded my way out front. The doorbell rang a second time just as I opened the door and revealed Lyssa standing on the stoop. The tightness of her eyes, the tension in her stance, and a thousand other little things told me in no uncertain terms that she wasn't here for a social call.

"Hey, Lyssa," I remarked. "Please, come in."

She jerked a quick nod and stepped through the doorway as I stepped back to vacate the space. She stopped just far enough inside the door, her hands clutching her elbows with her arms crossed across her midriff.

"What's wrong?"

"Is Gabrielle here?" She asked in an almost weak, defeated voice.

"Hey, Lyssa," Gabrielle said as she entered the room in just a robe like me while still toweling off her hair. Then, I watched her eyes take in Lyssa's posture, and she froze. For just a moment. The next moment, she pulled the lioness into a fierce hug, damp hair and all.

We stood like that in an almost-frozen tableau for uncounted minutes until Lyssa pulled away. She looked first to Gabrielle, then to me, and back again as she said, "I need the Huntress. Someone kidnapped my niece, and I think I know who it was."

"Tell me," Gabrielle said without missing a beat.

"My sister just trounced her... well, now-ex... husband in court. Aside from everything she didn't want, she also walked away with full custody of her daughter. He didn't even get visitation. I know; I know. But you don't know the guy. He's... he put the truth in every bad story you've heard about lions. I think he stole Jessie while Cindy was occupied elsewhere. Cindy—of course—is melting down. Megan—our other sister—is there with her and called me."

"Where is there?" Gabrielle asked.

Lyssa took a deep breath and shuddered as she exhaled. "Kansas. Hampstead, Kansas."

I turned and went to the master suite, retrieving my phone. I sent a quick text to my sister as I walked back to the parlor. On the first chirp of its ring, I answered and put the call on speaker.

"Hi, sis," I said. "You're on speaker with me, Gabrielle, and Lyssa."

"Hello, dear brother mine and ladies," Vicki replied. "How can I help you today?"

"I'm sorry to keep treating you like my travel agent, sis," I began, "but Lyssa's niece has been taken. She thinks the abductor is the niece's deadbeat dad who just majorly lost the divorce and custody court cases. They're in Hampstead, Kansas."

"From everything I've heard, the first forty-eight hours are the most important in an abduction case, shadowy organizations notwithstanding," Vicki remarked. "How long ago was she taken?"

Lyssa lifted her head and spoke toward the phone. "No more than five hours. My sister Cindy isn't too coherent right now, but my other sister—Megan—thinks it hasn't been more than five hours. She's there with Cindy."

"Wyatt," Vicki said, "I feel rather safe in assuming you're not about to let Gabrielle and Lyssa go off to hunt this guy down, so assemble your hunting party. I'll be there in fifteen minutes or less."

The call ended, and I slipped the phone into one of the robe's pockets.

Lyssa stared at me. "This isn't your fight, Wyatt. Megan and I will be hiring Gabrielle with our own funds."

Gabrielle pulled her into another tight hug. "Oh, Lyssa, did you really believe you could tell Wyatt what happened, and he'd just sit here while we go off to deal with it? You're one of us now, and even if you weren't, children are special to him."

Before I gave any thought to the idea, I was moving. Four steps—maybe five—and I pulled both Gabrielle and Lyssa into my arms. I leaned in and gave Lyssa a quick kiss. I started to say something, but the moment didn't feel right. I realized in that moment the lioness was now one of us, 'us' being my immediate family. I'd have to be sure she knew that... and soon. As much as I hated to break the moment, though, we had things to do.

"Come on, Gabrielle. We need to get dressed. Vicki will be here soon, and we still need our hunting party."

Lyssa followed us to the master suite and sat on the bed as Gabrielle and I chose 'working' clothes.

"You know who would be better than wolves for tracking?" Lyssa asked while we dressed.

"Who?" Gabrielle's voice wafted out of her closet.

"Bears," the lioness replied. "They have even more scent receptors than wolves."

Gabrielle chuckled. "Yeah… Buddy will just *love* hearing that, especially after he popped off to Vicki about how wolf shifters have the best noses."

I watched Lyssa shrug. "Bears don't usually make an issue of it, and besides, they're not exactly lithe hunters."

Nope. Not at all. Hank—our friendly neighborhood store proprietor—in his grizzly came close to making my Smilodon look small.

"Let's stop by the general store and see if Hank or one of his bears would mind going with us," I said as Gabrielle stepped out of the closet. Like me, she wore cargo pants and a more tactical-styled top. A knapsack hung from a strap over her left shoulder. "We'll take Buddy and his posse for the extra muscle. Gabrielle, do you know what happened to Karleen? She wouldn't like us leaving without at least giving her the option of going."

A grimace flitted across Gabrielle's expression. "She went for a run. Most wolves can travel up to thirty miles in a day, and since she's a dire wolf, there's no telling where she is."

"Did she take her phone at least?"

Gabrielle pointed to the dresser behind me, and turning to look, I saw Karleen's phone, keys, and purse. I fought the urge to sigh. I wanted to include Karleen—or at least give her the option of being included—but I wasn't sure we had time to wait for her.

"Right, then," I remarked. "Nothing for it. Let's go talk to Hank."

Lyssa stood as Gabrielle led us out of the master suite. Gabrielle said, "I've texted Gladys to prepare the usual hunters' rations. I told her she should plan for us, Buddy's posse, and possibly two bears. We may have to wait a couple minutes, but she's working on it."

Karleen knew how to access the house after a run, so we locked up on our way out.

. . .

THE BELL over the door jingled as we entered Hank's general store. A number of people looked our way. Hank glanced up from where he assisted a young lady with different fabrics, and a young clerk handled customers ready to pay at the counter. The various scents wafting our way told me Hank was the only bear shifter in the room.

I *hated* line-jumpers. Hated them with a passion. But every minute we delayed was one more minute Cindy's daughter remained abducted. Regardless of how little I liked it, the only choice was to interrupt Hank with his customer. So, I headed their way.

Both the young lady and Hank looked to me as I approached and said, "Pardon my interruption, please, but I need to speak with Hank for a few moments on a matter of some urgency."

The young lady smiled and accepted the bolt of cloth from Hank as she replied, "Of course, Alpha Wyatt. I don't mind waiting."

Hank stepped my way, and we walked a short distance for the illusion of privacy. After all, any shifter in the store would hear a fly cough in the rafters... assuming flies actually coughed.

"What do you need, Alpha?" Hank asked.

"I'd like to borrow one or two of your bears for a hunting party. Lyssa's niece in Kansas has been abducted. I'm going to round up Buddy and his posse for extra muscle, but I'd like to find the niece as soon as possible."

Hank smiled. "Normally, I'd go myself, but Earl has been doing an excellent job showing that Paul Burkett how to be a bear. My vote is take both of them. Earl can be your main tracker, and Paul gets some real-world experience."

I nodded my agreement. "Sounds good. Do you want to make the call?"

Hank shook his head. "Nah. You're Alpha around here; you can handle it." Then, he broke into huge grin. "Besides, I have a customer waiting."

I chuckled and made a shooing gesture as I thanked him and turned back to my ladies. As I crossed the store back to them, I withdrew my phone from my hip pocket and accessed the local directory. Thank goodness, I could filter by breed. Godwin County apparently had fifteen shifters named 'Earl,' but only one of them lived in Precious and was a bear. I fired off a quick text message for Earl to grab Paul and meet me at the diner for a hunting mission with Gabrielle as we left the general store for our next destination.

THE MOMENT we entered the diner, my eyes locked onto Karleen. She sat at our favorite table with two large platters sitting empty in front of her. She looked rather pleased. As we approached, I thought I picked up hints of bison, and understanding dawned as I remembered Gladys received one of her meat shipments today.

"You should really try the bison," Karleen said as we arrived at the table. "It's a good batch this time."

My mouth watered a bit at the thought. "I'd love to, but I'm not sure we have time."

Karleen frowned and sat a little straighter. "What's wrong?"

"Someone took Lyssa's niece. She thinks her deadbeat brother-in-law did it and came to Gabrielle to hire the Huntress. I'm organizing a hunting party. Earl and the new guy, Paul Burkett, are on their way to meet us here. Vicki should be arriving any second, and I'm looking for Buddy and his posse."

"Why are you looking for us, Alpha Wyatt?" Buddy asked over my shoulder.

I turned and saw Buddy and his posse walking toward us from the door. Apparently, I'd been so focused on Karleen that I hadn't noticed the diner's door opening.

"I'd like you guys to come with me as extra muscle for a hunting party. Lyssa's niece has been abducted. Earl and Paul Burkett should be meeting us here soon, so between you guys, those two, and Gabrielle, whoever has her shouldn't keep her long."

Buddy nodded. "Sounds good. We didn't have anything planned for today anyway, beyond sighting in our rifles. Where are we going?"

"Kansas," I answered. "Vicki should be here…" The imp in question appeared at my side. "…anytime."

Vicki wore working clothes, much like Gabrielle's, and carried her staff. Unlike the formal appearance before the state's Supreme Court, this time, the staff looked like the gnarled and worn piece of wood—almost like a hand-carved tree branch—I'd seen during our hunt for the abducted children.

"Hello, brother mine," Vicki almost purred. "Are we ready?"

"Waiting on two more, sis. Shouldn't be long."

About that time, Gladys and several of her helpers arrived with packs full of food. The diner's owner said, "Here you go. Everything I've packed is warm right now, but it'll reheat well if it comes to that."

Vicki grinned. "No need for reheating. While we're waiting for the last of us, I'll amuse myself spelling those packs to keep their contents piping hot and fresh."

Over the next few minutes, my sister whispered words in

an ancient language over Gladys's packs. She stood from completing the last one as Earl and Paul entered the diner.

"There they are," I said. "Excellent timing."

"So, we're ready to hunt?" Vicki asked as she stood from crouching over the last pack, and I nodded. "Good. It has been too long."

The appearance of a simple, gnarled tree branch faded from Vicki's staff without apparent prodding. In its wake, we saw the staff in its truth. The staff's wooden shaft was blacker than night, seeming to draw in color and light around it. A pointed ferrule that looked to be gold capped its base, and at the top, a ferrule shaped like a dragon's claw grasped a clear, crystal shard. The staff radiated an emptiness... no... a *hunger*. A hunger so deep and unfulfilled that even all the souls in the entire world might not sate it.

Each of us shouldered one of Gladys's packs, until only Earl, Paul, and Lyssa remained pack-less, and Vicki led us to the street. Apparently, creating a portal in the dining room of a restaurant just wasn't done. As soon as we gathered around her, Vicki took Lyssa's hand and asked her to concentrate on her sisters. Then, she recited a series of words in that ancient language. Within seconds, a portal once again graced the center of Main Street, and we stepped through it.

A s soon as I oriented myself after stepping through Vicki's portal, I had my first look at Hampstead. The town itself didn't seem *that* different from Precious. Main Street seemed to serve as the heart of the town. Vehicles ranged in both age and level of maintenance, and more than one local walking either sidewalk gave our group odd looks, if not the full-on hairy eyeball.

"Come on," Lyssa said, gesturing down the street. "We should say hello to Alpha Steve before going to my sister's place."

"Will he give us any problems?" Gabrielle asked, as the group followed Lyssa down Main Street.

Lyssa shook her head 'no.' "He shouldn't. Megan told him Cindy asked me to hire the Huntress."

"Maybe so, but you arrived with a little more than just me."

Lyssa smiled. "Yeah… I did. You have no idea how much it means to me that all of you came out to help find my niece."

Gabrielle pulled Lyssa into a one-armed hug. "This is restrained, as far as Wyatt's concerned. If he was really worried about our chances of getting your niece back, we would've arrived through a Magi assault rift with three-hundred-fifty shifters in a war party."

"That is still on the table depending on what we find," I remarked.

"You know, brother mine, we should probably discuss stationing a few Magi who are Master-certified in teleportation in Precious if you plan to make a habit of this. Otherwise, the law of averages will eventually catch up with you, and I won't be available when you call. Now, granted, I'd drop what I was doing if it were a true emergency, but if we had a... oh, I don't know; call it an embassy... in Precious, that would cut down on response time and almost guarantee availability of portals and assault rifts."

"An embassy, sis? Really?"

Vicki beamed her innocent smile. "Why, of course. I hear you've recently come up in the world, what with being named Consul of the Shifters of North America. A mere *office* would never do. No, no, no. Only a Magi embassy would show due respect to your new gravitas."

I gave my sister a flat look to which she replied with her bright, innocent cheerleader smile. Oh, well... maybe picking at the title the Shifter Council foisted onto me would divert her attention from scratching posts, litter boxes, and other feline-themed prank gifts. That was a fair hope, right?

As more people noticed Lyssa in our group, the expressions directed toward us softened. I fought the urge to smile. In towns like these, having a 'local' with you made *all* the difference. We walked down the sidewalk, and as we neared a tall, steepled building, I saw 'Loch County Courthouse' chiseled over the main entrance. A trio in sheriff department uniforms stood on the steps of the courthouse, looking our way.

"So, how far are we from Dodge City?" I asked.

Lyssa gave a one-shoulder shrug. "Oh… around ninety minutes north of it, give or take. It really depends on how you drive. Ah, there's Alpha Steve now."

Lyssa led us straight to the trio; the center person looked to be an older man. The wind carried three shifter scents to us, all lion.

"Alpha Steve," Lyssa said as she approached the foot of the steps.

The 'older' man gave her a flat look that carried hints of humor around the edges. "*Alpha Steve*, is it? I don't remember you calling me *Alpha Steve* while you and your sisters chased Sandy and Brian around the backyard."

That was all the prompting Lyssa needed. She almost launched herself into the sheriff's arms. "Hi, Uncle Steve. How is everyone?"

I watched Alpha Steve hold Lyssa in a tight hug, and the only way his regard for her would have been more obvious was if he carried around a large neon sign the size of a billboard.

"As well as can be expected, Lyssie. This mess has been tough on a lot of us."

After a few more seconds, Lyssa released her vise grip on the man, and she turned to face us. "This is Steve Westridge, Alpha of Hampstead and Loch County… and my uncle. These two with him are Mike and Sam, deputies and my cousins." She then proceeded to introduce our group, saving me and my sister for last. "And this is Wyatt Magnusson, Alpha of Precious and Godwin County and Consul of the Shifters of North America. Beside him is Victoria Magnusson, Heiress of Clan Magnusson, Heiress to the House of Merlin, and Bearer of *Requiem*, the Black Staff of Ruin. Did I get all that right, Vicki?"

Vicki smiled and added a nod. "Yes, you did."

Steve eyed me ever since Lyssa mentioned that 'Consul'

nonsense. After a moment, he scanned the faces around me, saying, "Welcome, everyone, to Hampstead and Loch County. Thank you for coming. I wish the reasons for your visit were better. Sam, call Kent and ask him to send a couple vans down here, please."

The female deputy withdrew a cell phone from one of her belt pouches and made the call.

"So," Alpha Steve said, his tone artificially nonchalant, "you finally pushed through your Consul idea, huh?"

What? My head turned toward Lyssa like a tank turret swiveling for target acquisition. She caught my movement, and her complexion blushed red. Not quite ripe tomato red, but certainly Gala or Honeycrisp apple red.

Steve noticed the byplay, too, and he quirked his eyebrow in silent question as he said, "From the looks of things, your acceptance of Consul was less than enthusiastic?"

I nodded once. "Much like being Alpha of Precious and Godwin County. Neither were my idea or preference."

Alpha Steve chuckled. "Ah. I see. Lyssa and a couple of her friends on the Council have been fighting for that 'Consul' business ever since word came in of a feline primogenitor." Lyssa let out a strangled squeak as Alpha Steve kept right on talking. "Seems there's some kind of old document or scribblings or something that predict the next feline primogenitor will be some kind of Grand Poobah or some such. Don't ask me if there's any truth to it, but a lot of shifter scholars have been digging through all the old archives ever since you showed up."

By now, Lyssa's cheeks *were* the color of a ripe tomato as she growled out, "Uncle, you don't *have* to tell everything you know. You realize that, right?"

A pair of white vans came down the street and made a U-turn to pull up to the courthouse steps as Steve shrugged and replied, "Ehh... I figure the boy needs a little fair warning.

You and your friends sometimes seem to treat people like pieces on a chess board."

Well, thank you, Alpha Steve. Glad I wasn't the only one to notice that little behavioral quirk.

A frowning Lyssa pulled me to the first van where Alpha Steve climbed into the passenger seat. Lyssa, Gabrielle, and I sat in the second row with me sandwiched in the middle. Vicki dismissed *Requiem* as she, Karleen, and Earl moved to sit in the third row. Everyone else piled into the second van, filling it to capacity.

As the vans rolled out, Alpha Steve turned a little in his seat to speak to us better. "Okay. So, here's what we know. Bonnie—Lyssa's niece—has been missing a little over four hours. At the time of the disappearance, her mother—Cindy —heard her scream for help, but by the time Cindy made it outside, there was no trace of her. Not even a scent trail. There is, however, a faint magical aura throughout the area."

When Alpha Steve paused, Vicki spoke into the silence. "Depending on the effect used to mask the trail, there's a chance that nothing will be there even *after* I break the masking. If it was a hedge wizard charm like the abduction cases back in Washington, everything will be there, but there are higher order protections that prevent tracks and scent trails and all that from being laid in the first place. Lyssa said Cindy believes her ex-husband took Bonnie?"

"Yes," Alpha Steve answered, nodding. "She's a clerk in the county records office, and everything there is public information. None of us can think of anyone with motive to take Bonnie *other* than that deadbeat Oliver Price."

"That's the dad and ex?" I asked.

"Yeah," Alpha Steve replied.

"And Cindy, Bonnie, and Oliver are all lions?"

Alpha Steve nodded. "Yes."

I looked to Gabrielle and said, "So, the first step is for Vicki to break the masking and see if anything appears?"

Gabrielle stared out the window and nodded in an almost absent-minded manner. "Yes. If it's like the abduction cases back home, breaking the masking will make this *so much* easier. Frankly, I'm hoping for that. Worst case, I'll track the magic. I've done it before."

"Is there any chance that breaking the masking will remove all magic traces and make it impossible to track them if no tracks appear?" Lyssa asked.

"No," Gabrielle answered, turning to lean forward just enough to make eye contact with Lyssa. "My first hunt for the Council involved a shifter and Magi working together, despite the tensions. The Magi used the more powerful protection, and I saw currents and eddies in the magic even after the Magi working with me broke the protection, which I used to track the bad guys."

"That's why they call her the Huntress," Karleen opined from the third row. "From what I've heard, that little ability is *beyond* rare."

I saw Gabrielle look away, turning back to the window, and it made me think she still wasn't used to having the reputation in shifter society that she did. Heh... I knew *that* feeling. But I didn't like her to feel embarrassed or anything like that, so I took the focus off her.

"So, how are you and your deputies going to run with us? And does Cindy have a scent article of some kind?" I asked.

Alpha Steve retrieved a plastic container of flavored toothpicks and popped one into his mouth. Then answered, "Cindy runs a horse farm. Stabling services, training, and that kind of thing. The deputies and I will mount up and ride with the crowd."

A thought popped into my mind. "And they're regular horses? Not horse shifters?"

He gave me a weird look. "Of course, they're regular horses. It wouldn't be fair for horse shifters to compete against regular horses in races and what not, and besides, that would just be demeaning to them."

"Didn't mean to step on anyone," I replied. "I should probably shift as soon as we arrive and test the horses with me."

"Why? They've been bred around predator shifters for several generations."

I pointed to my chest. "Smilodon. Sabertooth cat. Not a regular feline predator. I doubt I smell anything like lions or tigers or really any other feline predator shifter the horses have encountered. I'd hate for them to panic and hurt themselves or someone else."

The intensity of Alpha Steve's expression faded as his eyes unfocused, his entire demeanor advertising he was deep in thought. "Yeah... hadn't thought about that. Not a bad idea. I would run it by Cindy, but she's not having a good day. I'll ask Ted as soon as we arrive. He's the ranch manager."

THE CONVERSATION FELL AWAY as the vans left the town behind. I saw why Hampstead and Loch County appealed to families of lion shifters. It was probably as close to the Serengeti as a lion was going to get in North America. Hampstead itself was a small farming town surrounded by miles and miles and miles of wheat fields, broken only by highways and train tracks. Some of those fields laid fallow, covered with tall grass and other non-wheat plant life. Most did not, and those fields gave me a much deeper and more honest understanding of the 'amber waves of grain.'

We drove for about thirty minutes before we turned off the highway. Our new road split fields as far as the eye could see in either direction, but about fifteen minutes after leaving the highway, the fields fell away on the van's right side and revealed a horse ranch that was rather impressive in its size alone.

A gravel lane connected the road to the ranch house, and fenced pastures bracketed it. The lane ran a couple hundred yards before it opened into a courtyard with a roundabout that had a massive flower planter in the center. The main house was a single-story ranch-style dwelling with a porch. A large barn stood off to the left, and a garage and what looked like a small bunkhouse stood off to the right. Two women—who bore a resemblance to Lyssa—stood on the porch.

The van slowed to a stop, and Alpha Steve opened his door as Gabrielle hauled open the sliding door. She and I cleared the way with alacrity to permit Lyssa's urgent egress and dash up the steps to throw her arms around the two women I believed to be her sisters. Even from the short distance I stood, I could see how tightly Lyssa hugged them.

A crowd formed in the courtyard as the passengers vacated the second van and collected around us. Everyone in our group seemed to look to me for what to do next, and I fought the urge to sigh. This wasn't my circus. Either Lyssa or Gabrielle was the ringleader... or maybe both of them were. But I guess my people looked to me because I was their Alpha, so I should probably get to Alpha-ing.

After giving the sisters a couple minutes, I headed for the porch, Gabrielle and Karleen on either side of me with Alpha Steve on my far left and Vicki on my far right. My shifter hearing informed me that everyone else fell into a loose group that followed us. Lyssa broke the hug and stepped to one side as we approached, and she gestured to me like a game show hostess.

"Cindy, Megan... this is Wyatt Magnusson, Alpha of Precious and Godwin County and Consul of the Shifters of

North America. The lady on his left is Karleen Vesper, the North American dire wolf. The lady on his right is Gabrielle Hassan, the Huntress. The lady to Gabrielle's right is Wyatt's sister, Vicki. We brought two bear shifters to assist with tracking, plus a small wolf pack if we need extra muscle."

Lyssa's sisters' eyes widened just enough for me to notice when Lyssa introduced me, and those same eyes became tea saucers at the introduction of Karleen. As soon as Lyssa stopped speaking, the woman closest to her of the two took a half step forward as she said, "Welcome. I'm Cindy, and this is our other sister, Megan. I'm not sure I have the words for how much it means to me that all of you would drop what you were doing to come here and help us. 'Thank you' seems so insufficient."

I stepped forward and offered my most encouraging smile. "We'll do everything we can to see your daughter returned to you, ma'am. I promise you that."

Alpha Steve stepped to my side, saying, "Cindy, is Ted around?"

"No," Cindy replied, adding a shake of her head. "He had this week scheduled as vacation, but Rory should be around." She grabbed at her belt for something that wasn't there. "Drat... I don't have my radio."

Megan pivoted and strode into the house, saying over her shoulder, "It's right here, Cindy."

Moments later, Megan placed it in Cindy's hand, and Cindy summoned Rory to the porch at the roundabout. After clipping the radio to her belt, she asked, "Why do you need Rory?"

Alpha Steve gave a little cough as he answered, "We... uhh... have an unusual shifter breed as part of the hunting party, and we thought it might be best to test the horses around them before we head out. Come to think of it, we have *two*."

"While the three of you check the horses, is it okay if Vicki goes ahead and breaks the masking?" Lyssa asked.

Cindy frowned. "Breaks the masking?"

Vicki lifted her right hand, and *Requiem* in all its foreboding glory winked into existence within her grip as she stepped forward to join me. Both Cindy and Megan blinked as Vicki said, "I am Magi, and I can break whatever effect is masking the scents and tracks of Bonnie's abductors."

"Yes, please," Cindy replied as she gestured toward the house. "They took Bonnie from the backyard and fled west through the fields."

Rory arrived right about then, and it seemed to be time for me and Karleen to don our fur.

G abrielle, Karleen, and I stepped into a mud room as Alpha Steve waited outside with Rory, and everyone else followed Lyssa and her sisters through the house to the backyard. Karleen and I stripped and shifted, and Gabrielle collected our clothes into a duffel she had removed from her pack and unrolled.

As the Loch County sheriff, I thought Alpha Steve would've possessed decent skill at keeping his emotions from showing in his expression, but maybe Karleen and I were just that striking. As we padded off the porch, Alpha Steve gaped. Rory outright paled, and Deputy Mike took a step back as his hand went to his sidearm.

Nice to know we attracted attention.

I watched Rory take a cautious sniff and resisted the urge to smile as he shuddered.

It's good that the cougar recognizes a true predator, the growly voice opined. *Saves me spending the effort to educate him.*

Rory glanced from us to Alpha Steve and back again several times before he said, "Uhhh... I'm not sure how this will work out. Yeah... they scent like a wolf and feline respectively, but she doesn't scent *anything* like any other wolf I've ever met. And don't even get me started on him. Just the sight of those teeth makes my cougar want to look for the tallest tree and stay there until he leaves... the state."

Alpha Steve chuckled. "My lion isn't exactly calm, either. Might as well get this over with. Have your hands gathered the trail horses?"

Rory nodded and gulped a swallow. He turned to walk toward the barn and waved for us to follow him. Karleen and I trotted along in their wake, giving them about a ten-foot lead and then keeping pace with them. I didn't see either deputy move, but my ears told me they followed at a respectful distance.

The barn was a large structure that matched any ranch barn I had ever seen, whether in pictures or old Western movies or TV shows. Painted the stereotypical red with white trim, it had a set of massive doors at the front and back, and I saw both were open as we approached. Eight of Rory's ranch hands sat atop horses. Three of the horses had tan coats with blond manes and tails. Two had a blue-gray base coat with black spots. And the last three had coats that were deeper browns with black manes, tails, and 'boots.' Or did horse people call the different coloring on a horse's knees and hooves 'socks?' I wasn't sure. I never grew up around horses.

We were thirty to forty feet away when the wind shifted, and we were suddenly up-wind of the horses. Within seconds, all of the horses became restive. The ranch hands started trying to keep the horses calm as we continued to approach.

About ten feet later, the situation worsened. All the horses snorted and started making noises, and two of them— a blue-gray with spots and a darker brown with black boots —pawed at the dirt. The other horses started stepping forward and back or side to side, despite the best efforts of their riders to keep them calm.

We were maybe twenty feet away from the horses when one of the tan ones reared. The ranch hand kept his perch, but when the horse reared a second time, she hit the ground. The horse dropped back to the ground and pivoted, then hopped over its former rider and charged through the barn. The last I saw of it, the horse jumped over a fence and vanished from sight. My shifter hearing told me it picked up speed *fast*.

At least the other horses handled me and Karleen well enough. Oh, sure… they were restive, but none of them panicked like their associate just did. We stopped around fifteen feet away from them and sat on our haunches. Over time, with treats and calm assurances from the ranch hands, the horses even seemed to calm and steady themselves.

"How many horses did you need?" Rory asked.

"Just four," Alpha Steve answered. "Me and my deputies plus Wyatt's sister."

Rory nodded, then replied with a new question, "Does the sister have any experience riding?"

Both Alpha Steve and Rory turned to look at me, as if I could somehow answer them as a Smilodon. I did my best to shrug and hoped it conveyed something akin to 'how should I know.'

"Right," Rory remarked. "I'll see she gets the most sedate, well-behaved, and reliable horse we have. I'll also speak to Cindy about bringing along a ranch hand or two to help with the horses. She didn't say anything about hearing a vehicle, but they had to have something better than feet. We would've found them already by now, otherwise."

I felt *something* off to my right that made me think of Vicki, and I suspected she just broke whatever magical effect masked any tracks or scent trails the abductor left. Not seeing anything else to do at the barn, I stood and padded off toward the ranch house's backyard. Karleen soon arrived at my side, and my ears told me everyone else in our little group fell in behind us.

A rail fence—much like every other fence I had seen so far—blocked off the backyard from the rest of the immediate property. Karleen took off at a sprint and cleared the fence with apparent ease. The part of me that was always a big cat gave me the impression we could do the same, but the only thing I could picture in my mind was catching one of my paws on the top fence rail and bringing a whole section down. I didn't want to add fence repair to Cindy's already horrible day, so I trotted to the gate I saw further around the yard.

CINDY and her sisters led Vicki and the rest of Wyatt's hunting party into a substantial backyard that looked to be almost sixty feet square, enclosed by a rail fence. A small patio with a roof and outdoor furniture extended from the back of the house, and a permanent circle made of brick with a blackened grill on top occupied the far right corner of the patio from the house's door.

To Vicki, the magical effect blocking tracking smothered the area like a thick, suffocating blanket. She stepped past Gabrielle and the sisters and walked to the center of the space. She closed her eyes and concentrated on the magic. Yes... it was definitely created by some hedge magician's charm, and she fought the urge to sneer. Those pathetic street hustlers had no business playing on the same field as true Magi, but like her grandparents had waxed eloquent many times since Vicki began her studies, not everyone was fortunate enough to be born a Magi. Vicki suppressed a growl that would've gone well with the suppressed sneer, then took a deep breath and shook her head as she cleared her mind.

"Well?" Gabrielle asked *just* as she approached the calm serenity she preferred for casting.

Vicki opened her eyes and turned to her audience. She offered her perky, happy cheerleader smile, saying, "Oh, it's the work of a hedge charm. When I break the masking, there should be plenty of residual scent and trail to track whatever idiot did this."

Lyssa angled her head to the side, frowning. "Why do you say the abductor was an idiot?"

"Hedge work is third-rate magic at best, and whoever created the charm that did this…" Vicki clenched her jaw for a moment. "…there are Magi children just nearing puberty who could create a better masking effect than this. If the situation were not so grave, I think I'd feel offended."

Gabrielle and the lioness sisters shared a look before Gabrielle said, "So, it won't be any more difficult to break than the mask at the nanny's house?"

Vicki snorted. "I could break this with the cantrip they use to *teach* dispelling." Vicki's expression became thoughtful, and she tapped her chin. "Matter of fact, I think I will."

Without further ado, Vicki pivoted on her heel and lifted her staff until she appeared to be something like an odd mirror to the Statue of Liberty. She took a breath and rattled off a handful of words like a machine gun. The crystal atop her staff flared brighter than the sun for a split second, and in the blink of an eye, the backyard lost its pristine appearance. The grass and sod sprouted missing divots and gashes where Bonnie must have dug her feet into the lawn as she fought her abductor, and the gate lost its latch.

Gabrielle turned to the sisters. "Cindy, do you have a scent article for Bonnie?"

"Yes, of course." She darted into the house.

"Vicki," Gabrielle began, "would you gather our clothes into our packs, please? This duffel has Wyatt's and Karleen's with room for mine."

Vicki nodded and accepted the duffel, while the guys— Earl, Paul, Buddy, and his posse—stripped and shifted. Gabrielle followed suit, and just as Cindy returned with a pull-over hoodie, Karleen as a dire wolf leaped over the fence and trotted up to Gabrielle's jaguar and sat on her haunches. Moments later, a sabertooth cat nosed the backyard's gate open and trotted up to Karleen and Gabrielle also.

Lyssa's sisters gaped at Wyatt and directed incredulous expressions to her as they pointed at him. Lyssa just smiled and nodded as Vicki gathered Gabrielle's clothes into the duffel. Alpha Steve, his deputies, Rory, and the ranch hands arrived with the horses as Cindy approached Gabrielle with the hoodie. Earl, Paul, and Karleen moved in to take their own sniffs of the hoodie, too.

As the bears moved deeper into the backyard toward the gate, Rory said, "We lost Sugar. Wyatt came within about twenty feet of her, and she dumped Daisy to the dirt and bolted, tack and all."

"Is Daisy hurt?" Cindy asked.

Rory shrugged. "Just her pride, and maybe a bruise or two. Nothing serious. I figured we'd put Wyatt's sister on Mabel, since she's best with new riders, and I'd take a couple ranch hands along on the other horses."

Megan took the hoodie and zipper bag Cindy gave her and pushed the hoodie inside before sealing it as Cindy walked over to Rory.

"No, my sisters and I will take the other three trail horses," Cindy countered. "We all grew up riding, so we can keep an eye on Vicki and help her if she runs into trouble."

Vicki looked up from where she was putting a person's

clothes into the proper pack, saying, "Oh, you don't need to worry about me. I've been riding horses since I was little."

After she finished collecting the clothes, Vicki walked over to where Karleen and the two bears milled about near the gate. "Well, how about it, team? Do you have a scent trail?"

Both bears and a dire wolf turned to her and made obvious nods to answer 'yes.'

"So, we're ready to go?"

Another obvious nod to answer 'yes.'

Vicki turned back to the rest of us and said, "Well, folks, what are we waiting for?"

That set off a flurry of activity during which those still bipedal with thumbs moved packs to horses, and everyone gradually gathered outside the fence gate. As soon as Alpha Steve, his deputies, Vicki, and the sisters sat astride their mounts, Alpha Steve spoke in a raised voice, "Okay, let's go hunting!"

THE BEARS SET off a shambling jog that we had no trouble maintaining. Karleen trotted behind them, then Gabrielle and I, before the rest of our hunting party spread out behind us. The occasional equine sound told me the horses still weren't too comfortable with me, but I didn't hear any shouts of alarm. So, they must not have been too unhappy.

The tracks that even I could follow soon met tire tracks, and the bears stopped for a moment. One took deep breaths with his nose held high, while the other sniffed the ground. After a few moments, they turned to each other as if they somehow communicated before taking off at that shambling jog again.

The tire tracks were obvious as we progressed through

the ranch's fields and pastures, but we soon came to a creek or river. It looked to be about thirty feet wide but seemed shallow. One of the bears dove right in and splashed his way to the far bank. He walked that far bank for about twenty feet in either direction before coming back to us. He shook his head to communicate 'no,' and the bears set off on the ranch house's side of the waterway as it meandered in a generally southwest direction.

We followed the waterway—whatever type it was—for quite a while until we arrived at another crossing. This time, even I could see tire tracks on the far bank, leading out of the water, and I resolved myself to getting wet just as the bears sent huge plumes of water into the air as they charged across. The water barely covered my paws in most places, but I seemed to have inherited the near-universal dislike of being wet that most cats have. After climbing out of the crossing, I stopped to shake off the excess before running to resume my position beside Gabrielle.

THE BEARS LED us at a steady pace, relentless in their pursuit of the scent trail, and only the top quarter or so of the sun remained above the peaks of the Rockies far to the west when the bears slowed to a stop. One of them took the time to tamp down a circle of the brush that surrounded us before he shifted, and Earl motioned for us to gather around him as he crouched. The riders dismounted and fixed weights to one of the reins before joining the rest of us.

"Okay. The scent trail is getting really strong, and I think we're close. I'm also smelling wood smoke and hints of gasoline. I think there's a cabin somewhere close. But that's not why I stopped." Earl pointed to the south with his right arm. "I smell water that way. Is there a river or a lake over there?"

Lyssa and her sisters looked to one another as Alpha Steve pawed at one of the pouches on his duty belt.

Cindy said, "I don't know how far south we are, but we'll come to Pawnee Fork eventually. Could that be the body of water you're smelling?"

Alpha Steve produced a decent handheld GPS, and I heard it beep as he powered it on. After a few moments, he said, "You're right, Cindy. From the looks of the map, we're no more than a tenth of a mile north of Pawnee Fork."

"Didn't Oliver have a fishing cabin or something somewhere along Pawnee Fork?" Megan asked.

Cindy frowned, her brow furrowing with thought. "Yes, but I'm pretty sure it's in the next county over. Uncle Steve, we may be outside your jurisdiction."

"Doesn't matter," Lyssa interjected and pointed at me. "If we're not in Loch County anymore and the local sheriff gets wound up about it, he—or she—can take it up with Wyatt. The Shifter Council named Wyatt Consul of the Shifters of North America, so as long as we're between the Arctic Ocean and the southern border of Mexico, we're inside *his* jurisdiction."

Well, damn... maybe this 'Consul' thing wasn't so bad after all.

Without another word, Earl shifted back to his grizzly bear, and we set off on the scent trail once more. One thing I learned over the course of the afternoon and evening was that grizzlies can be *quiet*, no matter their size. Don't get me wrong; compared to me and especially Karleen or Gabrielle, they were noisy. But... I had to concentrate to hear them over the horses behind us. I was not expecting that.

The sun had well and truly set by the time we broke through the underbrush on the edge of a clearing. It looked to be seventy-five to a hundred yards on a side, and the centerpiece of the clearing was a cabin that someone converted into a rough, two-story house at some point in time. Its origins as a cabin were obvious, because the oldest lumber in the construction showed its age more than the rest. A chimney rose up the side of the structure closest to us, and it spewed a thick steam of smoke into the sky. Flickering lights through the windows led me to believe lamps or candles or something of the sort lit the interior. Each visible wall of the house sported at least two massive floodlights, large bowls or bells and looking like the massive lights used in the old-time school gymnasiums. A four-seat side-by-side sat in front of the house, and scattered throughout the yard within about twenty-five yards of the house, many posts supported even more of those floodlights, four per post.

We were still looking the place over—or at least *I* was—when motion above the cabin's porch drew my eyes. A window right over the center of the porch eased open, and a person clambered out and onto the porch roof. As the person moved more fully into the light from the overhead full moon, I decided the person was a female who was roughly adolescent in age.

"Bonnie," I heard Cindy gasp behind me, just as the teenager neared the edge of the porch's roof.

We all watched in silence as the would-be escapist's feet slipped out from under her. She hit the porch roof with a thud that even *we* heard—well, at least we shifters—before rolling off to land on the ground with a slightly more muffled thud. The young lady pushed herself to a sitting position and shook her head as she rose to stand. She had moved from sitting on the ground to kneeling with one knee on the grass when the house's front door opened to reveal a man's lanky frame.

The man looked over his shoulder and shouted, "Dammit, Ollie... she's free!"

22

I erupted into motion, and it took all my willpower to keep from roaring my challenge to the heavens. The non-aggression pact the horses and I enjoyed was still new enough that I wasn't sure it extended to them not minding if I roared. At my second stride, I approached the bears' hind quarters, and I extended all my claws, tearing up the sod with my extra traction as I shouldered my way between them.

As I ran toward the house, my shifter hearing picked up a faint, "Well, don't just stand there. Go get her!"

The voice was so faint that I decided it came from deeper in the cabin, and the man in the doorway charged across the porch and down the steps. In seconds, he was up to a full sprint, and I altered my course to intercept him. Bonnie risked a glance behind her and put on more speed, but I could tell she was now putting everything she had into her flight. It wasn't enough. The man ever so slowly closed the distance between them.

A thick mass of clouds occluded the moon overhead, plunging everything into a darkness nearing pitch black, just as Cindy shrieked at the top of her lungs, "Bonnie!"

The sprinting teenager looked our way, but shifters in human form didn't have much better night vision than humans. Still, one should never doubt a child's ability—regardless of age—to recognize her mother's voice. Bonnie cut a hard right turn, and I marveled at her ability to—first—complete such a maneuver and—second—not break an ankle or something regardless of being a shifter. She damn near turned on a dime and gave back a nickel in change.

I maintained my 'target lock' on the man chasing Bonnie, who now angled more toward us. I couldn't *quite* make out his facial expression this far away, but he seemed to recognize Cindy's voice, too. On the bright side, though, he didn't seem to react to me charging toward him with everything I had.

"Someone hit the lights!" the pursuer shouted as he ran. "It's blacker than a lawyer's heart out here!"

Seconds passed as the distance between me and the pursuer dropped by yards with every tick of the clock. I wasn't counting them, but I knew it wouldn't be too long before those floodlights came on and ruined my surprise.

My whole awareness became the man chasing Bonnie, my perceptions shrinking down to the most severe case of tunnel vision I could remember. Nothing else mattered. Not the house. Not my people behind me. Not even Bonnie. Just my full-body sprint and my target... no. My prey.

How in the world he never heard a thousand-pound cat charging at him across the yard, I'll never know. Maybe he did hear me but just didn't process the sound's true meaning. It didn't matter.

The distance closed to the point that my feline side roared, *Now!*, and I put every ounce of muscle into a leap toward the man. I was halfway to him when the floodlights came on, and I *loved* the sheer terror that claimed his expression when he saw me flying toward him.

He squeaked out, "What the hell," mere moments before my front paws touched his shoulders. I rode him down to the ground and forced my forelegs to fold with me as gravity reasserted its claim. I think every bone between the fifth cervical vertebra in his neck and his pelvis shattered in a single, ghastly *CRACK!* that mimicked a lightning strike and thunderclap no more than a hundred yards away. The gruesome cacophony even overshadowed the combined sound of the man striking the ground and my bulk landing on him.

My tunnel vision snapped back to full situational awareness, just as the first grizzly passed me in his lumbering version of a full sprint. I pushed myself to stand and roared my defiant challenge to the clouds and stars above as the rest of my hunting party charged past.

Heartbeats later, Alpha Steve charged past me on his mount, shouting at the top of his lungs, "Dammit, people... we need them *alive!*"

The lead grizzly jumped onto the porch just as another man came through the door and skidded to a stop. The grizzly—whether Earl or Paul—reared up on his hind legs and put his whole shoulder into an ursine haymaker that sent the man flying back through the doorway. I heard the crash of his landing even as far as away as I was, and it did *not* sound even remotely pleasant. The grizzly roared his triumph and dropped back to his paws.

"Earl!" Lyssa's voice cracked like a whip in the cooling night air, and the massive grizzly froze mid-step. "No bears in the house! You're too damn big. One of you go around back; one of you stay on the front porch. Wolves, split up; surround the place and watch for runners. Gabrielle and Buddy, clear the house. Wyatt, stay there and grab anyone who slips by us. Deputies, follow Gabrielle and Buddy to assist with clearing the house."

I was about to leave my first prey of the evening to his

pathetic, broken whimpers, but at Lyssa's instruction, I laid down on him once more, eliciting another groan or four. A horse clop-clopped past me at a steady walk while I watched the evening's festivities unfold, and I saw Cindy had intercepted her daughter and pulled Bonnie up to sit behind her. Bonnie stared at me as they passed, her expression blending awe, unsettled nerves, and a dash of fear.

A commotion off to my left revealed four wolves chasing a guy hauling tail away from the back of the house. If he was dumb enough to turn my way and managed to outrun his lupine pursuers, I'd intervene. But no. He wasn't that good… or that lucky. Two wolves brought him down, one in a flying leap that hit him between his shoulder blades and the second in a well-timed bite that severed his Achilles tendon. Either would've accomplished the goal, but both combined guaranteed whoever it was would not be escaping anytime soon.

Minutes later, I heard Deputy Mike shout, "First floor clear, suspect contained!"

Right on its heels, Deputy Sam echoed, "Second floor clear, suspect contained!"

"All clear!" Alpha Steve replied in his own shout before lowering his voice to a normal volume. "Bring everyone to the front yard."

Another scream off to my left drew my attention, and I chuffed my amusement at the sight of one of the wolves dragging the runner around front by simple expedient of sinking his—or her—teeth into the runner's wrist. The poor sod's screams and protests seemed fit to raise the dead five counties over, but I found myself unmoved by his plight. If he didn't want to be subdued, he should not have run.

Deputy Mike brought a muscled guy in shifter-grade handcuffs through the front door. The guy filled the night with his own profanity and heated invectives, many of them directed toward Cindy and her sisters. I was prepared to let the idiot shout himself hoarse, but he made the mistake of calling out Lyssa by name.

Nope! Lyssa was *mine*.

I pushed myself up to stand and charged off toward the cluster of people and animals surrounding the fool whose life expectancy lost decades every second he kept layering derogatory slurs upon Lyssa. Whether by conscious awareness or some kind of shifter-only sixth sense, the crowd between me and the blathering idiot parted.

I slowed to a steady walk as I neared the crowd and timed my shift so that one step in human form put me in the perfect position to drive an uppercut with all my weight and inertia behind it into his abdomen somewhere between his stomach and diaphragm. His speech ended in an eruption of air and a mist of bile, and he collapsed to his knees and spewed vomit onto the grass. He possessed sufficient awareness—or perhaps wisdom—to miss everyone's feet. I grasped a handful of hair and yanked his head back, making eye contact as I kept my right fist available if needed.

"If you desire even the slightest hope of seeing your next birthday, you will cease your disrespectful prattle and apologize to everyone for inflicting it upon them... especially Lyssa."

"What the hell, Wyatt?" Alpha Steve exploded. "He's in custody. You don't hit people in custody."

I lifted my eyes to meet his gaze for several moments, and I sensed more than one of my people stepping back to make room. I hauled the object of our disagreement to his feet, pulling out more than a few tufts of hair in the process to the accompaniment of pained shouts. I spun him around to put his back to me and wrapped my hands around the handcuffs at the mechanism's housings and the chain link that connected to them.

I need to snap this chain. I don't care what it takes, I sent to the part of me that had not been human since the cougar attack.

I felt a swell of power fill my body, and I *knew* my eyes shifted to full Smilodon. My shoulders tensed and arms tightened, as I clenched my jaw the muscles around my eyes tightened. For several heartbeats, the night was silent as a tomb. Not even crickets chirped or frogs croaked within earshot. With no warning whatsoever, a sharp *PING!* split the night, and the center link in the chain that secured the handcuffs snapped and flew into the darkness.

I maintained eye contact with Alpha Steve the entire time, and every facet of my psyche cheered when he looked away first, his entire demeanor radiating shock and fear. His deputies went whiter than bleached flour in the blink of an eye.

"There," I growled. "Problem solved. Now, back off."

I spun the man back around to face me, and my left hand wrapped around his throat. I met his eyes as I spoke, my voice calm and unemotional, "I still haven't heard an apology, prey."

His heart erupted into overdrive as the smell of urine and feces assaulted our senses. "Please, don't kill me."

"That remains to be seen, prey," I countered. "I will consider your plea after your compliance."

His eyes scanned the crowd with frantic abandon. I don't know who he sought, and he whimpered for a moment then near-shouted in a pleading tone, "I am so sorry. It wasn't respectful or kind for me to say those things, especially about Lyssa and her family. The Westridge family always treated me well, and I repaid that very poorly. Please, please, forgive me."

"Acceptable, prey," I remarked, then pointed at the ground. "Now, sit and stay. If you run, you'll only die tired."

His knees touched grass within a finger-snap. He bowed

his head and crossed his hands in his lap, still sporting the bracelets from the shifter handcuffs I ruined.

I returned my attention to Alpha Steve, asking, "What's next?"

Alpha Steve just stared at me. His mouth wasn't quite agape, but it was clear to me he still worked to process what had just transpired. When he found his voice at last, he chose his words poorly, "What the hell was that?"

A growl escaped my lips before I realized it, and I felt my eyes shift back to full Smilodon as the non-human portion of me took greater precedence. I felt the swelling pressure within my chest just before my cat bathed the area in pure, unadulterated alpha dominance. The two prisoners who hadn't voided themselves yet did so as they collapsed to the ground, terror dominating their expressions. The members of my hunting party in human form dropped to their knees, even if doing so required a dismount. The shifters in animal form bowed as best they could. Even the horses stepped back and did the weird kneeling that horses do.

"Overall, I am more than happy to let you chart our course in this," I said to Alpha Steve, my voice far closer to the growly voice I often heard in my head, "but *no one* will interfere when I correct disrespect to my people... especially disrespect to one of my ladies. I do not care in the least that you are Alpha, Sheriff, or her uncle. Do you understand?"

Alpha Steve jerked an assenting nod as he spat a rushed, "Yes, Alpha Primogenitor."

"Good. Now, what's next?"

"We should process the scene," Alpha Steve answered, his speech becoming more normal the longer he spoke. "Even if this case doesn't go to court—whether human or shifter—we should collect any pertinent evidence."

I nodded once, whether in agreement or permission I couldn't say. "Very good. Let's get started on that."

Everyone stood. Those in human form tied off their mounts, but honestly, I highly doubted the horses would wander if they didn't rear and flee at my burst of dominance. But I suppose it made them feel better. Alpha Steve and his deputies retrieved evidence bags and nitrile gloves from their packs. Deputy Sam retrieved a small camera as well. And the three set off to collect anything in the house they deemed 'evidence.'

After a few minutes of everything going well, I stepped back from my prey and shifted back to Smilodon. It wasn't fun standing barefoot on grass damp with dew and naked as the day I was born with a cool breeze blowing toward the creek or river or whatever it was Earl said was nearby. As soon as the shift completed, the smell radiating off my prey became even more objectionable, so I backed off a dozen paces or so. The added distance didn't really help all that much, but the patch of wildflowers at my front paws helped me ignore the stench.

I WASN'T sure how long we waited until Alpha Steve declared the evidence gathering complete. I fought the urge to growl that they took as long as they had, but I wasn't an officer. If they needed all the time they took, it wasn't my place to gainsay them.

But we discovered another problem. Transporting the prisoners. I personally favored some Old West justice; just tie one end of a rope around their torsos just under their armpits, and they could walk or drag as it suited them. Sadly, it was a major achievement if my first prey of the evening took a breath without bone shards shredding his heart or lungs. Walking—let alone traversing the distance back to Cindy's horse ranch—was a bridge too far. Then, there was the idiot runner with the severed Achilles tendon. If a blade or something similar had severed it, the guy would be well on his way to walking again... or soon would be at any rate. But that was not the case. A shifter delivered the injury with his or her teeth. Shifter healing would ensure he walked again without impairment, but he'd heal human slow. Which meant he wasn't walking anytime soon, either.

In the end, we rigged individual litters for the two who couldn't walk, pulled by the horses the deputies rode. I fought the urge to grin and scare our prisoners even more when Cindy and Lyssa looped ropes around their chests and secured the opposite ends to the saddle horns of the other two horses. My cowed prey made no move to divest himself of the rope, despite his hands enjoying relative freedom, but I was happy when Lyssa told half the wolves to take up a rear guard and watch for escape attempts.

Once we had everything gathered and everyone ready to move, we set out for the ranch at a fast walking pace for humans.

THE HUES of imminent sunrise colored the eastern horizon as we arrived back at Cindy's ranch. I felt a swell of pride at the successful hunt and retrieval of Lyssa's niece, but crushing fatigue soon overshadowed it. I paused at the back-yard's gate for a huge yawn, and I'm sure the display of my teeth in all their sharpness sent fresh ripples of terror through our prisoners.

Speaking of whom...

I shifted back to human and walked over to the prisoners gathered. Their exhaustion was even more apparent than mine. I made eye contact with each in turn as I said, "Listen up. I'm too tired to care what happens to the lot of you right now, but if you're not where they put you when I wake up, not even the deepest cave in the most remote mountain range on the other side of the world will be sufficient to hide you from me. Do you understand?"

All of them jerked choppy nods and whimpered, "Yes."

"Good." I turned and shifted back to Smilodon as I crossed the backyard to an oak tree whose shade looked rather comfortable. As I reached the trunk, I padded around in a circle before laying down, and I was asleep before my head touched my paws.

23

A chirping chorus pulled me from my well-deserved rest, and as the insipid, unrelenting songbirds pushed me ever onward toward consciousness, I considered climbing the tree to discuss my dislike of their poor timing in as direct a fashion as I could manage. Then, I processed that a warm weight pressed against me, and I forced my eyes open.

I was surrounded. To my left, a jaguar pressed herself against me. To my right, a lioness. Karleen must've lost the coin toss, because a dire wolf snuggled against my rear, sleeping peacefully with her head turned away from the jaguar's tail. Love and warm regard swelled within me at the sight, and I fought the urge to express my feelings toward them and ruin their sleep with licks that led to kisses and cuddles.

A great yawn stole my focus. Well, I suppose I could look on the birds' song as a lullaby. Might as well try, at least…

. . .

WHEN I WOKE NEXT, my ladies were gone, and the afternoon sun warmed me to the point of discomfort. Pleasant scents of food beckoned me toward the house, and I pushed myself to my feet. Then, I did a full-body stretch to work out the kinks, even fully extending the claws of each foot.

Okay. I was rested… well, mostly… and I was awake and on my feet. Time to investigate those wonderful smells.

My nose led me to an extra-large doorway with no doors that opened into a large dining room. I saw Cindy, Bonnie, Megan, my ladies, and most of my hunting party gathered around the table. They all possessed plates filled to varying degrees from the wondrous cornucopia that dominated the center of the massive table along its entire length. I don't know whether it was the savage growl my stomach produced or I wasn't as silent as I thought, but everyone at the table froze and looked my way, many of them holding forks or spoons midway to their mouths.

I took a step closer to the table and inhaled more of the lovely food smells. Lyssa shook her head and snapped her fingers as she pointed behind me.

"Nope," she said. "You're taking a shower first, just like the rest of us. Besides, none of us want fur in our food."

I backed up a couple steps and sat on my haunches before I gave Lyssa my best attempt at sad kitty eyes. I must've needed practice, because she just shook her head again and pushed back from the table.

"Don't try that with me," Lyssa said as she stood. "You know I'm right. Come on; I'll show you where the shower is. If you're nice, I'll even lay out your freshly laundered clothes, too."

Lyssa led me through the house as I padded along at her side until we arrived at a guest room. She pointed to a door to my right as she moved a set of clothes from the dresser to the foot of the bed.

"You can have food once you've showered and dressed. Don't worry; we'll save your share."

I trudged to the doorway and peeked inside. The room was a well-appointed guest bathroom. It only had a shower—no tub—but otherwise, the facilities were at least on par with the Alpha's house back home. Fair enough. I touched the part of my mind that stayed human no matter my form and willed the shift. Almost faster than one could blink, my human self stood in the bedroom. I turned to say something to Lyssa, but she was already gone. I guess I failed to impress in a contest with hot food after a raid the night before.

I snorted a laugh as I went to the shower and turned on the hot water. I wouldn't hang around with me either, if I had the option of food right now.

My hair was still damp to the touch when I returned to the dining room. I didn't have a stopwatch, but I think I may have set a record for the world's fastest but most complete shower… or challenged the record at the very least. At my entrance, Cindy gestured to the sole available seat, which just happened to occupy the head of the table.

By the time I touched the seat, a large plate heaped with food sat in front of me. My stomach protested my neglect once more, and I tucked into the food with a will. The plate was half empty before I realized someone was speaking to me.

"Huh?" I asked as I looked up, forcing myself to take the time to chew and swallow and *not* chase another fork full.

Karleen and Gabrielle both chuckled at my lack of focus while I ate, but they shouldn't have been surprised. They'd seen this side of me before.

"I said that I didn't have the words to thank you," Cindy

answered. "You'll never know what your help—everyone's help—means to me."

I nodded as a half-smile curled one side of my mouth. "You're welcome. I doubt any of us would've slept well, if we knew we could help and didn't. Besides, I'm a firm believer in the old saying that all evil needs to triumph is the inaction of good. I won't say that I'm good or your ex is evil, but his actions certainly were. Say… has he behaved himself?"

Cindy snorted her own laugh. "Oh, yes. They're all pliant as mice under the supervision of owls. Rory and a couple of the hands hosed them off shortly after we returned and put them in the barn. They each have their own stall, as we have a few vacancies at the moment. They haven't even squeaked and were *very* polite when the hands took them food."

"Good. I'm glad I don't have to repeat the lesson."

"Alpha Steve asked for me to inquire how you wanted to handle them before he and his deputies left," Cindy continued.

I blinked my surprise. "Me? Why? He's technically your Alpha, right?"

Cindy and Bonnie both bobbed a nod.

"Well, as far as I'm concerned, he can have them if you don't want them. As the saying goes, I don't have a dog in the fight, beyond reminding them to show respect where it's due. The only reason I'm here is to see Bonnie returned safe and sound, and like they say in the movies, it seems my work here is done."

Cindy looked deep into my eyes for several moments as she held her silence. When she spoke at last, I heard gratitude, regret, and hunger for something other than food in her voice, "Lyssa is a very lucky lion."

My eyes roamed across my ladies—all three of them—and I shook my head. "You're wrong. I'm a very lucky Smilodon."

· · ·

AFTER FOOD, we began the preparations to leave. It didn't require much effort, but I made a special visit before we said our goodbyes.

The man I now knew to be Oliver Price looked up as I opened his stall, and I watched the color flow out of his face like a river to the sea.

"Please…" he whimpered as he jerked his head back down. "Please, don't kill me."

"I didn't come here to kill you, Oliver. I'm leaving, but I wanted to be sure you understood the conditions of your reprieve before I left. I care not a whit what you do with your life as long as you never inflict harm—whether physical, emotional, or mental—on another living soul. As long as you walk the straight and narrow, as it were, you'll never see me again. But before you start thinking about your freedom, you should know that my sister is a Magi who is Master-certified in teleportation. All I need is a text that you're acting up again, and you will see me. I promise you won't enjoy the experience."

Oliver jerked a choppy nod. "I– I understand."

"Good. Now, Alpha Steve will be along after a while to collect you. As he is your Alpha—not to mention the county sheriff—he'll handle where things go from here. I hope you make smarter choices than you have thus far."

Before Oliver could respond, I turned and closed the stall behind me as I left. I hope he understood that this was his one and only chance to change his ways. If I had to come back here, he would not survive the visit.

I STEPPED through Vicki's portal and stood on Main Street in Precious once more. It felt good to be home. Damn good.

We cleared the street, and I pulled my sister into a strong

hug as I thanked her for everything she did and had always done for me… just not the litter box, scratching post, or flea collar that still decorated my room at my grandparents' estate. After Vicki vanished to her destination of choice, I spent several minutes expressing my gratitude to the members of my hunting party for their time, effort, and excellent work… especially the wolf who made the Achilles tendon strike on the runner. That was sheer artistry. Soon enough, only Karleen, Gabrielle, and Lyssa remained. I met each of their eyes in turn before I swept Lyssa into a one-armed hug and pulled her to my side.

"Gabrielle, do we have an available room at the Alpha's house?"

She gave me a small smile before she answered, "Why, yes, Wyatt… we do indeed. What do you have in mind?"

I turned to Lyssa and stole a quick kiss on her cheek before I leaned close to her ear and spoke softly enough not to hurt, "It's yours if you want it."

Karleen and Gabrielle both beamed as Lyssa turned, pulled me to her in a full-body hug, and assaulted my lips with a kiss thorough enough to leave me a senseless mass drooling on the concrete. When she felt the kiss sufficient, she released me and stepped back.

"Hell yes, I want the room."

I grinned, then pulled her back in for another kiss. Only this time, I dipped her low for the main event and transitioned into a slow twirl as I rose. As the twirl faded, her eyes looked a little dazed as a dreamy expression dominated her features. Now, who was the senseless one?

"Come on," I said, steadying her on her feet. "Let's get you out of the hotel."

. . .

A SHORT TIME LATER, we had Lyssa checked out of the hotel and moved into the Alpha's house with the rest of us. She fiercely protested paying for her room out of my personal funds, but I kissed her and kept kissing her until she stopped protesting. Karleen and Gabrielle watched with appreciative expressions, while Melody's expression implied she wanted her own kisses.

Sadly for her, she did not pique even the slightest interest in me. Yes, she was very attractive, but so were most female shifters. Yes, she was a strong woman; I harbored intense dislike and lack of patience for anyone who lived their life as a doormat, regardless of their gender. And she had a wonderful personality. I always enjoyed encountering Melody, but... she lacked *something* my ladies possessed. Something that almost called me to them. I had no idea what it was, and to be quite honest, I wasn't sure I'd tell Melody if I did. I liked women, but sharing my life with three of them was more than plenty, thank you very much... no matter how much I loved them and regardless of the fact that I wouldn't trade any of them for anything in all existence.

After delivering Lyssa's luggage to her new room, we gathered in the family room... or as some would call it, the den. An L-shaped sectional sofa dominated a portion of the family room, and I sat in the very corner of the L. I watched the ladies determine through some method beyond my male understanding who would sit where and fought the urge to smile in satisfaction when Gabrielle and Karleen both indicated for Lyssa to sit on my immediate right. Lyssa didn't sit beside me; she snuggled into me as tightly as she could as Karleen did the same on my left. Gabrielle followed suit on Karleen's left, and I had to admit it felt good to be sitting in my home with my ladies around me.

"So, what's next?" Lyssa asked after several moments of the four of us just enjoying being close to one another.

That... was a very good question. I hadn't heard anything from Hauser about the two cases we dropped in the government's lap, but honestly, I didn't really expect that I would hear about the case Vicki brought them. That was a Magi matter and not any of my business. Sloane's situation, though, was very much my business.

"We should follow up with Hauser or Burke about the status of Sloane's case in Nebraska. I would've thought they would update us if they made any progress, but they may be waiting to give a post-case summary."

Gabrielle leaned forward far enough to look across Karleen to me and Lyssa as she said, "Why don't we call them and *ask*? I'm sure Sloane's slowly going out of her mind after the long silence. Sure... we told her about handing the situation off to Uncle Sam, but there's been no news since then."

I shrugged and fished my phone out of its resting place in my thigh pocket. I thumbed through my contacts until I found Hauser's entry and tapped the button to call her. It rang three times before a woman who *wasn't* Agent Hauser answered, "Special Agent Hauser's phone. Special Agent Burke speaking."

Ah, okay. My rising concern faded. "Hello, Agent Burke. This is Wyatt Magnusson. I was just calling Agent Hauser to check in and see how everything was going."

Silence extended on the call for several moments as I heard a door close and footfalls. Burke soon said, "Sorry. I had to find somewhere I could speak. We're in Podunk, Nebraska, right now. Hauser's explaining the facts of life to the county sheriff and regional state police commander as we speak."

I swallowed a laugh with some effort. "Uhm... I'm pretty sure the town's name isn't 'Podunk.'"

"I'm pretty sure it isn't, either, but when you've seen as many of these one-stoplight towns as I have, they all kind of blend together." A brief pause. "Except Precious. There is zero chance of Precious ever being 'Podunk, Washington,' in my mind, and I've only seen the town in passing. After all, a damn big and terrifying cat lives there."

I could hear Burke's teasing smile at that last bit. "Well, I'm glad to know we made an impression on you."

Before I could say anything else, Burke interjected, "Oh… hold, please."

Silence returned for a moment, but I heard Burke whisper that it was me on the call. Then, Agent Hauser said, "Hello, Wyatt. How is my favorite Smilodon today?"

"Wait… you know *another* Smilodon?" I asked, playing along.

"Of course not, which means you don't have to work too hard to be my favorite," Hauser replied, and I heard faint sounds in the background that made me think they were walking, like doors opening and closing and the like. "So, I think the county sheriff and state police here in Nebraska finally understand the situation. They weren't happy about it, and I had to lie that Sloane is an informant on a federal case to get them to back off. They didn't want to believe that someone else murdered the Higgins couple and burned their farmhouse to the ground. Do you mind handing over those two along with their confessions?"

"Not at all. Should I make sure they understand their situation prior to the hand-off?"

"No. Please, don't," Hauser was quick to say. "If the court gets even a whiff that they may have been coerced or intimidated, the judge will dismiss the case faster than Vicki vanishes in a teleport. Burke and I will come pick them up, and we'll discuss their options and our recommendations on the flight back to Nebraska. While we're in town, I'll take the time to inform Ms. Martinez that she is no longer a person of interest in the case, with any and all warrants, bulletins, or other notices rescinded."

I heard what sounded like car doors close as I asked, "So, when would you like to retrieve the miscreants to face Nebraska's justice?"

An engine revved in the background of the call before Hauser replied, "We're heading to the airport now, and we'll fly to Spokane. I think that's the closest airport to you. I'll give you a call once we're on the road to Precious. An agent from the closest Resident Agency will meet us at the hangar, and we might have to take him back to the office before heading your way."

"Alrighty. It sounds good to me. If you time it right, I'll put you up in the town's hotel for the night as guests of the Alpha and give you the nickel tour of town."

"I'll mention that to Burke, and we might just take you up on the idea. See you in a few hours, Wyatt."

"Bye, Hauser. Be safe."

I thumbed the button to end the call and looked to my ladies. Shifter hearing was such that I knew they heard both sides of the conversation.

"I'm glad the matter has been resolved for Sloane," Karleen said, filling the ensuing silence. "What do you think she'll do now?"

I arrested my reflex to shrug, mindful of Lyssa's head on my shoulder. "That's up to her. For the first time in a while, she's free and clear to chart her own course."

Karleen nodded her agreement, and we settled into a comfortable silence. Since Sloane's situation was resolved, I could check off the most pressing item on my agenda, but I didn't doubt that something else would rear its head and demand my attention. And probably rather soon. So, I took the soft win of spending the evening with my ladies while I waited for the next 'emergency.'

24

Hauser and Burke rolled into town late that night. We met them at the hotel, and the wheels went off the wagon when I informed the night manager that they were my guests.

"Uhm, no," Hauser countered. "Absolutely not. We have regulations against accepting gifts over twenty-five dollars. I know you mentioned it when we spoke earlier, but it's just not ethical for us… especially when we're here to pick up criminals for a case. Uncle Sam will cover the bill."

I sighed. As much as she had a point and I didn't want to make trouble for them, I considered them *friends*. One of the few perks of being Alpha of Precious and Godwin County was doing little things for my friends, like… oh… paying for hotel rooms or dinners. I felt like getting Nathanson on the phone to get his okay for what I wanted, but my conscience reminded me that wasn't fair either. Then, I noticed dark circles under their eyes artfully obscured with makeup, and a more thorough look-over revealed other signs of fatigue.

"Okay," I conceded in a carefully neutral tone of voice. "When was your last day off?"

Hauser and Burke looked to one another, their expressions indicating the deep thought of long-time road warriors trying to remember the last time they were *not* working.

"Errr…" Burke vocalized.

Hauser added her own contribution. "Uhm…"

"Wasn't it right before we went to New York for the Magi case?" Burke asked.

"Yeah, that sounds right," Hauser answered. "So, maybe three-ish weeks ago?"

Yeah, these ladies needed a couple days. So, while they proceeded to get settled in their rooms, I enacted my nefarious plan. I texted Deputy Director Nathanson, asking if he was awake and available for a call. When my phone rang, I accepted the call and stepped outside the hotel, leaving my ladies to wait for Hauser and Burke to return or send a 'goodnight' text.

"What do you need?" Nathanson asked.

"I apologize for contacting you so late, but I wanted to ask you to pass a word to Hauser's and Burke's supervisor that they need *at least* one day off. They just told me they've been going non-stop except for sleep since handling the Magi case in New York."

Silence extended on the call to the point that I wondered if it dropped. At long last, I heard a heavy sigh before Nathanson replied, "We've *told* Hauser about that. She tends to go all out until she crashes from fatigue, and that doesn't do anyone any good. Neither her nor the agency. Her work has never slipped, even at the extreme end of exhaustion, but it's rare that she can find anyone else who can keep up with her. I'm now worried she has found a kindred spirit in Agent Burke. What are your thoughts?"

"Well, they're here in Precious right now to retrieve and transport the black ops agents responsible for the Higgins farm fiasco back to face Nebraska's justice. The whole team that was pursuing Sloane has been just fine in our jail, and they have no chance of escaping the town where the Huntress lives. Never mind the fact they're vanilla humans, which puts them at an even greater disadvantage. I'd like for Hauser and Burke to stand down for at least a couple days, and while they're here, I want their meals, their rooms, their entertainment to be on me. I tried paying for their rooms already, but Hauser cited ethics issues if I did."

"Yeah, that's a thing. People in government jobs—regardless of what level—are supposed to be impartial. If they are viewed as having been compromised by you, that won't be good for them in the long run." He fell silent for a few moments. "I'll send word to their supervisor to put them on a mandatory seventy-two-hour stand down and dispatch another team of agents to transport the black ops crew. Hauser and Burke can spend their three days exploring the wilds of Godwin County."

"Thank you, sir."

Nathanson chuckled. "You realize that Hauser will be pissed as hell with you, maybe even Burke as well?"

I noticed my ladies exit the hotel and join me where I paced. "Well, they can get glad in the same pants they got mad in, sir." All I heard was laughter from Nathanson. "I consider them friends, and I value my friends' wellbeing."

"Damn, Wyatt," Nathanson said once he regained his composure. "I have half a mind to apply for the SAiC position of the Paranormal Branch Resident Agency we're going to put in the consular office the State Department wants to establish in Precious. I get the feeling I'd have a blast."

Wait... what? I closed my eyes and pushed the tidbit Nathanson shared out of my mind. No one from the State Department had said anything to me about putting a consulate or embassy or whatever the proper term was in Precious, beyond the idle discussion during the meeting with the President. And quite frankly, I *did not* want to think about it right now, given the past forty-eight hours.

"You're always welcome, sir," I chose to reply. "That was my only reason for calling, so unless you have something, I'll let you get back to your night."

"All right, Wyatt. You can expect the storm to make landfall as soon as Hauser and Burke wake up in the morning. Have a good night."

Nathanson ended the call, and I turned to my ladies as I slipped the phone back into its pocket.

"Hauser and Burke are settled into their rooms," Gabrielle said, "and they said they were going straight to bed when they came down to thank us for meeting them. They asked about you, but we told them you had to make a call."

I grinned. "Well, at least you didn't lie to them. Let's head home and get some sleep ourselves."

The walk back to the Alpha's house passed without incident or excitement.

~

I AWOKE the next morning to fierce pounding on the front door of the Alpha's house. The house was large enough, its walls thick enough, and the door stout enough that it was only my shifter senses that allowed me to hear the pounding in the first place.

My sleepy mind processed that someone was pounding on something right about the time I heard someone shout, "Dammit, Wyatt! Open this door right now! Don't make me get the ram out of the SUV!"

Well, I guess Hauser and Burke received their standdown order. Lovely. I did my best to leave the warm bed without waking any of my ladies and pulled on a robe before almost sleep-walking out to the front of the house. I opened the door mid-strike and caught Hauser's fist before it knocked on my nose.

"You know, I'm pretty sure you're allowed to sleep in on your days off," I grumbled in a voice that told anyone who heard me I was half-awake at best. "Come in if you want to, and close the door either way."

I turned and ambled back through the house to the kitchen with Hauser and Burke following close behind me. I devoted my full concentration—what I had of it so far—to measuring out loose leaf tea into the reusable cup before dropping the cup into the device.

"Do either of you want coffee or tea? I can manage either without a four-alarm fire, but anything more advanced, you'll have to wait."

"The hotel offers a continental breakfast," Burke replied, "but thank you."

Oh, yeah… I did vaguely remember something about that when I first moved to Precious. Excellent! Less work for me and more time to wake up. I withdrew a cup from the cupboard and added enough honey to it I could be mistaken for a bear shifter. I slid the cup under the brew nozzle, closed the device's lid, and pressed the 'Brew' button.

I shuffled over to the conventional coffee maker and started the process of brewing my ladies' preferred nectar of the gods. I couldn't stand the stuff, myself. Yeah… certain blends of coffee smelled kind of nice—while others smelled downright heavenly—if you didn't burn it like it was damned, but I never found the right combination of additives to make it taste appealing.

And I've always been of the mind that any drink people called an 'acquired taste' wasn't worth acquiring in the first place.

As soon as I set the coffee to brewing, I turned back to my cup and retrieved it from its brewer, then joined Hauser and

Burke at the bar that divided the kitchen from the family room. I pulled myself onto a barstool and swirled a stainless steel stirrer to distribute the heat and honey in a semi-even manner. Then I chugged half the cup. Yum. Pure ambrosia. Those coffee heathens didn't know what they were missing.

I felt life and awareness begin growing in my mind, and I no longer had to spend effort to remember who these guests were. A huge yawn interrupted the moment, and I took another swig of tea.

"So, Nathanson said you'd probably be a bit unhappy that I called him last night," I remarked as the first hints of coffee reached my nose. I gave my ladies no more than ten minutes before their blessed brew brought them shambling like zombies to the kitchen.

My comment re-awakened Hauser's ire, and she glared at me. "Damn right I'm unhappy. My work habits are none of your business, *Mister* Magnusson. I'd like to know just what gives you the right to interfere in my professional life."

"You're my friend, Hauser, and I don't want you to get hurt because you're exhausted. We've shared a few adventures, and I think you're a good person. I like knowing good people. Same goes for you, too, Burke. And no, I don't mean anything more than just a friend. Three women have already staked a claim on me, and I don't really need any more."

By the time I reached the end of my rambling answer, Hauser lost her ire. She slumped on her barstool and frowned. "That's so not fair. No one has ever been able to guilt me into taking time off like that."

"What... it's not fair that I want you alive and well among humans as long as possible? Or it's not fair that I'm not afraid to tell you?"

"Either. Both."

I chuckled as I dove in for another swallow of tea. I started to say more, but Karleen leading my ladies into the kitchen interrupted me. They all wore robes, so I assumed they heard us talking when the coffee woke them. Or maybe they were easing Lyssa into her place with us. I know Karleen, Gabrielle, and I never worried about robes when it was just the three of us here.

Each of my ladies retrieved a mug and doctored their brews to their respective satisfaction before joining us at the bar. After a few cautious sips, Gabrielle looked to the agents, asking, "So, came to read Wyatt the riot act for butting into your business?"

"Yeah, but it didn't work. He pulled the friend card."

All three of my ladies beamed. Karleen said, "Yeah, he's a master at fighting dirty when he chooses."

"So, what's your plan?" I asked, the severe lack of a transition or segue brought on because I still worked through my morning wake-up procedure and didn't feel fully personable yet. I abandoned my barstool to prep my brewer for another cup of tea.

"Our supervisor instructed us to report to you for three days of low-stress rest and relaxation," Burke supplied, as my brewer refilled my cup with *my* ambrosia. "He said he would be—and I quote—quite wroth if we did otherwise—end quote."

Huh… I wonder if Nathanson or his supervisor called him after being woken up in the night. That thought made me chuckle a bit as I returned to the bar while I stirred my tea. As I ascended my barstool, I pondered the stray thought of whether walking while stirring my tea provided ample evidence that I could walk and chew bubble gum at the same time.

Guess I still had a ways to go before I was 'awake.' That kind of nonsense didn't usually intrude once I completed my daily boot-up cycle.

"So, what do you have in store for us?" Hauser asked.

I finished my first swallow of tea from the second cup and considered the question. "Well, I suppose that depends entirely on what you like to do that isn't work. We could go hiking. We could introduce you to some pups and cubs, if you've ever wondered what it's like to pet a baby wolf or lion or whatever; we'll have to be careful about that, though. It's second nature for the kids to play fight, and we don't want them biting or scratching you. I'm sure your boss would prefer you return rested, healthy, and... *not* a shifter."

Hauser and Burke shared a look before Burke said, "You know, the regs don't explicitly state that agents have to be human, and the Secret Service is openly trying to recruit shifters. Do we have any in Paranormal Branch?"

"I don't know for sure," Hauser replied, "but it wouldn't surprise me. And I'm not sure anyone could say anything if you wanted to become a shifter. As long as you put in for sick leave or vacation or however they wanted you to record the time off, I'd think it would be your personal choice."

I watched a thoughtful expression take over Burke's face, and I suspected I'd be getting yelled at by someone in her chain of command at some point in the future. I wasn't going to be the one to turn her, though. Nope, not at all. The end result if I—as a primogenitor—turned someone was too much of an unknown subject for my liking. Based on how things usually went, she'd come out a primogenitor like me, but that meant I should have been a cougar. And I wasn't.

It was simply too much of a risk in my eyes to try turning someone into a shifter.

"Well, first things first, we should probably update Sloane on her situation," I interjected.

"That is an excellent idea," Karleen opined, "but let's do it after breakfast."

When both Gabrielle and Lyssa added their support to

Karleen's statement, I exercised my nascent wisdom and asked them what they wanted to eat.

~

SLOANE LOOKED at the handwritten note she found slipped under the door of her hotel room.

Please, join Alpha Wyatt in the town hall at your earliest convenience after nine tomorrow morning.

The penmanship of the note approached the decorative and artistic quality of calligraphy, and the notecard itself was premium card stock, heavier than normal paper by a considerable margin. Perhaps just thin enough to fit between the door and the carpet. The reverse side of the card was blank. There was no signature, no mention of a delivery time.

She turned, and her eyes locked on the clock hanging on the room's far wall. Ten minutes after nine. Damn. Sloane heaved a sigh and crossed to the suitcase that served as her closet, retrieving fresh clothing that she laid on the bed. A brief shower later, she dressed as quickly as she could without risking mishaps and pulled a brush through her hair a couple times.

The reflection staring back at her out of the mirror wasn't ready for any red carpets or award banquets, but it was the best she could do in the time she had. Sloane double-checked to ensure she carried one of the two keycards for the room, then left to find out what awaited her.

SHE STEPPED out of the hotel and into a bright, sunny day. She afforded a quick glance at the sky as she crossed the sidewalk to the curb and did not see a single cloud anywhere. Glancing both ways, Sloane crossed the street and noticed that this was not one of the busier mornings she'd seen since arriving Precious. Whereas some days cars lined either side of Main Street, parked vehicles merely dotted the parking spaces that morning.

A young man sat behind the reception desk when Sloane entered the lobby of the town's administration building, and she crossed the short distance and presented the card. He read the note and pointed to the hallway on his right.

"Go all the way down the hallway and through the double doors at the end."

Sloane thanked him with a nod and a smile as she moved to follow his directions. The double doors opened to reveal a space that looked very reminiscent of a courtroom. A gallery of benches occupied two thirds of the room with a wide aisle down the center, ending at a decorative wooden balustrade. A few chairs sat just beyond the balustrade, and an oval-shaped conference table with chairs along the back faced the gallery. Wyatt, Karleen, Gabrielle, Lyssa, and two women Sloane didn't know occupied seats at the table.

"Someone slipped this card under my door," Sloane said as she arrived at the table's edge.

Wyatt grinned. "Yes. That was Melody, acting on a note I left for her after she went off-shift last night. We have an update for you. The new faces are Special Agents Winnifred Hauser and Edwina Burke."

"Hello, Ms. Martinez," the lady introduced as Agent Hauser said. "Special Agent Burke and I visited Nebraska to speak with the officers in charge of the Higgins case. It took quite a bit of talking, because Deputy Marks seemed rather fixated on you for some reason, but all warrants, bulletins, and/or advisories involving you in relation to the Higgins case have been revoked. You'll still appear in the case file of course, but otherwise, you're free and clear."

Relief. That was the only word that came to mind for the complex cocktail of emotions that surged through Sloane's psyche. Her legs trembled, and she staggered to one of the chairs against the balustrade and sat—pretty much fell—into it. It was over. She could visit a town or city or anywhere she chose now without fear of being arrested if someone ran her identification.

She pulled her eyes back to the people in front of her and offered a weak smile. "Thank you. Thank you so much."

It was time to decide what came next.

The morning after Hauser and Burke left town, I started my day with the usual tea. In my quasi-awake state, the desire for an egg and cheese sandwich on toast with lettuce, ketchup, and mayonnaise dawned bright and clear in my mind. So, with the courage buoyed by my conviction that I could *surely* figure out making such a sandwich if I could setup complex data networks, I proceeded to prove my thesis by creating a masterpiece of edible perfection.

It seemed like a good idea at the time...

"WHAT THE HELL WERE YOU THINKING?" Karleen shouted over the shrieking alarm as each of my ladies worked a separate task to achieve the overall goal of eradicating the cloud of smoke dominating the top three inches of the kitchen's air space, thereby silencing the rude alarm intended to save our lives in the case of an uncontrolled fire... or a half-asleep Smilodon trying to make breakfast.

The offending skillet now lay in the backyard where

Karleen chucked it before grabbing a large dishtowel to fan the alarm's sensor. Flames no longer reached skyward from the blackened mass of (possibly) organic material coating the (supposedly) non-stick surface, but it hadn't quite cooled. A column of smoke about as thick as my wrist continued to waft upward even yet... as if life in general chose to thumb its nose at my well-laid plan.

"I thought we had a *deal*, Wyatt," Gabrielle growled amid coughs as she placed a large box fan on a stand in the open doorway that led to the back deck. She plugged it into a nearby outlet and switched it to its highest setting. The roar of its motor did little to drown out her continued speech. "You make your tea however you like it and start a pot of coffee brewing for us, and one of us or more handles everything else. That's how breakfast—well, any meal around here, really—has always worked. Yes... you may touch the toaster, too, but that's it!"

Lyssa arrived with a second box fan, and Gabrielle opened a window to receive the fan while I looked on from my perch atop a barstool on the opposite side of the bar from the kitchen. The two times I had attempted to enter the kitchen to assist in cleaning up my own mess, both Gabrielle and Karleen gave me *very* firm looks and pointed at the stool where I now sat. They also informed me in no uncertain terms that they revoked my kitchen privileges until further notice.

Over the next few minutes, the near-permacloud above our heads faded to the point that the alarm felt safe in ceasing its rude wailing, and each of us expressed our relief at the progression toward residential peace. Karleen stopped fanning her dishtowel, and just as the towel left her hand on its way toward the countertop, there was a knock at the door.

"Is everyone okay in there?" Sheriff Clyde asked, his voice almost a shout.

So much for the morning's achievement remaining a secret in the family...

I pushed off the barstool and trudged to the front door. I opened it and waved for Sheriff Clyde to follow as I went back to my barstool.

Sheriff Clyde stopped a few feet from the bar that separated the family room from the kitchen and examined the scene with his keen eyes, honed across decades of small-town law enforcement in shifter communities. After assessing the visible evidence around the scene, he grunted his conclusion for peer review.

"Huh... Wyatt tried cooking unsupervised again?"

"Yes," Gabrielle and Karleen answered almost in unison while shooting me a glare that threatened dire consequences for any future culinary experiments.

"Anyone hurt?"

"No," Karleen answered.

Lyssa interjected, her tone dancing the crest of the fence between normal speech and growl, "Unless you count rudely interrupted sleep."

Gabrielle and Karleen both admitted the accuracy of Lyssa's qualification and nodded their agreement.

Sheriff Clyde nodded. "Well, a couple people called in the smoke and the alarm, so I thought I should check. Good luck with your morning."

I walked him to the door and thanked him for checking on us. Before he left, Sheriff Clyde extracted a promise from me that I wouldn't try cooking without supervision again for the sake of the town and ambled down the walk to his waiting SUV. I watched him pull a U-turn in the street and head back toward his office before I closed the door and returned to my perch.

· · ·

As SHORT TIME LATER, the four of us walked into Gladys's diner after quick showers to remove the worst of the smoke. It seemed to me like everyone sent accusatory stares my way, but that was probably just my embarrassment talking. While we debated our table preference, a hand shot into the air and waved us over, and we found Sloane sitting by herself.

"Wanna join me?" Sloane asked when we neared her table.

The ladies were already in motion to pick their seats before I could twitch my shoulders in an answering shrug, so I simply followed suit.

"How are you doing on deciding what's next?" I asked as my ladies gave their drink orders and accepted menus for us.

Sloane gave me a sheepish half-smile. "That's kinda why I wanted to talk with you. I want to try living here for a while. It's been so long since I had roots of any kind, and I've never really lived in a shifter community."

My immediate thought was to wonder why she'd need to talk to me about it. I mean, she was her own person. Then, my mind caught up with reality and the nature of the shifter world. *Of course*, she wanted to talk to me about moving to Precious... because I was the Alpha of Precious. Damn. I was still a sleep-idiot. I should have done a better job of waking up before venturing out into polite society.

I was just glad I didn't actually *voice* my thought process that time.

"Sure," I answered. "You'll have a place here as long as you want one, as far as I'm concerned."

Sloane smiled her response.

The server returned with our drinks, but we'd been too invested in the conversation with Sloane to make any decisions about food. So, we asked for a few more minutes. As the server nodded and moved off to check on another table, the bell over the diner's door rang. Sheriff Clyde entered the diner with someone sandwiched between him and one of his deputies. The trio approached our table, and the sheriff stepped aside to reveal Thomas Carlyle.

An irrational surge of anger filled me, and I frowned. Was it really that irrational? The minute Doc said Carlyle was healthy enough to be on his own, we shipped his ass out of town. Where'd he go? Don't know; don't care. I hadn't said that he wasn't welcome back in Precious, but I kinda thought that was implied in the manner of his send-off.

"Well, I can't say that I expected to see you again," I remarked. "What brings you back to Precious?"

"Alpha Wyatt," Carlyle began, his voice tentative and cautious, "may I have a moment of your time?"

"You're speaking. I'm listening."

"Uhm... maybe in private, please?"

I snorted. "Whatever you have to say, you can say here or shout from the county line. Your choice."

Carlyle scanned the dining room with his eyes, and it was plain he hadn't expected to have an audience. Tough shit. He should be thanking whatever deity he worships that I didn't just drag his mangy ass back through the diner's door and rip out his throat for him to die in the street.

When it became apparent that my answer wasn't changing any time soon, he sighed, then squared his shoulders. "I came to beg your mercy, Alpha Wyatt. In the weeks since I left here, I have found no place I have been welcome. Not even with my family. I've spent most of the time living in my vehicle. I have no right to ask this, I know, but I thought... I thought maybe I could earn my way back to at least acceptance among shifters here."

I wanted to smart off to him about how he maybe should have paid a little more attention to the people he passed on his way up the social ladder, because he saw those same people when he came sliding back down. But I didn't. As I sat there, considering what he said, I spent the seconds looking him over. The signs of being at the end of his rope became apparent when I paid any attention to his clothes and hygiene... instead of who he was.

As his situation sunk into my awareness, a part of me wanted to feel bad for him. I had not wanted to ruin his life with our fight. I just wanted him to be a better person to others. I guess the people he stepped on were not as forgiving as I was and had chosen to express their true opinion once I proved he wasn't invincible. Come to think of it, he wasn't filling out his shirt like he used to, either.

"Have you been eating enough?"

"That..." Carlyle glanced toward the kitchen. "That doesn't really matter right now."

So, no then. Dammit. I don't mind kicking a rabid mutt who needs it, but the idea of kicking a man when he's already beaten just did not sit well with me at all. And dominant wolf or not, the longer I looked at the man Thomas Carlyle had become, the more certain I was that he was one or two steps shy of being a beaten, broken man.

There were three seats available at our table... well, technically *Sloane's* table. Shit. Fine. Maybe buying Sloane's breakfast would be a sufficient apology for commandeering her table.

"Sheriff, have you and your deputy eaten yet?" I asked.

"We were just on our way over when we found Mister Carlyle."

I shot a semi-apologetic glance toward Sloane. "Sorry to steal your table out from under you. Gentlemen, this table has three open seats. Sit down; breakfast is on me."

Sloane, Sheriff Clyde, and even his deputy immediately protested my decision. But Carlyle looked like he wanted nothing more than to sit, but he waged a war with his pride about being the only one of three—Sheriff Clyde, Carlyle himself, and Clyde's deputy—to accept my offer. I locked my eyes on Clyde's and, while doing my best to maintain a non-expression, tried to will him to understand my intent. After several seconds of no progress, I lost my patience.

"Fine. Sheriff, take your deputy and get lost. Carlyle, pick a chair."

I think my words and tone *finally* communicated to Sheriff Clyde that he'd missed a cue somewhere, but I no longer cared. This was keeping me from my food, and I was only going to tolerate that for so long. The sheriff took his deputy to another table just as the server swung by to ask if we'd decided what we wanted. I passed Carlyle my menu and told her the bill for this table was *mine*, even going so far as to weave a minuscule amount of alpha dominance into the statement. She jerked like I'd just goosed her with a hat pin and nodded. I think Sloane finally figured out the situation, because she didn't say a word. Either that, or she felt the dominance too and chose the better part of valor.

The ladies and I ordered, and when the server turned to Carlyle, his expression proclaimed to the world he was afraid to order anything while being hungry enough to order *everything*.

"I… uhm…" Carlyle stammered.

I did my best to give him a neutral but welcoming expression. "Pick your three favorite dishes, and order them. If Gladys's crew doesn't do it better than you're used to, you'll eat here on me for the next three months."

Truth be told, I was slowly coming around to the idea that I'd be helping him get back on his feet anyway… which meant covering his meals… which meant paying his tab here at the diner. The incident this morning proved to anyone who could smell smoke and hear thunder that I have no business *cooking* anything.

Carlyle must have seen how serious I was, and he did indeed pick three dishes from the menu. I smiled my thanks.

He gave me an answering smile of his own, but it was cautious, almost like he asked for permission.

The picture I slowly built of who Thomas Carlyle had become was not a picture I liked. People—whether Magi, shifter, or human—should stand tall. Stand up for oneself. Not be a doormat with shattered self-worth like I was starting to think Carlyle had become.

I fought the urge to sigh. It wasn't my responsibility to fix it. For that matter, I *couldn't* fix it. Only Carlyle could do that. But he needed a place to start. A foundation to build on. And right now, he didn't have that. He came to *me*—the guy who shattered most of the bones in his body and started his downward spiral—and begged mercy.

Our food arrived. The sheer mass of edible goodness coming to the table required three servers to deliver. I was fine with that. If someone copped an attitude, they could speak to me. My ladies chatted with Sloane while we started our meals, and Carlyle tore into his like he hadn't eaten in a very long time.

I tried setting everything aside to concentrate on my food, but my mind swirled and splintered across multiple trains of thought. Well, not really. It was more like several trains of thought spawned idea after idea after idea. Rapid fire. Like those tiny firecrackers all bound to one fuse, except several sets. No rhyme or reason which train of thought spawned an idea next. Just pop-pop-pop-pop across all the different strands.

I hated when my thoughts were like that. Made it damn difficult to concentrate.

The idea crossed my mind before that I should maybe carry a notebook to write down as many of the thoughts as I could. But at times like these, writing down the cascade of thoughts would majorly interfere with my eating. Most times, it wouldn't matter... but eating was important.

The ladies were still halfway through their orders when I finished mine. Carlyle was about halfway through his orders, too, but that was okay. After all, he ordered three breakfast *platters*.

I waited until Carlyle finished. A quick glance showed me the ladies were still going. I think they were chatting more than they were eating. Ah, well... not my circus, not my monkeys.

As the server topped off his coffee, I leaned back against my seat and asked, "So, how would you contribute to Precious?"

Carlyle had the refilled coffee cup about halfway to his lips when I asked, and the cup froze. He stared at me like a deer in a semi's headlights.

"Dude, drink. It's okay. Use the time to consider your answer."

He moved his eyes away from me to look at the tabletop as he sipped and I waited.

After a few more seconds, he said, "To be honest, I'm not really sure. Most of my past experience with packs and shifter communities has been as an enforcer or Beta."

Yeah... that wasn't going to happen until he proved to me that he wouldn't abuse any power or authority I gave him. But I also realized that *I* wasn't the person to say he could stay. Not by a long shot.

I nodded my understanding as I replied, "I think it's safe to say that won't happen for a while, so some re-training is in order. But I just realized that I'm not the person who should approve your settling in Precious."

Carlyle—and possibly other people at the table—blinked in confusion. "But... but I thought you were Alpha here."

"Oh, I am, but in this instance, that doesn't mean I have the *final* say, just the first. The person who will ultimately decide your fate is a young lady named Melody. Cute, sweet girl. She works day shift at the hotel's front desk. I think you've met her."

By the time I stopped speaking, Carlyle looked whiter than the coffee cup he held.

26

The ladies and I left Thomas Carlyle in the care of Sheriff Clyde and his deputy with instructions that they escort Carlyle to the hotel where he would plead his case to Melody after giving me twenty minutes to speak with her. If they came to the hotel and I was still in the lobby, they were to go for a walk around town and check back later.

THE BELL over the door rung as I led the way into the hotel's lobby. Melody exited the back office and beamed upon seeing me and my ladies.

"Hi, Alpha Wyatt," she chirped.

"Hi, Melody. I have a favor to ask."

Melody's smile faded only long enough to allow her to speak. "Anything, Alpha."

"Thomas Carlyle came to me in the diner and asked if he could try living in Precious. He looks… well, he looks bad. According to him, he's been run out of every place he's tried to settle, and if it's true, I'd say he was a bigger shit to people on his rise to power than what we saw a few weeks back. So, here's the deal. I told him that I'm not the final say in whether he has a chance to start over here. *You* are the final say. The sheriff and one of his deputies will bring Carlyle here after my ladies and I leave, so Carlyle can plead his case. My favor is that you listen to what he has to say. If he tries to coerce, threaten, or otherwise manipulate you into saying 'yes,' my answer will be somewhere between 'no' and 'you can have a ten-minute head-start before we hunt your worthless ass.' If you won't feel safe living in town with him here, then he will not be here. End of discussion. But I'd like you to hear him out and see what you think. Are you okay with that?"

By the time I finished speaking, Melody lost a little of her glow. She didn't *quite* look fearful, but her expression betrayed increased anxiety. She dropped her eyes to the counter that served as the front desk and slowly nodded her head.

"I'll do it," she said, her voice meek and not even a shadow of its former happiness.

Damn and blast. I had never wanted to see *this* Melody again. And I definitely didn't want to be the cause of her reappearance. Helping Carlyle get back on his feet was *not* worth dimming the radiance of Melody's bright soul.

"Okay. You know what... don't worry about it. I'll call Sheriff Clyde and have him send Carlyle down the road."

I was halfway into my turn to leave the hotel when Melody said, "Wait... please?"

I turned back and saw less anxiety in her expression. It was still there but less than it was.

"You said he looked bad?"

"Yes," I answered. "I told him to sit at my table and order his three favorite dishes from the breakfast menu. His clothes hang off him like there's not as much of him as there used to be. He's been living in his SUV. We walked by it on the way in, and the third row of seats is missing to make a large enough space for his wolf to curl up and sleep. I saw no sign of food wrappers or trash or anything like that, so I think he's been eating only what he hunts. And if people have been running him off, he might not have had permission to hunt. So, he's probably been poaching rabbits and groundhogs."

At this, Melody's expression curled into a frown of disgust, and I didn't really blame her. No shifter I'd ever spoken with claimed groundhogs as worth eating, no matter their predator form or their hunger level.

"I really think he's only a day or two away from being at the end of his rope, Melody."

Melody held her silence for several moments more before she lifted her head and met my eyes. Her expression and demeanor bore no trace of the anxiety she'd held just moments before as she said, "I've been where he is. I've been the shifter no one wanted. When I came to Precious, I had my mind made up that I was going to kill myself if I didn't find a place here. Alpha Jace was the first to give me a chance in I don't know how long, and I'm still here. It would be very poor repayment if I didn't give Thomas Carlyle a chance when no one else will. I'll hear him out, Alpha Wyatt."

Karleen stepped up to the desk. "Would you like me to be here when you do? Just in case?"

"I want to say you don't need to worry, but I'm not going to say that," Melody answered. "Thomas Carlyle was the scariest wolf around for more years than I know, and I'm honestly a little afraid at the idea of facing him alone. I understand Sheriff Clyde will be here, and one of his deputies... but Carlyle is just *that* scary to us, you know? More than one of us wondered why you never took him down."

"No one came to me. I mean, it's one thing to hear a

bunch of people say such-and-such Councilor is a jerk, but how are you supposed to know it's just not talk? All I needed was one person to come to me and *tell me* what he did, how he behaved. It's no one's fault; I'm not trying to say anything like that. But at the same time, I never felt good about basing those kinds of decisions on hearsay alone. It could've just been a bunch of assholes grouching around because he caught them being assholes, you know? I'm sure Wyatt here isn't universally liked across all shifters, regardless of just or unjust. So, I'll buy a paper and go sit in the lounge where I can hear everything that happens at the front desk and read it. Will that make things better?"

Melody's infectious smile was back, and she bobbed her head in an eager nod.

Karleen turned to the other ladies and me, saying, "I'll catch up to you."

"Fair enough," I replied with a nod. Then I turned, and Gabrielle, Lyssa, and I left the hotel.

No more than a hundred feet separated us from the hotel's entrance when my phone buzzed its vibration in my pocket. I retrieved it and saw the caller was Deputy Director Nathanson, and I thumbed 'accept.'

"Wyatt here."

"Thank you for taking my call, Alpha Wyatt," Nathanson said. "Do you have a couple minutes?"

"Of course, sir. How can I help you?"

There was a slight pause before he answered, "I'm doing something I promised I'd never do. I'm checking up on my agents. Hauser's and Burke's supervisor just told me it's been thirty-six hours since he has heard from them. I want to say that's not uncommon, and on the one side, it kind of isn't. But to paraphrase so many movies, I have a bad feeling about it. At their last check-in, they were maybe an hour from the coordinates the black ops team gave us for the entrance to their group's facility. This isn't the kind of work where we wouldn't hear from them. Digging around in the agency's archives for a week? Sure. No one wants regular updates on that, but approaching a black site that has sent people into the field—into America—that have proven themselves willing to kill and burn... I just can't help but feel they need help."

I agreed with everything he said. There was just one problem. "Are you asking me to investigate a United States government facility that is in United States territory and not shifter territory?"

Nathanson responded with a heavy exhalation. "And there's the rub, isn't it?"

"Oh, I'd say it's more than a 'rub,' regardless of the literature allusion. I have no problem taking a shifter war party up there and hiding them in the trees while I approach the gate. Matter of fact, Hauser and Burke have stored up sufficient goodwill with Vicki that I wouldn't be surprised but what she activates the 7th Magi Expeditionary Unit and drops an assault rift or two if she learns they're in trouble. Come to think of it, I've heard Grandpa and Grams talk about how Hauser and Burke impressed them. I doubt they would come to the party, but if they do, who needs a Magi expeditionary unit at that point? *But...* I don't think it's wise for *any* of us to make a move without official governmental sanction. Anyone with an axe to grind—whether against us or against the current administration—would happily charge out of the woodwork to make more hay than Nebraska or Kansas if we or the Magi move to assist without that official approval."

Another heavy sigh. "Right. You're right. I wish you weren't, but you are. Okay. I'll take this to the Director and ask for both of us to take it to AG and hopefully the President."

"How did the 'we have shifters and Magi' conversation go with the new AG?" I asked.

Now, Nathanson chuckled. "As the Deputy Director in charge of Paranormal Branch, I had to have that conversation, and it would be very impolitic to carry tales. But I will say that she was not prepared at all for the idea we have people inside the country who can become lions, tigers, or even an extinct sabertooth cat. And when we came to the part of the conversation where I said Merlin did exist and might possibly still be alive... well... let's just say it was a very educational conversation for her."

"Fair enough. So, go have the conversations you need to have. Regardless of the outcome, I'd appreciate knowing."

"I'd say that's the least I can do, after asking you to break a treaty that has existed since 1789. Thanks for taking my call, and you'll hear from me when I know something."

I tried to say 'goodbye,' but the call ended before I could. I didn't even consider giving Gabrielle and Lyssa a recap of the conversation. Shifter hearing being what it is, they heard it all in real time. I slipped the phone back into its pocket and looked to each lady in turn.

"If you don't mind, let's wait until the house to discuss this. I'd like to turn it over in my mind a minute or two."

The ladies nodded, and we continued our walk to the Alpha's house.

"You made the only decision you could make under the circumstances," Lyssa said the moment the front door closed. "Frankly, Deputy Director Nathanson shouldn't even be calling you directly. It should filter through either the State Department *or* the local office... except that we don't have a

State Department representative or a local office yet. After all, there's such a thing as the chain of command."

I didn't *quite* grimace. "I'm not sure I like the idea of Nathanson needing to go through eighty-seven people to talk to me, especially if he *needs* to talk to me... such as the situation we have now. There has to be a better way than the normal international relations bullshit."

Lyssa closed her eyes and pinched the bridge of her nose. She might have even groaned. "Wyatt... if you want to be respected as a head of state, you need to *act* like one, even if that means someone like Nathanson having to go through eighty-seven people to talk to you."

Gabrielle's eyes shot wide, and she slipped around Lyssa and walked to the hallway. I wasn't sure if she was fleeing the field or what, but she knew me well enough to know the minefield Lyssa just found. And it seemed she wanted no part of it. I heard the door to the hall bathroom close and felt a little better. I definitely wasn't about to ask to see if it was an honest need or just avoiding the discussion.

"You have a point, Lyssa. But help me remember something here. *Who* wanted me to be a head of state for the shifters? Hmmm?"

Lyssa's eyes flicked toward the hallway where Gabrielle disappeared, and the slight uptick in her heart rate led me to believe she finally realized her whoopsie.

"I... I see your point."

"Thought you might."

She swallowed and licked her lips as if they were suddenly very dry. "So, how would you like to handle this? I mean... yes, I pretty much forced the position onto you. I... I suppose you could always repudiate the decision. The Council hasn't made an official announcement yet, so we could—"

Lyssa stopped speaking when I pulled her into my arms

and buried her face against my chest. "Oh, my silly lioness. Just what makes you believe I would *ever* consciously do something that would embarrass you in front of your peers on the Council or all the shifters of North America?"

She turned her head and took a couple breaths before she replied, "Well, it would be your right, and… and I suppose I deserve it."

I kissed her forehead before placing my hands on her shoulders and extending my arms just enough to look her in the eyes. "I don't care what you do. I don't care how pissed I am. I don't care how much you might feel you deserve it. I will *never* consciously embarrass one of my ladies in public. Nope. No way. Not gonna happen."

Lyssa's head dipped down as she held my gaze, and a shy smile curled her lips. "You mean that?"

"Silly lioness," I said, pulling her back into a tight hug and adding another kiss to her forehead. "Of course, I mean that. I'm not in the business of saying stuff I don't mean. I'm pretty sure that's what liars do."

Lyssa's arms tightened around me as she whispered, "You are too damn good to us, Wyatt. You really are."

I kissed her head again. "That's not true. I'm not good enough, and I don't ever want to start feeling like I am good enough."

The door of the hallway bathroom opened, and I thought I heard the toilet filling post-flush. Footfalls padded down the hall until Gabrielle returned to the sitting room. She dried her hands with a towel as she walked.

"So, I guess you two kissed and made up?"

I felt Lyssa smile against me as I answered, "I'm not sure we were ever really fighting. Lyssa did reach a wrong conclusion, though."

"And just what was that?" Gabrielle asked as she arrived at our side.

"She said I'm too good to the three of you."

A small smile tugged at one corner of Gabrielle's mouth. "I… think we're going to have to agree to disagree there. You are so damn good to us, Wyatt. So good."

Unwilling to re-hash my argument to the contrary, I just snaked my arm around Gabrielle and pulled her to us, kissing her as soon as she came within range.

I DON'T KNOW how long we stood there, holding each other and trading the occasional kiss. We still hadn't moved when Karleen came through the door and charged in to get her share. After a few minutes of welcoming Karleen home, she stepped back so she could see us.

"Well?" I asked.

"Melody said he could stay," Karleen said simply. "He actually impressed me. He started the conversation with the most heart-rending apology I think I've ever heard. By the time they finished talking, Melody didn't show any skepticism anymore, and at no point did she act like she felt uncomfortable or afraid for her wellbeing."

I nodded as I considered the matter. There were so many ways to handle the situation now, and the difficulty became trying to predict which choice was the best. "Do you mind taking him under your wing, so to speak?"

"Hell yes, I do," Karleen shot back before her serious demeanor dissolved into a huge grin. "If you want wings involved, you'd better call Sloane. But yes, I don't mind being his mentor for all that is Precious-related. I already asked Melody to put a room at the hotel on my tab until we can get him situated a little better."

Gabrielle sighed. "That may not be as soon as we—or he —might like."

She then proceeded to update Karleen on my conversation with Deputy Director Nathanson. By the time Gabrielle finished, any trace of joviality was long gone from Karleen's demeanor.

As Gabrielle fell silent, Karleen stood in silence for a few heart beats until she huffed a sigh and shook her head. "Well, damn. That's gonna be a mess."

Understatement of the month, right there...

27

President Olivia Williams tossed her glasses onto the desk's blotter and leaned back against her seat as she pinched the bridge of her nose. As much as she chose her job and as much as she wanted to do it and felt she could do it better than 'the other candidate,' she grew less enthused about attempting to work with Congress as days passed. She needed more 'fun' days... like having a thousand-pound Smilodon standing in the Oval Office.

The last time she spoke with Lucy, her best friend since elementary school—who also happened to be the Secretary of State—informed her that plans progressed toward establishing an embassy in Precious. To some, establishing an American embassy *inside* the borders of the country would sound ludicrous. Okay... it would sound ludicrous to most people. Unless they knew about shifters. Frankly, Olivia wanted an embassy with the Magi, too; she felt that was an untapped relationship just like the shifters. But... all things with time.

There was a quick double knock on the door leading to

her executive assistant's office moments before the door opened to reveal Clara Wilkins, said executive assistant.

"What do you have for me, Clara?" Olivia asked. She and Clara had been a hugely successful team for years, since her very first term as a city assemblywoman back home. No matter where she went or what job she held, Olivia didn't want anyone else for a right hand.

"Ma'am, the Secretary of State, the AG, the Director, and the Deputy Director are here. They claim to have a matter of some urgency and would like you to weigh in. From what they said, it's not their place to make the choice for you on this one."

Olivia's eyes went to the frightening stack of bills sent to her for signing or veto. Part of her said it was her civic duty to work through them and respond with a certain amount of alacrity. But... the top of the pile was an utterly atrocious bill she did not want to be a law. She didn't even want to touch it without nitrile gloves, and believed she'd want a shower as soon as she finished reading it. At least she had a good excuse...

"Send them in. They wouldn't say it was urgent if it wasn't. In fact, it would not surprise me if they understate things at times."

Clara nodded once and returned to her office, leaving the door open. Moments later, she led the petitioners into the office. As Olivia stood to greet them, Clara slipped back to her space and closed the door on her way.

The Attorney General was new... in more ways than one. Mina Vickers had just three years on a federal bench with an impressive case record as prosecutor when the Attorney General's position became available. She came to Olivia's attention as a brand new judge who handled a gruesome case that had all kinds of national coverage, and she did it with aplomb, skill, and fairness.

"I'm sure you would not ask to jump the schedule unless it was a matter of importance, so please, tell me what we have."

AG Vickers nodded to Deputy Director Nathanson, who proceeded to outline the situation with Special Agents Hauser and Burke. He even included a transcript of his call with Wyatt. Olivia eyed the transcript and wondered if Wyatt knew or even suspected Nathanson recorded the call, but that was a matter for another time.

"For such a young guy, Wyatt has a remarkable grasp of the realities of modern politics. If we didn't live in the Information Age, he could just take a war party and go sort it out. By the time anyone learned of it—assuming someone ever did—it would be so old news at that point as to be immaterial. Of course, without the modern information infrastructure, they wouldn't have *known* Hauser and Burke might be in trouble, so it's a bit of a double-edged sword. Like almost every other facet of the human experience. Right, then. Has anyone looked at the treaty with the shifters? Is there any precedent in there that will give us even a fig leaf?"

Lucy laid the relevant document on the coffee table between them. Well... not the original. It was a modern transcription. The original occupied a shelf in a secure vault in the National Archives set aside for top secret but nationally significant documents. Olivia had it on very good authority that the shifter treaty shared space with the Magi treaty.

"Article Two, Paragraph Seven, states that either party may request the assistance of the other for as long as the treaty stands and goes on to delineate precisely *how* to go about requesting assistance," Lucy answered.

Olivia blinked. "That... is remarkably open-ended. I thought treaties were a little more specific than that."

"I think it has a lot to do with the fact that they're *also* considered American citizens. They pay taxes. They register for selective service, but none of their registrations go into the 'normal' database. Can you just imagine the fallout if a Drill Instructor or Sergeant pissed off a young shifter enough that he or she lost control and shifted right there in the training formation?"

Mina frowned. "Why did shifters get special treatment when the Native Americans didn't?"

"Power," Deputy Director Nathanson answered without missing a beat. "Same thing with the Magi. At the time we ratified those treaties, a company of shifters could have obliterated over half the Continental Army. Magi might not need even that many. Beyond that, I've seen certain records that indicate Magi and shifters were *very* helpful with certain aspects of the War for Independence, and it was almost a quid pro quo situation. Wherein they helped us and we left them the hell alone. In modern times, the balance of power is much more... balanced, but it wasn't back then. I'm sorry to say that the Native Americans simply were not the threat and power that shifters and Magi were... and still are today."

"I'm sorry, but I just can't see it. I mean... sure, I understand the briefing on the two groups, but I don't see how sleight of hand tricks and chanting gives a group of people equal respect with the federal government. And the idea that there are people who can turn into animals? Sorry. I just having a hard time believing it, classified briefing or no."

Olivia met Lucy's gaze and saw a playful smirk coloring her friend's features. Olivia could only imagine what outlandish scheme dominated Lucy's thoughts but couldn't deny her own curiosity. Their current stature in society precluded the kinds of jokes and pranks that built their reputations in youth.

"What's on your mind, Lucy?" Olivia asked.

Lucy began her reply with an artful shrug of nonchalance.

"Well, if you feel it's important that the members of your Cabinet who will have the greatest chances of interacting with Magi and shifters be on the same page, why don't I volunteer to personally carry our request to Wyatt and invite Mina to accompany me?"

"Absolutely out of the question," Mina shot back. "I'm not even a month into the position. I can't afford the time even a government flight would require."

Lucy's eyes twinkled, and she lifted her mobile as she raised an eyebrow in silent question.

Olivia fought the urge to sigh and won. If the job had been even slightly fun over the past few days, she probably would not have given in. But the job *hadn't* been fun, so she did. And gave Lucy one nod.

Lucy unlocked her phone and made a call while the Director and Deputy Director Nathanson looked from the President to the Secretary of State and back again, confusion writ large across their expressions.

"Hi," Lucy said, "I'm Lucy Perez, the Secretary of State for the United States, and I was hoping to speak with Victoria Magnusson." Lucy paused, seeming to listen. "Why, thank you. Please, call me Lucy, Vicki. So, we have a matter involving Special Agents Hauser and Burke, and the President has directed us to formally request the assistance of the Shifters of North America. As Wyatt is their Consul now..." Another pause. "Oh, that would be just lovely. Yes. Can you come straight to me? Perfect. Thank you, Vicki. Bye."

Lucy thumbed the control to end the call and returned the phone to her purse, then leaned back against the sofa's back as if waiting for something.

Hearing Lucy's half of the conversation must have been sufficient for the Director and Deputy Director Nathanson that they no longer sported confused expressions, and they leaned back against their seats as well.

With a crack like that of a static electricity discharge—just multiplied by a thousand—and a faint tang of ozone, Vicki Magnusson appeared in the Oval Office. Before Olivia, Lucy, or anyone else could greet the new arrival, Mina leaped to her feet and stood between Vicki and Olivia in a heartbeat, shrieking for security at the top of her lungs.

The door leading to the West Colonnade, the door leading to the hallway, and the door leading to Clara's office burst open. Suited agents with sidearms drawn charged into the room, eyes flicking about the room as they sought the threat. Mina pointed at Vicki with her left hand, while her right clenched into a fist at her side and she worked her jaw as if to speak.

"No threat," Olivia said as she stood, making calming gestures with her hands. "There's no threat here."

Mina pivoted on her heel. "How can you *say* that? That... that woman appeared out of thin air! She could kill you at any time. That's a *threat*, Madame President."

"I thought Magi were just people with sleight of hand tricks and chanting," Lucy interjected.

Immediately, every armed agent relaxed, and the senior agent—Gloria Miller—lifted her sleeve mic toward her mouth. "Stand down. Everyone, stand down. No threat. Ms. Perez and the President were educating the Attorney General about Magi. Sound the all-clear across all sectors."

As the agents filed out of the Oval Office, Mina pivoted back to Lucy, glaring and clenching her jaw. "I do not appreciate being the butt of someone's jokes. That... that was so far beyond unprofessional I can't even think of an appropriate word for it, especially with subordinates present."

"Oh, lighten up," Lucy groaned. "No matter *what* we said, you never would've believed us, and frankly, this isn't something where you can stick your head in the sand and go on with your day any time the topic arises. You're the Attorney

General for crying out loud. You need to understand the world's a lot more complicated than whatever childhood fantasy you've been living."

Vicki lifted a hand to draw attention and said, "If I may, that was over the line just a little bit. The beliefs she has about how the world works are precisely the beliefs we—both the Magi *and* the shifters—want her to have. We don't *want* to be known to the world, especially when you consider that shifters are effectively immortal. Can you even imagine the mob that would descend on every shifter enclave if people learned becoming a shifter will cure—totally *cure*—all the untreatable diseases and afflictions humans fear? And usually within the first twenty-four hours? Oh, sure... there's a chance the person won't survive the change, but if they're already dying of Stage Four brain cancer or something, does that really matter?"

By now, Mina gaped at Vicki. "Are you serious? What about Batten disease?"

Vicki gestured at Mina like a gameshow hostess. "Your Honor, I rest my case. And to answer your question, yes, becoming a shifter will cure Batten disease... as long as the person survives the change."

Mina's eyes flicked to the people surrounding her for a moment before returning to Vicki. "What does it take to become a shifter?"

Vicki glanced from Lucy to Olivia to the Director and Deputy Director Nathanson. Then asked, "Is this really something we should discuss here and now?"

"No," Mina replied, her voice defeated. "It isn't. I'm sorry."

Olivia approached and placed a hand on Mina's shoulder. "It's okay. With the possible exception of Vicki, there isn't one of us in the room who doesn't understand the love a parent has for a child... and how far we'd go to save them."

Mina's shoulders slumped. "I'll have my resignation for you by the end of the day, ma'am."

Olivia fought to maintain a non-expression. "I don't understand. Why?"

"I… I'm compromised, ma'am. How am I supposed to be impartial when I know there are people out there who could save my son? And how can I ask to plead my son's case when so many other children can't? How is that fair?"

"I understand what you're saying, but answer me this. If I accept your resignation, where will you go from here?"

Olivia couldn't see Mina's expression. Didn't know the war between pure honesty and protecting the possible cure for her son that raged within her.

Vicki eyed the woman with a shrewd expression as she spoke in a calculating tone, "You'd go to Precious, wouldn't you? You might even take your son there."

Mina flinched as if Vicki had slapped her.

"Yep," Vicki remarked. "Thought so."

"How long does your son have?" Olivia asked.

Mina swallowed hard, then almost whispered, "Mid-twenties, maybe. But that's the extreme outside of the range from what the specialist said, given my son's case. His cognitive impairment isn't too bad, yet."

Olivia looked up to see Vicki staring at her. The President thought Vicki wanted to say something—the words hovering right at the tip of her tongue—but the young Magi stayed silent.

"Okay," Olivia said, feeling like she didn't know how to get past the awful turn the conversation had taken. "Vicki, would you mind delivering a formal request for the shifters' assistance to your brother?"

The young Magi beamed. "Don't mind at all, ma'am."

"Very well. If you don't mind waiting, I'll write it up now."

~

MY SHIFTER SENSES picked up the sound of Magi teleportation mere moments before Vicki strode into the Alpha's house from the backyard. She seemed her usual live-wire self as she crossed the space between us like a cutter with its engines locked at 'flank speed' and almost hit me on the nose when she thrust an envelope in my face. I accepted the envelope and betrayed my surprise at seeing it held a piece of the President's personal stationary. After skimming through it, I smiled that it was a formal request from the United States to investigate the disappearance of two agents from their Paranormal Branch just a few miles north of Jackson Lake in Wyoming.

"Okay, then. I guess it's on," I remarked as I passed the note to Gabrielle.

"There's something else," Vicki said as her perky demeanor faded.

I frowned at the sudden change in my sister. "What's wrong? Are you okay? Is it Grandpa or Grams?"

"No, Wyatt, they're fine," she answered, shaking her head. "Look, it's a long story, but I can't—I just *can't*—keep this a secret. The Attorney General's son is dying."

I *loved* kids, and those words hit me like a body blow. "Do you know how old he is?"

"I'm sure I could find out," Vicki answered.

I turned to my ladies, saying, "Talk to me about turning children."

Gabrielle and Lyssa shared a *look*. I had no idea what it meant, but I could tell they knew something.

Lyssa said, "It can be tricky. It doesn't always work out well."

"What are we talking, here? Sixty-forty odds that it'll work?"

"More like twenty-eighty." Gabrielle's voice was soft and somber. "Children aren't exactly robust, Wyatt."

I nodded as I turned the matter over in my mind. No... I didn't want shifters to become known in the world any more than any other shifter did. But a dying child?

"Thank you for telling me, Vicki, and I'll decide what to do as soon as we've located Hauser and Burke. Vicki, do you mind handling the transport again?"

Vicki smiled, though it wasn't up to her usual brightness. "Not at all, brother mine. They're my friends, too."

I looked to each of my ladies in turn and saw nothing but calm and steadfast support. I took a deep breath and released it in a gradual exhalation. "All right, then. Let's assemble the war party."

I stepped through Vicki's assault rift to a hilly, forested area that didn't look too different from the terrain I was used to seeing. The group gathered just out of sight from a local road but not so far that I couldn't hear the occasional vehicle pass us.

"That's Mount Berry," Gabrielle said, pointing to a distant peak. "I ended a rogue hunt about ten miles west of it a few years ago." She fell silent as she scanned the area. "If I had to guess, we're on the north side, pretty much where the foothills give way to the actual run up to the peak. That graveled road is probably the road mentioned in the case-file notes Nathanson sent."

I closed my eyes and concentrated on a slight draw on the Smilodon, focusing on my senses and specifically my sense of smell. Then, I inhaled through both my nostrils *and* my mouth. Trees. Lots of trees. Pine, spruce, and other conifers. But my sense of smell wasn't so acute that I could pick out specific scents like… say… two human federal agents.

Earl approached and stopped a respectful distance from my side. "So, is this the place?"

"I think so. I guess you won't stick out so much, this time."

Earl snorted. "Yeah… but we could be in trouble, too. There's a momma grizzly and a couple cubs around here somewhere. They're not close, or maybe the scent is old… but it's something we need to keep in mind."

I nodded my thanks. "Any scent of Hauser or Burke?"

"Not so much, but that perfume Burke loves passed this way. It follows that gravel road, there."

Damn. How did I not smell that, too? Burke *bathes* in the stuff.

Earl must've read something in my expression, because he snorted a laugh and made a dismissive wave. "Don't feel too bad, Alpha Wyatt. Number one, you're a cat. Cats are not known for their senses of smell. Number two, they've had some weather around here the past couple days. High winds and…" His voice trailed off as he took a deep, slow sniff of the air. "…and I think a thunderstorm or two."

"Okay," I asked. "So, how do you know they've had high winds? That almost sounds like you're making this up."

"All the normal scents are jumbled and mixed together. I'm smelling deciduous trees and mints from those conifers over there, and I smelled the conifers when we first came through the portal or whatever Vicki calls it, which was nowhere close to the deciduous trees. The only time you get ambient scents *that* messed up and chaotic is in the wake of high winds, and the winds were probably not too long ago, either."

That made sense. At least to me. No idea if a forester or naturalist would say the same. I still pondered the idea when Vicki, Karleen, and Lyssa arrived.

"We're all accounted for," Lyssa said. "Ready to proceed when you are."

"Let's move out," I replied, turning toward the gravel road and putting actions to the words.

THE GRAVEL ROAD steadily climbed the burgeoning slopes that would lead to Mount Berry, and Earl stayed at my side, serving as a kind of co-leader for the hike. After about ninety minutes, we came to a fork. Earl held up his hand in the signal to hold position as he walked a few dozen feet down each path. After visiting both, he pointed to the right-hand path from my perspective and signaled for us to continue.

Another thirty minutes of walking delivered us to a chain-link fence with razor-wire at the top. Large signs proclaimed the land beyond the fence to be U.S. Government property with unauthorized access punishable by several years in prison, a rather hefty fine, or both. A large gate extended a couple feet beyond each edge of the gravel road. There was no keypad, intercom, or even a lock on the fence's gate. No one reported a camera anywhere within range sight.

"Burke's perfume leads that way," Earl said, pointing beyond the fence.

"That's all well and good, but how did they get through the fence?" I asked.

Earl shrugged. "I'm a grizzly bear, not a clairvoyant."

That said, he ambled to the gate and touched the back of his hand to the metal. No zap, spark, or otherwise noticeable electrical discharge, and he nodded then turned back to the group.

"Let's get some hands on this gate," he called out, and I—along with several others—joined him.

Earl looked to me, saying, "Okay, there's a trick to this. Concentrate on your animal's strength flooding your body. Don't shift, but will the greater strength you have as your cat to saturate your human form."

I nodded as I closed my eyes to concentrate on the part of my mind that was no longer human. I pictured the strength of my cat surging into my human body, making myself as strong as my form would allow.

My human form is too weak for my full strength, and I think I've integrated enough to achieve synthesis, the growly voice informed me. *Should I try?*

I mentally shrugged and replied, *Sure... let's do this.*

I felt myself grow. Taller. Broader. My muscle mass almost tripled. And I felt my incisors lengthen and curve. I suddenly became aware of my clothes being *very* tight. I opened my eyes and found Earl and everyone around me looking up at me, their mouths agape. More than one scented slightly of fear.

"What?" I asked, and my voice wasn't mine... not completely. More guttural. Rougher. Almost a perfect blend of my normal voice and the growly voice I'd heard in my mind since becoming a shifter.

Jaws worked, but no one spoke.

We did not have time for this. I shook my head and returned my focus to the gate. I did not like the thought of shredding my fingers on those tiny chain-links, so I trudged over to the pipe that served as a frame for the gate. The group who responded to Earl's call parted around me like a sea. I clamped my hands around the pipe, then considered my position. Pushing against the gate's mechanism sounded better than pulling, the more I thought about it. So, I reversed my stance, rolled my shoulders, and put my entire body into a pushing the gate open.

My shoulders tightened and bunched. I squatted slightly and leaned into the effort. As I clenched my grip on the pipe I felt familiar muscles flex in my fingers, and claws extended from each finger and thumb.

As the seconds transitioned to minutes, a faint groaning grew louder and louder. I kept pushing with everything I had, and soon enjoyed the reward of watching the pipe within my grip give a little and bow out in the direction I pushed. After what felt like hours of straining against the gate—but was probably no more than five minutes or so—a shriek of tortured metal pierced the air, and a massive *SNAP!* followed on its heels as something broke inside the gate's mechanism. All resistance to the gate's motion vanished in an instant, and I almost fell.

The gate was now a horizontal yo-yo, and a five-year-old human could open or close it at will.

I turned to my people and found everyone staring at me still. It was like no one noticed the gate was now open. I sighed and fought the urge to shake my head. It was a good thing, too. With my saber-teeth out, I would probably have shredded the top of my straining shirt. And that was another good point.

I need to be human again, I sent to the home of the growly voice.

No, the growly voice shot back. *I need to return to human form. I haven't been human in a long time and never will be again.*

I felt myself shrink as a lot of strength left my limbs. My incisors returned to their 'normal' size, and the whiskers and fur seemed to withdraw back into me as it vanished. I rolled my hands back and forth as I flexed my fingers; everything seemed back to normal. Except that my clothes now felt a little looser than they had. Even my shoes. I knelt and tried tightening the laces and re-tying them, and that helped. But it wasn't perfect.

Ah, well… I resolved myself to a long conversation with the growly voice about this new synthesis I achieved. *And* I wanted to look at myself in the mirror. I suspected it was a kind of Smilodon-human hybrid, a cat-man, and that had to look damn cool.

"Okay, people," I said, and I fought to control my surprise. My voice was just like it had always been for the most part, but it seemed to carry a gravelly undertone that hadn't been there before. I sounded about twenty years older... if I'd spent those twenty years shouting across a parade ground or battlefield. Something else to consider, but not now. "Show's over. Let's get a move on."

AFTER PASSING THROUGH THE GATE, we dispatched the war party for maximum coverage and camouflage. A mass of bears, wolves, cats, birds, and more following a graveled road would stand out only slightly less than an honest person in politics. Soon enough, only Earl and Vicki walked with me, and I had to devote my full focus and strain my senses to get even a hint of the war party moving through the forest around us.

We walked for another thirty minutes or so, but only traveled about a mile. We weren't trying to cover a lot of ground in a short amount of time, and frankly, we were checking the road for traps. Land mines, trip wires, laser trip wires... any of these and more would not have surprised me at all.

But we found nothing.

VICKI CONCENTRATED as much on the ambient magic as she did the path. If there were any magical traps laid along the road, they'd resonate against the ambient power regardless of whether they had any visible component. Part of her still wanted to freak out a little bit at seeing her brother shift into some kind of sabertooth, furry man... not to mention how he broke the gate mechanism all by himself. But she couldn't afford the distraction. Not at the moment. It was, however, something to discuss with Grandpa and Grams. They would have the best chance of knowing what *that* was.

The road ended in a small man-made clearing formed around the entrance to a massive cave. The highest point of the opening's edge looked half-again the height of a tractor-trailer. About thirty yards or so back into the cave, concrete bunker doors blocked further access.

There. Ripples in the magic. A ward existed somewhere nearby, but it wasn't active at the moment. Vicki closed her eyes to concentrate on the ripples. Trace them. They were... elusive. Maybe masked somehow? Protected from detection? All at once, understanding snapped into perfect clarity. The wards protected the entrance. Not a fortification like a fortress's walls. No. Once active, it would turn the clearing into a prison, keeping everything on one side of the ward separate from the other side.

Vicki opened her eyes and took in the scene before her. Wyatt walked ahead some thirty feet in front of her. Earl lagged behind, probably staying close to protect the boss's sister. *Snort.* As if she needed that. But Wyatt? Wyatt was too damn close to the ward where it waited silent and primed, a stalking predator in an overgrown forest.

She opened her mouth to shout a warning... just as Wyatt set foot on the concrete that lined the floor of the cave entrance. The ward flared brighter than the sun as it activated and became solid to Vicki's arcane senses. No wall was perfect, though, and Vicki closed her eyes once more and devoted her full focus to her perception of the ambient magic.

There. A figurative crack.

Vicki opened her eyes and allowed her sense of the ward to guide her focus as she squared her shoulders and went over the Greater Dispelling that was the first Master-level spell Grams taught her. Concentrating on the weakness, Vicki called her staff, then recited the spell.

Requiem's crystal grew in brightness the deeper into the spell Vicki went—and the more power she drew into herself. As she spoke the final syllables that completed the casting and unleashed the power on the object of her focus, the crystal atop her staff shone bright enough to light a small gymnasium.

Vicki closed her eyes as soon as she completed her casting and watched the spell hit the ward with what should have been the force of an exploding Howitzer shell against a crumbling castle wall.

But that didn't happen.

She watched as the ward absorbed the Greater Dispelling and split that power between strengthening the ward even more and generating a massive shock effect. Vicki rattled off a quick elemental protection spell and felt it take hold, just as the ward spawned a lightning bolt... that struck Wyatt square in the center of his chest.

An anguished scream of helpless rage tore from Vicki's throat as she watched her brother collapse into a twitching heap. Her perspective shifted downward as a tidal wave of impotent tears washed her cheeks, and it wasn't until Earl began pounding on solid nothingness that she realized she had fallen to her knees.

Earl had no hope of physically breaking through the ward. She *knew* that. But that didn't stop a part of her from hungering to race to his side and add her effort to the endeavor. No. Rash, emotional reactions were not the way to defeat this challenge. Analytical calm utilizing the finest arcane education in the world would carry the day.

Vicki wiped her face as she pushed herself to stand once more. Her mind racing in its consideration of the problem. The ward was protected from dispelling, but what about teleportation?

Her eyes went to Wyatt's chest. After a few moments of concentration, she saw he still breathed, and a rush of joy and relief surged through her.

Yes. Teleportation was a risk, but if she didn't target the ward itself, that should bypass its protections, right?

Vicki took a deep, steadying breath. Then a second. She closed her eyes and focused on that sense of Wyatt she'd always had, even when he was just her brother with no Magi talents. She cleared her mind, took another deep, calming breath. Then, she recited the teleportation spell, still focused on Wyatt.

She jerked her eyes open as she neared the final syllable of the spell to watch him disappear from within the ward and appear at her feet. She couldn't wait to razz him about charging forward.

The power surged within her as she completed the spell, and she felt the effect take hold, recognizing the feeling of a near-perfect casting. Yes! This was going to work. It was going to…

Vicki's silent cheering stopped as icy claws of fear surrounded her heart when she watched Wyatt vanish from where he lay and *not* re-appear at her feet. What happened? How?

She wanted to rage again, but the fear that her brother was well and truly gone was too strong. She clamped her eyes closed once more and sought the connection—the bond —between them. Heaved a sigh of relief when she still felt it.

Except it felt like Wyatt was *deeper* into the mountain bunker now.

Crushing despair drove Vicki back to her knees as understanding dawned in her mind. She had just handed her brother—her best friend and the *only* feline primogenitor—to the vile people who sought Sloane to experiment on her.

29

Despair and self-loathing were Vicki's reality as she knelt on the grassy center strip of the graveled road they'd followed to reach the bunker. Her brother was gone. Delivered to people who would make whatever time he had left a cruel agony... and delivered by *her* hand. The ward that blocked access to the bunker's entrance was impenetrable and freakishly protected; she had no way of breaking it to have even a hope of saving Wyatt.

Her life was over. There was no coming back from this. Ever. And she wasn't sure she wanted to.

She was supposed to *protect* him. That's what her grandparents always told her when they were little. She'd have to protect Wyatt as they grew older, because she was Magi and he wasn't. It wasn't until a week or so before the cougar attack that made him a shifter that she realized fate cursed her to watch Wyatt age and die while she looked no older than thirty or maybe a very-well-preserved forty. Yes, Magi aged and eventually died, but they aged at a rate glaciers envied. Her grandparents *lived through* the Renaissance.

Noise reached her ears, but she didn't care. Why did

anything else matter now? The noise became more insistent, and something grabbed her shoulders and shook her... forcefully.

Vicki blinked her eyes and found Gabrielle, Karleen, and Lyssa standing around her... all nude. They looked at her with intense expressions, and it took a couple repetitions before she realized they were asking what happened to Wyatt.

Grams always said she had to own her failures before she could have any successes, so she wiped her face and pushed herself to her feet once more as she fought to control a heaving sob that tried to tear through her.

"I don't know what happened," she said. "There's a ward protecting the bunker, and it's centuries beyond *anything* I've ever seen. It took my Greater Dispelling and used it to strengthen itself *and* shock Wyatt. Then, it warped my teleportation to send him somewhere inside the bunker. From what I know of wards, that's not possible."

Karleen's fierce gaze bored into Vicki as she grasped Vicki's shoulders. "So, what do we do? How do we get Wyatt back?"

"I don't know that we do," Vicki answered and fought the sobs that tried to overtake her again. "I can't get through the ward."

"What about your grandparents?" Gabrielle asked, and Vicki felt the blood drain from her face.

No. She couldn't tell her grandparents. Just... no. She already hated herself for what she'd done. She couldn't add her grandparents' disappointment to it as well. But they'd have to be told eventually, and if anyone told them, it should be her.

Own her failures, right?

"You might want to shift back to animals," Vicki

remarked. "I'm going to use the Magi equivalent of a video call, and they'll see everything in my immediate area."

By the time Vicki finished her first deep breath hoping for something resembling calm, a lioness, night-black jaguar, and a dire wolf surrounded her. One more deep breath. Okay. Time to face them.

She recited the words to the spell she wanted, and an oval-shaped image appeared that was frayed and wispy along its fringe. The image was a window to the destination of the 'call,' and showed the back deck at her grandparents' estate. Both her grandparents stood at one of the staircases that led from the deck to the garden. They were talking with Miles— the oldest groundskeeper on the property—about something before they noticed the spell.

"Vicki, dear," Grams gushed, "whatever is the matter? You look a fright?"

Vicki started to speak, but the sobs surged again. She clenched her jaw and took a couple breaths to drive the sobs back from whence they came. A faint surface calm descended on her mind, and she tried again.

"I... I'm in trouble, Grams. I lost Wyatt." She couldn't meet their eyes. She didn't want to see their disappointment.

"Tell us everything." Grandpa said. It was odd. He didn't *sound* disappointed.

"We're tracking Special Agents Hauser and Burke. They disappeared while investigating the black ops organization that hunted Sloane."

Grams interjected, "Those were the federal agents we met during the abductions case?"

Vicki bobbed a nod. "We found their bunker, but Wyatt triggered a ward that feels like it's designed to keep people *inside* it. When I tried Greater Dispelling, the casting strengthened ward and shocked Wyatt into unconsciousness. When I tried to teleport him out, the only thing I can think of is that the ward corrupted the teleportation and sent him deeper into the facility."

She still stared at the ground as she spoke, so Vicki missed the look of recognition that flitted across Miles's expression.

"I... can't break through the ward," Vicki continued. "I... I failed to protect Wyatt, Grams. I'm... I..."

"Och, lass," Grams said, her accent slipping out, "ye haven't failed. We'll get him back. I promise."

"No, Maeve, you won't." Shock obliterated Vicki's despair and soul-crushing sadness, and she jerked her head up at the sound of Miles's voice. It was calm, certain. His brogue coming out in full force. "That working is beyond even yer mastery, the both of ye combined. *I* will handle this."

Vicki watched as Miles whispered a word as he took a step and vanished... only to step out of nothingness twenty-odd feet away from Vicki and farther from the ward. His gait was steady, relentless, inevitable as the sea against the shore. As he passed Vicki's position, he lifted his left hand toward her, his hand cupped as if holding a cylinder... or perhaps a staff.

Before she could fully process what happened, Vicki felt a swell of... happiness? ...from the staff as it ripped itself free of her grasp and flipped end over end like a twirler's baton until it struck Miles's palm with a clap.

The moment *Requiem* touched Miles's hand, its crystal erupted kaleidoscopic incandescence, and all semblance of the kindly old groundskeeper vanished in the blink of an eye. The white, bushy beard almost touching his sternum remained, as did his full head of snow-white hair. But his gait bore no trace of infirmity whatsoever, and a black robe embroidered with all manner of runes and symbols hung from his shoulders.

Those runes flared brighter than the sun for the span of a

finger-snap, and sheer *power* unlike anything she'd ever felt before struck Vicki like the leading edge of a tsunami. Not even the entire Magi Assembly radiated that much raw power. And suddenly, Vicki *knew*.

The kindly old groundskeeper who ambled around her grandparents' estate was the greatest Magi to have ever lived. The *founder* of the Assembly. The author of its guiding tents and the Arcane Laws.

He was *Merlin*.

Vicki pulled her focus away from her spiraling thoughts in time to see Miles—no, Merlin—stop just short of the ward. He lifted his hand, fingers and thumb splayed wide, and power crackled around it like the globe of a Van de Graf generator as he touched the ward. He stood motionless and silent for several heartbeats. A frozen tableau.

At last, he withdrew his hand as he shook his head, and Vicki thought she heard him say, "So be it. I *warned* her."

Her? Her who?

Before Vicki could voice her confusion, he stepped back from the ward and lifted his face to the sky.

"Mab! Did you really think you could interfere again without my notice? Release this ward at once!"

Holy... did he mean Mab, as in Queen of the Winter Fae? The Queen of Air and Darkness? What did *she* have to do with this? Wait... wasn't she a myth?

"Answer me, Mab. I know you can hear me."

Vicki didn't know how long her runaway thoughts spiraled into the dark recesses of her mind, but however long it was, it was long enough for him to run out of patience.

"Very well," he said, shouting into the wind. "I gave you the chance."

He rolled his shoulders, then took a step forward. As he stepped, he thrust *Requiem* toward the ward, crystal first, and the moment it touched the ward, he spoke a *word*. It didn't sound like any word Vicki had ever heard, and the power it released would have staggered the Himalayas.

The ward stood *no* chance.

The spell shattered, releasing a thunderclap, as lightning erupted from the ground all around the cave entrance. Arcs reached out to kiss the cavern's walls, and a couple even reached a camera and keypad closer to the doors. A cascade of sparks exploded from those devices, and faint alarms began to blare deeper into the mountain.

He swept *Requiem* in a side-to-side wave—as if wiping a squeegee across glass—and the lightning dancing across the ground vanished. The way clear, he turned to *Requiem*.

"Thank you, old friend. It was good to work with you once more, but it's time to return. Serve my great-great-granddaughter as you would me, and protect her. I fear a sea-change is on the horizon."

With that, he released the staff, but it didn't fall. It flew unerringly back to Vicki and came to rest in the grip of her right hand, just where she always carried it. When she pulled her astonished gaze away from the staff, Merlin was gone.

Before she could revel in the absence of the ward, the huge doors to the bunkers began a ponderous slide down into the ground. Within moments, people in tactical gear with weapons stormed through the entrance, and the fight was on.

MY CHEEK PRESSED against something cold. That was the first understanding I processed as I woke. Then... I felt twitchy. Why did I feel twitchy? Why did I feel sore all over?

I opened my eyes. I lay in the center of a room no more than fifteen feet square. The floor was concrete, the walls the same. Industrial fluorescent lights buzzed above my head.

One wall held a door; it looked to be made of metal. As I pushed myself to my feet, I saw that I stood inside some kind of circle with weird inscriptions. Runes, maybe? Glyphs?

Where the hell was I?

After some quick stretches and squats to loosen up the tension that seemed to saturate my body, I walked toward the door. I thought I remembered Vicki and our grandparents talking about circles or something during one of my visits recently, but I couldn't remember what they said. Containment or protection, maybe? It didn't seem smart to just walk toward the door full steam ahead, so I proceeded at a cautious pace, my hand in front at about half an arm's length.

My hand touched *something* right over the outer line of the circle. But there was a spongy-ness to it that felt odd. I wasn't sure it was supposed to be springy like a trampoline or the like. I placed my hands side by side and pressed against the springy spongy-ness, and the harder I pressed, the more it gave. Until I both heard and *felt* a *POP!* and all resistance vanished. I took a falling step forward, and I felt static or needle-points all over my body as I stepped past the edge of the circle. But I was free. Of a sort.

My eyes moved to the door, and I couldn't help but wonder. Did the people responsible for the circle also lock the door, or did they rely on the circle to contain any arrivals? Time to find out...

My fingertips just brushed the doorknob when alarms blared and wailed beyond the door. They were so loud that they hurt my ears... and I mean *hurt*. It would be a minor miracle if my ears didn't start bleeding soon. Was it because of me touching the door? Was that it?

I couldn't hear *anything* with the awful racket beyond the door, and I hated the idea of just opening the door and stepping into whatever lay beyond. But at the same time, I didn't like the idea of staying put like a good Smilodon. Until I knew where I was, there was no *good* Smilodon.

The doorknob didn't zap my fingers as I brushed them against it, so I took hold and tried it. The knob turned without impediment, and the door swung into the room as soon as the latch fully retracted into the door. Huh…good for me, but kinda stupid for them. Too much faith in the circle, I guess.

I stepped into a hallway maybe six feet wide. Concrete construction all around. And I promptly brought my hands up to cover my ears, because I stood directly under a speaker for that damned alarm siren. No signs anywhere to be seen, but down the hallway to my right, I saw people in tactical clothing running past. I wasn't sure I was up for confronting all the people I saw running past that end of the hallway, so I turned to my left. And found a dead end about sixty feet away. Two more doorways broke off from the hallway before the end, but again, no signs.

Damn. This was getting me nowhere.

Something had to give about that alarm, too. I could barely force myself to think with it blaring as loud as it was. I stepped back inside the room with the circle and slammed the door shut. With that minor reprieve, I unbuttoned my shirt and removed it. I then set about wrapping as many layers of cloth as possible between the outside world and my ears. It wasn't perfect. It wasn't going to *be* perfect. But it muffled that wail enough that inside the room I could barely hear it, which led me to hope I could step outside and *hopefully* think even with the horrid wailing.

Well, no time like the present to find out…

I opened the door once more and smiled when the sheer tsunami of sound didn't immediately assault my ears. I stepped into the hall and took a couple breaths. That alarm was still loud, but it wasn't the eardrum-splitting wail that prevented any and all hope of coherent thought it was just a few moments before.

Good enough.

I didn't see anyone running past the intersection to my right anymore, but I still felt a little leery about heading that way without checking those two doorways. When I reached the first, I found a steel door with all kinds of strange symbols carved into the metal. They pulsed with a silvery light at a steady cadence, fading in and out with a complete cycle every second to second-and-a-half. There was one of those observation slits covered with a piece of metal that slid to the left, and what looked like a cuff and tray port sat lower down the door.

Huh... just who was so special they rated a metal cell door inlaid with magic? And were they good people? Not for the first time, I wondered if I was inside the bunker where Hauser and Burke disappeared. But if I was, how did I get there?

I fought the urge to growl as impatience swelled within me. I needed to stop thinking, stop debating, and *decide.* Either check the room or don't, but the dithering had to end if I wanted to go home to my ladies.

That thought bore a striking resemblance to the tone and feeling of the growly voice, but it didn't *sound* like the growly voice. I wondered if that was part of the integration and synthesis it mentioned.

Regardless, I opened the observation port. I'm sure it made a sound as I slammed the sliding cover against its stop, but who would know with the alarm wailing overhead? The room on the other side of the door was indeed a cell, and it held an occupant. A young woman lay on a concrete cot with wafer-thin pad between her and the concrete; she held her pillow folded around the back of her head and pressed against her ears. She wore orange scrubs with a white t-shirt under her top, white socks, and white tennis shoes. One wall held one of those steel toilet-sink combination units you see in pictures of jail cells, and the floor angled down to a large grated drain that looked at least four inches across.

I closed the observation port and moved to the next doorway. It held a door just like the one before, complete with pulsing symbols. I opened the observation port and found an empty room. The concrete slab didn't even have a thin mattress pad.

I returned to the doorway with the occupied cell. Several rods of steel rebar—almost an inch thick—prevented the door from opening, but only one of those rods sported a padlock and hasp to prevent the rod from being removed. I crouched and looked closer at the padlock and fought the urge to snort. It wasn't even a high-security padlock; it didn't look any different than a padlock one might find at the local hardware store.

Damn, people… overconfident much?

I willed the shift back to the synthesis form—the Smilodon-Human hybrid cat-man—and took hold of the padlock with my right furry hand, threading one finger through the arch of the padlock—which barely fit—and pressed my left hand against the hasp with the padlock between my index finger and thumb. It was all about strength, now.

I squatted down just a little bit to lower my center of gravity as I widened my stance, making sure to press my left foot against the bottom of the door. I tensed my muscles and pulled on the padlock's base with everything I had. Several moments passed before I felt something weaken. Then, all at once, the lock's mechanism broke free of the arch. I dropped the 'box' that housed the lock's mechanism and removed the arch-piece from the hasp. I was sure breaking that lock made all kinds of noise, but again, who'd know with that insufficiently damned alarm that *still* blared.

I held the hasp open and slid the rebar out of the wall, then slid the rest of the rebar rods back to free the door. Then, the door swung open of its own accord. Part of me hoped for some kind of grand, heroic entrance like you see in the movies, but with the pillow wrapped around her head to block out the alarm, she had no idea I was there. I couldn't even see her face.

There was no telling how soon someone could come to investigate that circle, so I didn't really want to take my time. But I just couldn't leave her. Sure... there was the chance she was some kind of criminal, but if this *was* the bunker we originally sought, I really doubted that. Which left me with only one decision. How to get her attention without scaring the daylights out of her. I approached her bed—such as it was —and tapped my finger against her ankle.

Her entire body flinched as she scrambled into a sitting position and threw the pillow at me before she crab-walked backward as far as she could. She stared at me with wide eyes.

Her mouth moved, but I couldn't hear her over the alarm. I gestured that I couldn't hear her and stepped closer until I leaned in front of her with my hands clasped behind my back, trying to present an aura of safety... or at least no imminent threat.

"Who are you? You don't look like one of the guards," she shouted into ear.

I moved to lean close to her ear, and I couldn't keep from grinning as I said, "I'm Wyatt Magnusson, and I guess I'm here to rescue you."

30

Hauser lay stretched out on her bunk, watching Burke pace their tiny cell like a caged predator. Every time her circuit took her to the metal door, Burke gave the offending item a solid kick before resuming her pacing. Anywhere else—any*when* else—Burke would have worn Hauser's nerves beyond fraying. But in their captivity, the pacing and resistance Burke displayed served to bolster her own resolve.

It didn't help that they both sported orange scrubs like inmates, and the process they'd endured before donning them hadn't been great, either. After all, *they* were not the bad guys. They stopped the bad guys.

Ever since taking up their current place of residence, they followed a strict regimen of exercise as best they could, in between being taken to an interrogation like some kind of maximum-security mass murderer. Yep. Anytime one of them left the cell, it was hands cuffed behind the back with shackles at their ankles. Not fun at all. If they stayed 'on schedule,' someone would arrive to take Burke sometime in the next thirty minutes or so.

Suddenly, the lights flared super-bright then flickered... and kept flickering. A loud *BANG!* shook their cell, and the lights—along with the door's magnetic lock—died.

"Hurry!" Burke hissed.

Hauser heard the door open, and she saw Burke's silhouette framed in the glow of the hallway's emergency lighting. Never one to look a gift horse in the mouth, Hauser launched off her cot and hustled out the door. As soon as she stepped past Burke, Burke pushed the door closed... just in time for the lights to start flickering and the mag-lock to reactivate.

A shrill alarm siren filled the hall and assaulted their ears. Hauser didn't know if they caused it or if it related to whatever that *bang* was, but she had no intention of being a good, little prisoner and waiting for these people to eventually kill her. She pivoted to Burke and leaned close to her ear to be heard.

"You know they'll kill us eventually, right?"

Burke replied with a grim nod as she winced against the auditory assault.

"You willing to go out like a sheep led to slaughter?"

Burke shook her head.

"Okay. Let's see how far we get."

IT WASN'T long until they encountered the first contingent of armed personnel. A small squad charged past an intersection up ahead of them, and they darted into a recessed doorway. It didn't seem like they'd been discovered. While Burke watched the hallway, Hauser checked the door. No joy. Locked. She tapped Burke's right shoulder and gave the hand signal to move on.

Five more recessed doorways between them and the hallway intersection...

The next was locked as well. So was the one after that. The third door after that first one was *not* locked, and Hauser edged it open to peek inside. It looked like a mechanical room of some kind, and her eyes keyed in on three people standing around what looked to be an electrical panel. At least the one section throwing sparks all over hell and gone led Hauser to believe it was an electrical panel.

Hauser eased the door closed and tapped Burke's left shoulder. When Burke glanced her way, Hauser flashed the signals for an open entry and three people. Burke nodded. Hauser opened the door just far enough to squeeze through, keeping her eyes on the trio clustered around the panel. Just as she feared the increased volume of the alarm would give them away, a speaker on the wall opposite the electrical panel warbled to life and began blaring.

Hauser and Burke hustled through the door and closed it while one of the trio crossed the room, lifted a crowbar, and ripped the wires out of the speaker. They crouched behind a stack of large spoils of cable.

Ah… blessed silence. Well, except for that sparking panel…

"Thanks, Nate. Those damn fools in the security office must've reset the broadcast network or something. I had that speaker turned off," one of the people—a man with a high nasal voice—said.

"So, what the hell happened?" another man asked, his voice reminding Hauser of the rumble of thunder.

"Well, the effect appears to be a fried transfer switch that prevented the generator bank from taking the bunker's load. I had to rig this cable just to get us back up and running. As for the cause, I don't know. Obviously, a power surge of some kind, but I'm not sure even a lightning strike could have done this," Nasal Voice answered.

"What about that ranger station we're using as a cover to

get power from the grid?" the third guy asked, and as he turned Hauser saw a gruesome scar running from his right temple to his jaw line.

Nasal Voice shrugged. "Again, I don't know. Weather's been clear all day. We're not even supposed to have clouds overhead until tomorrow. I've never seen *anything* blow a transfer switch like this. Whatever it was fused the switch. Fused—like welded it together or something."

"Whoa," Scarface opined. "Now, that's some power."

Nasal Voice turned and just stared at Scarface. Hauser couldn't see the man's expression, but she figured it communicated an utter certainty that Scarface was an idiot. "That's what I've been saying! Have you not listened to a word I've said?"

Hauser shook her head. She'd had enough of this. A quick series of hand signals informed Burke to take Scarface while she took Thunder Voice. Burke nodded her agreement, and they moved to have a clear path for a charge.

Burke signaled 'ready,' and Hauser replied with the 'go' signal.

In a contest of strength—and *only* strength—no woman can compete with a man, especially if the man maintains his body and trains with weights. Of course, most confrontations involve more than just strength. Such as... Hauser was a soccer star in school and had focused on her fitness since then. Just as Burke delivered a knife-hand strike to Scarface's throat, Hauser put all her power and momentum into a kick to Thunder Voice's groin.

Scarface went down, clutching his throat. Thunder Voice hit a new octave and collapsed to his knees, then doubled over as a high-pitched (for him) keening escaped his lips.

Nasal Voice made the mistake of gaping at the new state of affairs. He had not even moved when Burke pivoted and kicked the back of his knee. Hauser timed a rabbit punch to his throat to arrive a split-second before his knees hit the floor, so the combined force was much greater than it otherwise might have been.

Okay. They were safe—for the moment.

Hauser pulled a set of side-cutters from Thunder Voice's belt, passing them to Burke as she said, "See if you can find some cable like phone line or something to tie these guys up with. I'll make sure they don't rally."

Burke pointed to Scarface as she accepted the side-cutters. "I'm not sure rallying is in that guy's cards. His lips are turning blue."

Hauser set to searching their captives for anything they could use while Burke went in search of improvised restraints. She didn't like the idea that one or more of these guys might die, but she truly felt in fear for her life. Which made all this self-defense... at least, she *hoped* it did.

By the time Burke returned with some cordage, Hauser had three wallets, three keycards, some pocket change, a couple key rings, a handful of what looked like phone connectors, and two pocketknives. One was a spring-assist with a locking blade. *That* would help. Any weapon was better than *no* weapon. Hauser paused her efforts to assist Burke with restraining their prizes, and as they turned to Scarface, Hauser saw the point was largely moot. He still struggled to breathe, but it was a mere shadow or minuscule fraction of what it has been. As much as Hauser wanted to offer him at least a little dignity at the end, she couldn't bring herself to leave a potential threat behind her. Nasal Voice wasn't far behind him.

Over the next few minutes, they consolidated what they were taking—the two knives, the keycards, and all the cash and coinage—then headed for the door. As they left, only Thunder Voice remained alive, and he shouted imprecations and threats at the top of his lungs... for all the good it did.

Even to their mere human senses, they could still hear the alarm wailing through the door.

As they closed the door to the electrical room behind them, Hauser leaned close to Burke's ear and asked, "Were you ever in the military?"

Burke only shook her head to answer 'no,' rather than fight to be heard over the alarm, and Hauser felt like cursing. She hadn't gone to the military, either. They could have really used some hand-to-hand combat training beyond what their respective police academies and Quantico taught.

With a tap to Burke's shoulder and a hand signal, they moved. The remaining doors between them and the intersection had no immediately useful items. They were storage rooms for the electrical room and maybe a machine shop somewhere. Yes, if either of them had the proper training and knowledge, those rooms probably held a wealth of items for improvised weaponry, but nothing Hauser saw brought any good ideas to mind.

They cleared the intersection as best they could and didn't see anyone. They also didn't see any signs, either. Hauser hated the idea of following the people they saw, but she had no idea how to get *out*. They'd brought them both into the bunker wearing thick felt hoods. The exit could be *anywhere*.

Still not liking the idea at all, Hauser signaled for Burke to head the same way they'd seen the people running.

MINUTES PASSED WITHOUT FURTHER CONTACT. No sign of anyone. An eerie feeling settled around Hauser's shoulders and steadily grew the longer they crept along without further encounters. She just *knew* they waited around a corner somewhere in a massive ambush with machine guns and grenades. And that damned alarm didn't help.

They crept through a hallway that gently curved to the right and found a doorway with a red placard beside it. No words. Just a slightly off-square piece of metal painted red. Hauser pointed to the placard and door, eliciting a shrug from Burke. Awesome communication, there. Well, the nameless security guys on Star Trek always wore red shirts, so maybe this was the security office?

Hauser fought to keep from snorting in amusement. *That* was not a proper decision-making paradigm, but she feared the adrenaline and stress was getting to her. What the hell… the only way to know was to try. The door was locked, but one wall of the doorway held a keycard reader. She fished the keycards out of her pocket—thank goodness the scrubs had them—and tried the first one. Red light. Second? Red light. But the third? The reader's indicator flashed green with a chirp, and Hauser tried the door again. It swung open.

Two people—one man and one woman—sat at a curved console that faced a wall of borderless monitors. They had microphones on the console in front of them, and they both turned toward the door.

"Oh, shit," the man said. "They're loose!"

Well, no time to waste. Hauser erupted into a charge as Burke followed close behind her. Both people jumped out of their seats and pawed at the holsters on their belts. Hauser reached the guy before he drew on her and made a jumping lunge at him. Her impact staggered him to shuffle backward, and something *snapped* when his back struck the edge of the console. All fight left him in a finger-snap as he screamed and fell to the floor.

A gunshot to her left drew Hauser's attention, and she turned just in time to see the guy's fellow staffer—the woman—roll off of Burke. She held a semi-automatic pistol in her left hand that ended up pointed toward the far wall as she settled on her back. Hauser had no desire to let the woman get her feet under her again, and she charged across the space stomped on the woman's left wrist with her heel. The woman screamed as something snapped, and her grip on the pistol slackened. Hauser kicked the pistol away and turned to Burke. Then froze.

A slowly expanding imperfect circle of red dominated the center of Burke's torso.

Hauser kicked the woman in her left temple, not caring if she died or just fell unconscious, then rushed to Burke's side. Burke's eyes fluttered open as Hauser lifted her hand.

"It's bad, Winnie," Burke gasped, her speech flecking her lips with blood. "I can't feel my legs... and it hurts to breathe. I don't think... I don't think I'm going home... this time."

Hauser felt tears welling in her eyes. "Stay with me, Eddie. Don't give up yet."

"I'm not... not sure I have a... a choice."

Hauser searched the room with her eyes as she held Burke's hand. Looking for something—anything—she might use to move Burke safely and seek help. As much as she wanted to believe there was still time, the icy claws of dread digging into her heart told her the truth. But either way, she was not leaving her friend and fellow agent behind.

"Come on. This might hurt, but I'm not leaving you."

Burke made a gagging, wet cough that only served to coat her lips with blood even more. "You can't... carry me and... escape, Winnie. Leave me. I know... I'm dying."

"You stop that crazy talk right now, Agent. We're getting out of here... both of us." Hauser hauled Burke up and threw the woman's left arm around her shoulders while she wrapped her right arm around her waist, pulling Burke tight against her. "I'm not leaving you."

Hauser could tell Burke tried to take as much of her own weight as she could, but Hauser knew it wouldn't last. She just wasn't ready to admit it. As she moved them both toward the door, Hauser's eyes landed on a button labeled, 'Master Alarm Shutoff,' and she released Burke's hand at her shoulder long enough to slap it. The alarm outside the room cut off, and Hauser couldn't believe the relief she felt at that.

Now, to get out of this place…

A SECOND SWIPE of the keycard released the mag-lock holding the door to the security room, and Hauser cleared the hallway as best she could while holding Burke. She wasn't more than ten feet into the hallway when a massive, deep-throated roar echoed down the hallway. Holy crap… she *knew* that roar.

She eased Burke to the floor and met her friend's eyes. Saw the life slowly fading, but still present.

"Stay with me, Eddie. Please, stay with me. Looks like you get your wish after all." Then, she stood, took a deep breath, and shrieked at the top of her lungs. "Wyatt!"

I had to admit that the lady following behind me looked a little... odd... as she walked with the pillow from her cell wrapped around her head. I didn't look too snappy, either, but I hoped any roguish good looks I may have possessed as a shirtless guy with eight- or maybe even twelve-pack abs offset that a bit. Likewise, she might have been pretty enough that I would've paid no attention at all to the pillow, but the orange scrubs performed an excellent job of masking whatever curves she possessed.

HEY... don't knock it. I *am* a guy, after all, and I appreciate women.

WITH THOSE THOUGHTS leading the way, I approached the intersection with extreme caution. No sign of anyone. And no *signs*, either. Did these people capture others with such regularity that they *planned* for escapes? Would it have really hurt them to throw up a road-sign-like placard every once and a while?

I still didn't relish the idea of following after all those armed people I saw jog by the intersection, so I led my fellow escapee to the left. This section of the hallway only had a couple doorways branching off from it for quite some distance, and as we reached the first, we found it wasn't a doorway but another intersection.

I pointed to the next potential doorway down our original hallway and then gestured at my eyes before pointing at the potential doorway again. When my companion didn't walk past me, I turned to find her looking at me like I was an idiot. I rolled my eyes and leaned close enough for her to reveal one ear long enough for me to say, "Go check that other possible doorway, please, and nod if it's a door."

The woman nodded as understanding dawned, and she hissed back, "You need to work on your hand signals. I thought you wanted to chop something and get poked in your eyes."

I frowned at her back as she fast-walked to the next alcove but schooled my expression before she turned. She nodded in a very obvious way, and I jogged to catch up to her. This door held the first 'normal' latch I'd seen so far. A rectangular grip under a thumb lever. A keycard reader hung on the alcove wall next to the door, and I figured the door itself was locked. But I tried it anyway. It wasn't.

Edging the door open, I peeked and saw barracks-style beds. Bunk beds—one on top of another—lined one wall. Lockers lined the other. It did not appear to be occupied, but there was another door at the far side of the room. I entered, waving my hand for my companion to follow, and the alarm faded to a tolerable cacophony as soon as the door latched. I removed my shirt from my head, and I figured the faint rustle I heard came from lowering the pillow.

"Okay. Let's search these lockers. With that alarm, I doubt we'll find anything immediately useful, and if we are where I think we are, I have people right outside the bunker, so we don't need money."

I heard a delicate snort behind me. "Speak for yourself. These creeps pulled me off a crowded street in broad daylight. I have no idea how long they've held me here, but it feels like it's been a long damn time."

Even her voice sounded beautiful.

I wanted to argue with her. But at the same time, she wasn't one of mine. As much as I might prefer otherwise, I had no right to dictate to her.

"Okay. You do you, but if you weigh yourself down to the point you can't run, I'll leave you here," I said, turning to face her. And oh, damn. Wavy, flaming red hair. Emerald green eyes that shone with a vibrant zest for life. Yeah… she was so gorgeous I missed my ladies.

She looked up at me, holding her silence for several seconds before she snorted and shook her head. "No, you won't. You're one of those boy scouts who never leaves a damsel in distress. Otherwise, why free me? It's not like we have time for a roll in the hay, nor have you tried. I'll admit… that's kinda nice. But all of that shows you're a decent guy. You won't leave me here to face whatever fate holds for me, and you know it."

Dammit… she was right. The only way I'd leave her to her fate was if she attacked me.

"Fine," I almost growled. "But you're responsible for your pilferage. I'm no sherpa. You won't be loading *me* down with a bunch of stuff of no immediate use that we could replace later."

"Now, *that* I believe."

I shook my head as I turned and started my search.

· · ·

BY THE TIME I worked my way to the far side of the room, I considered that the time had been wasted. No weapons. No cell phones or anything like that. Nothing that could help me get word to anyone that I was alive and in need of help.

I turned to my partner in pilfering and quirked an eyebrow. "Well? Find anything you want?"

She scrunched up her face in a classic moue of distaste. "No. I have no interest *or need* for smelly jock straps and even smellier boxers and briefs. This room holds nothing of value for me."

"Well, grab your pillow. Back out we go."

I re-wrapped my shirt and checked that she had retrieved her pillow before I pushed open the door... and stepped into another hallway. No one in sight, but there was another alcove about sixty feet to my right that was either an inter-section or a door.

I headed that way, trusting my companion to follow, and wished that blasted alarm would die a rapid and painful death. I couldn't *hear* anything but my heartbeat the way it blared, and if I unwrapped my shirt from my head, I wouldn't even hear *that* much. I was maybe ten feet from the alcove that I was pretty sure was another hallway when a woman in tac gear and carrying a shotgun stepped into my hallway.

She froze at the sight of me, her eyes going wide. Her jaw worked like she said something, but no telling what it was. When she didn't get the response she wanted, she whipped the shotgun to her shoulder and pointed it at me, her mouth frantically moving all the while.

I still had no idea what she was saying, but she didn't seem to care.

She stroked the trigger of the shotgun, blasting me square in the chest... just as the alarm suddenly cut out. She worked the slide, sending a spent shell flying out of sight, but I saw her hands and arms shaking. I smelled her fear. I just took the full brunt of a twelve-gauge shotgun blast—presumably double- or triple-aught buckshot—and didn't go down.

I flexed my mind to produce the synthesis form... and became a seven-foot-tall furry humanoid Smilodon. I flexed the proper muscles in my fingers and thumbs to extend my claws, just to add insult to injury.

The acrid scent of urine proclaimed her terror as I took a step toward her and said, "Drop the shotgun and surrender if you want to live."

She remained frozen. Her eyes wide. Her whole body shaking with barely controlled atavistic terror. I didn't want to kill her if I didn't have to. I never wanted to kill *anyone*. So, I spread my arms wide, took one (hopefully) menacing step toward her, and roared at the top of my lungs.

The blood drained from her face faster than I've ever seen as her eyes rolled back in her head. Her knees buckled. Her arms slackened. I lunged and pulled my claws back inside. I grasped the shotgun by its receiver with my left hand and snaked my right arm under her left and around her torso. In my synthesis form, I barely noticed either weight.

As I lowered her to the floor, I spied a set of handcuffs on her belt. Perfect. I rolled her over and cuffed her hands behind her just as I heard someone shriek, "Wyatt!"

Hauser? Why did I hear such frantic urgency in her voice? I no longer had time to worry about double-locking the cuffs and surged to my feet. I shifted back to human and cast a quick glance back at my companion, as I growled, "Follow if you want to."

I took off at a run.

I STOPPED at each intersection and shouted for Hauser. Each time, she shouted my name. If I hadn't been so worried, I would've laughed at such an absurd game of Marco Polo. The occasional ping of metal buckshot hitting the floor accompanied my running search for Hauser; my body seemed to push it back out of me as I healed. It wasn't long until even my sense of smell detected the tang of blood in the air, and I opened my mouth to improve my scent response as I surged forward.

I barreled around a corner and skidded to a stop at the sight of Hauser kneeling over Burke.

"Oh, thank heavens," Hauser gasped. "She's dying, Wyatt. She's almost gone."

"Have you found anything sharp enough to cut with?"

"I have a knife," Hauser answered, fishing it out of a pocket and extending it to me.

I ripped open Burke's top and t-shirt underneath. Then, accepted and opened the blade before liberally slicing my wrist several times. When the blood tried to drip or my wrist healed, I jabbed the blade back in and opened up an artery. I bathed Burke's wound with my blood and fed her a liberal amount as well. Then, just to be sure I did everything I could, I shifted to my synthesis form—eliciting a startled scream from Hauser—and bit deep into Burke's forearm.

I shifted back to human and watched for several moments without any change, and I feared I was too late. Tears flowed down Hauser's cheeks as she whispered, "Please work… please work," over and over.

Then, my bite on her arm *started to heal*. When Hauser kept whispering, I looked and found her eyes closed. I nudged her shoulder, and when she opened her eyes, I pointed to Burke's arm where my bite now looked like red needle tracks.

A little cheer escaped Hauser's lips as she threw her arms around me and hugged me tight.

"Thank you, Wyatt. I don't know what I would've done if

I'd lost her." The immediate concern removed, Hauser focused solely on Burke and noticed the woman behind me. "Who's she?"

I shrugged. "No idea. I found her in a cell next door to the room where I appeared. Since these people want her for some reason, I figured I'd spring her."

"Only you, Wyatt," Hauser sighed as she shook her head. "Only you would free someone you didn't know—and probably never questioned—just..." Guilty as charged, Your Honor. "...to deny your opponents the person."

"Well, not *just* to deny them holding her. I do believe in personal freedom, you know."

Hauser chuckled. "Of course, you do. So, how do we get out of here?"

"Again, no idea. I've kinda just been following my instinct. Not to jinx us, either, but I'm starting to get a little worried about how empty this place has been. We encountered one person so far."

"Five for us, but yes. It's eerie."

A faint sound reached my ears, and I grinned.

Hauser eyed me like a veteran schoolmarm facing an unrepentant rapscallion. "And just why are you grinning like a fool?"

"Because I'm pretty sure I just heard a grizzly bear roar."

I gathered Burke into my arms, and we set off toward the sound of the roar I thought I heard. The bunker was a twisting maze of hallways and corridors, and we collected the woman I scared into pissing herself when we passed her.

THE FARTHER I LED US, the louder sounds of a fight became. But I wondered at the lack of gunshots. Everyone I had seen was armed to the teeth. There should have been lots and lots and lots of gunshots, right? Thank goodness for the solid walls, floors, and ceiling that served as an excellent resonance chamber… when there wasn't an ear-shredding alarm wailing throughout the place.

We continued the follow the sounds as we sought the exit. Well, *I* followed the sounds. Hauser and the former prisoner didn't hear anything yet. After several minutes, though, the sounds of fighting faded. But by then, the air held the tang of blood strong enough that even I could smell it.

After uncounted intersections, the hallway we followed ended in an 'L' and I saw daylight, about two dozen people in tactical gear on their knees, a horde of animals I called friends, and my sister in the distance.

Now, all that remained was to call in the cavalry and get Burke back to Doc's infirmary in Precious…

32

A week had passed since I led a war party to a black site bunker in the Grand Tetons of Wyoming. After securing the facility, we called in the Feds to deal with the survivors. We apologized for any breakage, and Hauser reported that she and Burke had killed two people during their escape. As Burke was still unconscious from me saving her life, their agency's Internal Affairs department decided to postpone the inquiry until Burke came out the other side of becoming a shifter.

I SAT on the back deck of the Alpha's house in Precious. The house faced east, and I enjoyed sitting on the back deck and watching the line of sunlight creep its way down the mountains and hills. The sun line's slow, stately progression reminded me of an ancient scanner. Which took my mind back to my old day job. A lot had changed for and with me since I was a dead-end tech for an IT company barely treading water, financially speaking. I was no longer the socially insecure, mostly out of shape geek. I was now the socially insecure, incredibly fit alpha shifter, serving as Alpha of Precious and Godwin County and Consul of the Shifters of North America.

I was not wild about that 'Consul' business, but such is life. The Shifter Council just made the announcement to all the shifters on the continent the other day, and I expected the fecal matter to start hitting the rotary air impeller forthwith. Nothing had… *yet*… but it was only a matter of time.

Part of me still felt a little blindsided—not to mention jealous—that Vicki got to see Miles… that is, *Merlin*… in all his glory, and I couldn't help but wonder what the history was between him and *Requiem*. From what Vicki said, he spoke to it as if it possessed an intelligence. Not gonna lie; *that* freaked me out a little. How does a staff possess intelligence?

Hauser has almost been living in Doc's infirmary, and more than once, either the ladies or I have brought her food or forced her to go to the diner with us to eat. She seemed *extremely* reluctant to leave Burke's side, and I hadn't forgotten her statement back in the bunker, either. More than once since then, I wondered if Hauser thought of Burke as more than just a fellow Special Agent. If she did, the question *then* became what Burke's thoughts on the matter were. Did she even *know*?

Sloane seems to be settling in just fine. I think she's still in the "I can't believe it's finally over" stage, since word around town is that she spends most of her time on the wing. I think she'll ease off in time, once she truly integrates the idea that she's not hunted anymore. Emotional awareness of something like that always lags behind intellectual awareness.

The lady I found in the bunker accepted my invitation to come back to Precious with us. I finally learned her name when she checked into the hotel as a guest of the Alpha: Moira MacCallan. The day after Moira checked into the hotel, the ladies and Vicki whisked her off to one of the state's larger cities, since she 'needed some things.' She seemed nice enough, but I still didn't know any more about her than her name and the color of her eyes and hair.

Well, that's not *quite* true. Back in the bunker, when I shifted to my synthesis form to bite Burke? *Only Hauser* reacted. Which meant she had seen a synthesis form at least once before. Yay… more pending surprises!

Still, though, things have—mostly—returned to normal around town, which has brought the matter of the former Attorney General's son to the forefront of my mind. Her resignation after only a month or so on the job was one of the first headlines I saw upon my return. I was going to need to make a decision about that soon, but I felt I could take a day or two to decompress.

Goodness knows, it wouldn't be long before Murphy delivered his next gift…

WHAT'S NEXT?

Have you read "Lone Wolf," Karleen's origin story?

If not, sign up for my newsletter to get it:
https://kfplink.com/tps

"Consular Times," Book 3 of the Primogenitor Saga, is
available for pre-order now.

Visit the book's page to choose your vendor:
https://kfplink.com/consulartimes

RATE THIS BOOK

Did you enjoy this story? If you did, please consider leaving a review.

Reviews are the lifeblood of visibility for independent authors, especially on the eBook retailers. The more reviews a book has, the more visible it will be on the retailers' sites.

I appreciate all reviews…good, bad, or indifferent.

AUTHOR'S NOTE

14 MAY 2021

First and foremost, thank you for reading...both the novel and these notes! I hope you enjoyed *Roc*!

I first jotted down an idea that became *Smilodon*, Book 1 of this series, in April of 2020. I had not intended to start writing this series when I did, but I'm glad I gave into the temptation.

Roc was as much of a joy to write as its predecessor was, and I am looking forward to *Consular Times*.

Some of you may have noticed that this book carries a dedication page, the first of my publications to do so. Earlier this morning (i.e. the morning of 14 May 2021), a dear friend of my friend and editor lost his grandmother. I have never met the friend of my editor. I never met his grandmother. But I did know *my* grandmother... well, one of them. She and my grandfather were fundamental parts of my life, almost cornerstones if you will. I lost my grandmother on 20 August 2000, six months and thirteen days after my grandfather, and it's rare that a week goes by without thinking of her or my grandfather in some way, even 20+ years into her loss. (And yes, I still know these dates by memory.)

We are who we are—at least in part—because of the people who touch our lives. For good. For ill. And everything in between. I don't think any of us will ever *know* all the people we have touched as part of our passing through this world. And I for one would rather try to leave my little corner better for my journey through it.

Thanks again for reading *Roc*! And an even greater thank you for wading through this note.

I hope the days have been treating you well, and I offer my best wishes for the future.

—Rob

THE NOVELS OF ROBERT M. KERNS

For a complete and accurate listing of all publications, both
currently available and forthcoming, please visit Knightsfall Press.

Knightsfall Press - Books

https://knightsfall.press/books

SO...WHO'S THE AUTHOR?

Robert M. Kerns (or Rob if you ever meet him in person) is a geek, and he claims that label proudly. Most of his geekiness revolves around Information Technology (IT), having over fifteen years in the industry; within IT, he especially prefers Servers and Networks, and he often makes the claim that his residence has a better data infrastructure than some businesses.

Beyond IT, Rob enjoys Science Fiction and Fantasy of (almost) all stripes. He is a voracious reader, with his favorite books too numerous to list.

Rob has been writing for over 20 years, and *Awakening* is his debut novel.

facebook.com/RobertMKerns

amazon.com/author/robertmkerns

bookbub.com/authors/robert-m-kerns